NO FOOTPRINTS IN THE BUSH

Arthur W. Upfield

NO FOOTPRINTS IN THE BUSH

A SCRIBNER CRIME CLASSIC

Previously published as *Bushranger of the Skies*

COLLIER BOOKS

MACMILLAN PUBLISHING COMPANY

New York

Macmillan Publishing Company
866 Third Avenue, New York, N.Y. 10022
Collier Macmillan Canada, Inc.

Library of Congress Cataloging-in-Publication Data
Upfield, Arthur William, 1888-1964.
    No footprints in the bush.
    (Scribner crime classics)
    "Previously published as *Bushranger of the skies*."
    I. Title.   II. Series.
PR9619.U6B8   1986   823   86-13641
ISBN 0-02025940-9

10 9 8 7

Printed in the United States of America

NO FOOTPRINTS IN THE BUSH

CHAPTER 1

MIRAGE AND BOMBS

ONE of Nature's oddities was the grove of six cabbage-trees in the dense shade of which Detective-Inspector Bonaparte had made his noonday camp. They grew beside an unmade road winding like a snake's track over a range of low, treeless and semi-barren hills; and, so close were they, and so virile their foliage, that to step in among them was not unlike stepping into an ivy-covered church porch on a brilliant summer morning.

A more inviting place for a noon camp in late spring, away out on the edge of Central Australia, is seldom offered, and thankfully Bonaparte made a little fire within the shade and boiled water in his quart-pot for tea. With contentment bordering on ecstasy, he began to eat a lunch of damper and hard-boiled duck eggs whilst reclining against his swag.

Thus he was able to see a picture made extraordinarily vivid by the clear sunlight beyond the shade, a picture roughly framed in the shape of a Gothic arch. In the foreground of the picture passed the unmade road he had been following for four days. The road went on to fall sharply downward and skirt a hillside two hundred feet above a boulder-strewn gully. Beyond the hill it disappeared only to reappear on the side of yet another hill, beyond which it again vanished and reappeared before becoming lost amidst the tiny foothills washed by a still white mirage sea covering a valley ten miles across.

Beyond the mirage-covered plain could be seen the scrub on the distant higher land, scrub appearing to Bonaparte like an inch wide dark-grey ribbon supporting the northern rim of the burnished copper sky.

Four days earlier Bonaparte had left Shaw's Lagoon, situated beyond Queensland's western border, a very small township offering no excuse for its existence other than that it marked the terminus of a motor mail route. Shaw's Lagoon was roughly eighty miles to the south-east of the cabbage-trees where he was now camped, and since he had passed through the gate in the State Border Fence he had passed through no other, had met no traveller, seen no house or hut. And now, down there on the plain, yet another twelve miles to walk to the McPherson homestead, could be seen the first hint of human life, the dust cloud raised by a moving vehicle.

Traffic on this road was rare. Eight days previously it had rained, and since then no wheel or hoof or human foot had marked it. It led to the Land of Burning Water, from which reports had drifted of strange happenings. There it lay beyond the hills, shimmering with yellow opalescence beneath the sun: burning water—the mirage.

From his high elevation on the edge of the hill range, Bonaparte idly watched the moving vehicle. On the basis of its speed, as indicated by the dust cloud it raised, he guessed it to be a car, and further, he guessed it was being driven by Sergeant Errey, as he was aware that the senior police officer stationed at Shaw's Lagoon was visiting McPherson's Station.

When the vehicle was hidden by the hills its progress still could be traced by the dust raised by its wheels, and presently it again appeared rounding a hillside, an ant running along an ant road. Calmly, and without haste, Bonaparte moved his body, brought the swag round to lie across his legs, and then began to remove the straps. It was certainly a car and the odds were in favour of its being driven by Sergeant Errey, for whom Bonaparte had a letter signed by the Chief Commissioner of the South Australian Police Department.

He had removed one strap, and his long fingers were engaged with the other, when with singular abruptness there burst into the silence about the camp the roar of an aeroplane engine.

Immediately following the arrival of this sound two crows, cawing in fear, almost fell into the branches of the cabbage-trees. Hidden from the man seated on the ground, they proceeded to vent their defiance on the plane, which passed over the camp, thence to follow the road to Shaw's Lagoon.

Bonaparte did not see the machine. It had come from the west, possibly skirting the northern edge of the hill range. Had it come from the north or north-west, he could not have failed to see it in the picture framed within a leafy arch of Gothic type.

The sound of the aircraft engine had faded to a low buzz, but the crows in the branches above Bonaparte refused to leave, although they must have known he was not more than twelve feet beneath them. They continued their noisy defiance of the machine, which had been to them an even greater terror than a human being could be.

Bonaparte removed the letter from his swag and began its restrapping, his hands working automatically, his gaze directed at that part of the road where next the car would appear.

The car did appear, and at the same time Bonaparte heard the aeroplane returning. Its pilot could not be searching for a landing otherwise he would have selected the plain. He could hardly be lost, for there was the road to follow. The machine certainly had come from the west, yet westward stretched hundreds of miles of open semi-desert country, empty of settlement. Why fly in the direction of Shaw's Lagoon for perhaps twenty miles, then turn and come back?

The frightened crows clung determinedly to their sanctuary. Bony lifted the swag from his legs to put it aside. His action was too much for the birds. They cawed and fluttered among the branches, but still were too frightened by the oncoming plane to leave. Their cawings were shut off by the thundering menace rushing towards them in their own element. They saw the vast hawk swooping upon their retreat, clung to the branches and shrieked defiance as it passed low above them. They saw the steel egg it dropped.

Fortunately for Bonaparte it was a small bomb. Fortunately for him, too, he was holding the swag in front of his body whilst seated on the ground. The bomb burst on the site of the now dead camp fire. Its explosion filled the shelter with dust and fumes, and sent outward steel fragments that lanced upward and severed leaves, to drop them through the dusty air.

Stunned by the noise, flung backward by the explosion, Bonaparte gasped in dust-laden air and fumes. His mind was divided: one part wildly angry because of the outrage, the other registering the fact that the crows had left their sanctuary, and fleeing as though pursued by ten thousand hawks. Twice the plane circled the grove of trees before flying on along the road to McPherson's Station.

Bonaparte saw it for the first time when, having lurched to his feet, he peered with semi-blinded eyes along that same road. It was a monoplane, small, extremely fast, painted a silvery-grey. He saw, too, the oncoming car which now was less than half a mile away and traversing the steep hillside. The aeroplane was flying low to meet it, so low that its landing-wheels appeared to threaten the car.

Bonaparte saw the bombs drop—two of them. They fell

together. The car, spurting red flame, gave birth to a growing ball of white smoke, and swerved off the road as though its driver was trying to escape the flame clinging to its roof. It ran up the hillside for several yards, then stopped and appeared to shrink inward into a heart of fire. The fiery heart rolled back to the road, rolled across the road, began to roll down the hillside, began to bounce as it gathered momentum. A central explosion increased the flames, and like a meteor it rushed down to the gully bed, where it lay and spouted upward a column of writhing black smoke. The aeroplane swooped and circled low over the burning wreckage. It bore no markings. There was only one man in it. His head could be seen behind the curved windshield. He was looking overside.

Within the black shadow cast by the cabbage-trees, Bonaparte crouched on hands and knees. Grey dust whitened his dark-brown face, rimmed his blue eyes, now brilliant and agate hard. The fine lips were drawn taut, revealing his white teeth in what was almost an animal snarl of fury. The zooming of the plane's engine was distorted in his ears, still feeling the shock of the explosion. His hands rested on the ground and his fingers dug constantly into its softness.

That the pilot had flown here with the specific intention of destroying a car and its driver was as evident as the shade cast by the trees. Doubtless the pilot had watched the car crossing the plain. He knew, without doubt, just where the road crossed the hill range, and before making his attack he had flown over the road for many miles towards Shaw's Lagoon to be certain there were no travellers upon it who would observe his subsequent act, or see his machine, and afterwards connect it with the destruction of the car.

The only cover near the road for many miles was that provided by the grove of cabbage-trees, and, to make doubly sure he would escape observation from a chance traveller camped in the shade of the trees, he dropped his bomb among them.

Bonaparte was tempted to run from the trees down to the blazing wreckage. To have succumbed to the temptation would have been stupid. For one thing, the car had come to rest at least half a mile from him; and for another there was no possible chance of rescuing its occupant, who must have died from the exploding bombs.

Having partially recovered from the surprise and stunning effect of the "exploratory" bomb, Bonaparte thrust the letter into a pocket and leaned back against his swag to watch and wait.

There was more than a hint of determination that none should escape the attack on the car as the aeroplane continued to circle low above what was a mass of blackened metal, enveloped by fire. For several minutes the plane circled. Then the pilot turned the machine westward, skimmed a hill-top and vanished from Bonaparte's vision.

Without movement, Detective-Inspector Bonaparte listened until he could no longer hear the sinister noise controlled either by a maniac or an ice-cold killer. The silence that had preceded the arrival of the two crows returned.

Bonaparte went down to the wreckage, lying on its side. The door in the top side was still closed, but no glass remained in it or the windscreen. The tyres were burned away. He could not get near enough to peer through the distorted steel skeleton to ascertain how many people had been inside.

Still with taut nerves and governed by a most natural horror, Bonaparte walked up the hillside, following the trail made by the blazing car. He had no hope of finding anything identifying the driver, for he had seen nothing detached from the vehicle during its descent, and now not even its numberplate was decipherable. Nevertheless he was mistaken; for, a few feet up the hillside from the place where the car had been bombed, he found a small leather attache case, on which the embossing remained to tell that its owner was Sergeant A. V. Errey. This jetsam, freakishly preserved from explosion and fire, was all the searcher found.

With hearing still tensed to receive the noise of an approaching aeroplane, Bonaparte stepped down to the road and slowly walked along it to the cabbage-trees, the case tucked under an arm. His mind was concentrated on the mysterious purpose of the outrage. It was a time when his eyes were much less active than normal, so much so that he came within two yards of the camp before his mind accepted the motionless shape of the tall, grey-haired, clean-shaven aborigine standing just within the edge of the trees' black shadow.

The man's physique was magnificent. His age was probably less than fifty. He wore no vestige of clothing save the pubic tassel, arm bands made of kangaroo fur and a forehead band to which was glued white birds' down and which raised his hair to a plume of grey web. In his left hand he carried a spear having a fire-hardened point, and in the right a heavy club fashioned from a mulga root.

"Hullo!" exclaimed Bonaparte, compelled to look upward into

the expressionless face. "Who are you? What your name, eh? How you bin called?"

Clearly, without accent, in English came the reply.

"I am the Chief of the Wantella Nation. I am Writjitandil, meaning Burning Water. This is the Land of Burning Water."

Black eyes opened wide, and in them blazed red anger. Bonaparte had spoken with superiority. Now he heard masterful pride in the voice of this naked black man.

"Who are you, half-caste? What is your business in the Land of Burning Water? Tell me, quick."

Swift movement of a sinewy arm followed the demand. The long spear became horizontal, its point aimed at Bony's heart.

CHAPTER 2

CHIEF BURNING WATER

THERE are men of every colour and race who stand high above their fellows by reason of the greatness of spirit lifting them to positions of leadership. In the affairs of the aboriginal tribes of Australia, no less than in the affairs of the allegedly more civilized white and yellow people, such men are found.

This was Burning Water. There was no mistaking the quality of leadership in his poise, in his facial expression, and especially in his eyes. Bony instantly realized that he was confronted by no ordinary aborigine. He saw with clear vision his own standing based on his unfortunate birth, saw clearly how he appeared to this regal man, and knew himself physically inferior.

"I am waiting," said Chief Burning Water, no whit abashed by the steady stare in Bonaparte's blue eyes, the lithe cat-like stance of the man born of a black mother and a white father, dressed neatly in serviceable bush clothes, veneered heavily with the white man's civilization. He saw only a despised half-caste, fruit of a woman who had broken a law.

"Put down your spear and we will talk. You are standing in my camp."

"I stand on my own land, not your land."

"Yet you are in my camp. However, you are welcome. Put down your spear, and we will make a fire and talk!"

"There is no time for frills, half-caste. You were here when the aeroplane destroyed Sergeant Errey's car and killed him. I saw it done. I saw you go down to the wreck. I saw you track up the hill to the road. I saw you pick up the Sergeant's dillybag. You have it now. All this happened in the country of the Wantella Nation. Further, you travel alone, and you walk when a man would ride a horse or a camel or drive a car or truck. Sergeant Errey was a good white man. Talk."

There was no mistaking the unbreakable will in the black eyes boring into his, and yet Bony without haste unbuckled his belt and removed his shirt and singlet. Then, turning his back to Burning Water, he said, speaking over his shoulder:

"Would you drive your spear into the sign of the square and the moon when it is full? I have stood on the square of squares facing the east and the full moon. My tribal father is called Illawalli, and he lives beside the northern waters. He has spoken to me of the Wantella Nation."

As Bony turned again to face Burning Water, the Chief's spear and club were dropped to the ground, and he advanced with his hand out-stretched:

"You bear the sign on your back of the great ones among us. I, too, have it on my back. I, too, have spoken with Illawalli who is as superior to me as I am to the tick on a cockatoo's back. Your name?"

Bonaparte now was smiling upward into the smiling face of Chief Burning Water.

"I am known as Bony," he replied. "I am on my way to visit Mr Donald McPherson, and to look for the cause of strange happenings reported from the Land of Burning Water—your land. I have seen a strange happening today. So let us make a fire and talk."

Bony put on his vest and shirt. He combed his hair and put on his felt hat. Burning Water picked up his club and spear, with the latter pointing downward to the gully. Bony turned and saw advancing up the bed of the gully towards the burned out car a party of nine aborigines.

"They are of the Illprinka Nation," Burning Water explained. "They have come from the great desert country towards the west, and not for years have they been friendly. We are but two: they are nine. We have seen what we should not have seen. We must go, quick and fast."

"How comes it that they are on your land and so far from their own country?" asked Bonaparte.

"I don't know, but I think many things. Perhaps The McPherson might tell you."

"The McPherson is a long way away," Bony said grimly, looking upward from the task of re-strapping his swag after having placed inside it the recovered attache case. "That being so, I will myself ask these Illprinka men what they are doing here on your land."

Burning Water stared into the abruptly cold blue eyes.

"They are nine," he pointed out. "They are enemies of the Wantella Nation. As you can see, they are well armed. You are a stranger to the Land of Burning Water. It would be wise for us to go, and to go fast."

To be discreet in the face of adverse odds is to be wise, not fearful. The present certainly was not opportune for questioning or probing into problems presented within the last hour, for a situation was developing demanding preparation to meet it.

For the third time at this temporary camp, he unrolled his swag and this time took from it an automatic pistol and two boxes of cartridges containing twenty-five.

"Where did you learn to speak English so well?" he asked whilst loading the pistol.

"I am The McPherson's tribal brother. He is my father and my son."

This physical impossibility was due to the intricate relationship accepted by any white man sealed into an aboriginal tribe. Bony offered no comment. In fact, he was feeling himself out of depth, as though he was in a strange country, when he was actually in his own. The prefix "the" before McPherson's surname was, indeed, odd.

"The McPherson taught me to speak his language properly, to add numbers, to read from books. The McPherson and I were young together. When Myerloo, the chief of the Wantella Nation, was killed, it was The McPherson who had me become chief in his stead. When that was done I discarded the white man's clothes which I wore for many years."

"The McPherson must be a great man," Bony said, pocketing the pistol and cartridges.

"He is both great and just. He owns four thousand square miles of land, and something like seven thousand head of cattle."

"Oh! Well, the enemy, I see, have discovered my tracks beside the wrecked car."

The aborigines below in the gully were running about like hounds on the scent. One pointed up the hillside with his spear. They were not unlike dogs unleashed in a course as they ran up the slope, shouting each to the others, moving with fascinating relentlessness of purpose. Bony could see that they were not following the marks made by the rolling car but those made by his boots.

Reaching the road, they ran straight to the place where he had discovered and retrieved the attache case. Without doubt they saw the mark on the ground made by the case when it fell from the car.

Bony squatted on his heels just outside the tree shadow. He motioned to Burning Water to draw farther into the shade, and it was noteworthy that Burning Water obeyed. Bony placed the automatic beside his right boot, and he picked up a twig and began idly to draw pictures on the sandy ground. Not for a moment did he cease to watch the party of aborigines advancing along the road.

When distant a full hundred yards from Bony they saw him and abruptly stopped. Excitedly they pointed at him and talked, a plump fellow with extraordinarily skinny legs evidently being the leader.

Native etiquette demanded that, on seeing a man in his camp, they must stick their spears into the ground as a sign of peace, and then squat beside their weapons until invited to enter the camp. These fellows ignored etiquette. They continued to advance, albeit at a walking pace.

Bony took up the pistol, aimed with care and fired. The bullet raised a spurt of dust at the edge of the road to the left of the party. Another bullet raised a spurt of dust to the right. The men halted. Bony shouted, using the Worcair dialect:

"What d'you want?"

There followed a conference at which the leader advised one thing and the majority another, resulting in the leader winning his point. He now advanced, leaving the others to retreat a little way and sit down facing the camp. The leader came without his weapons. Bony pretended to be gravely interested in his drawing on the canvas of the ground, the pistol lying beside his right boot. The Illprinka man came to squat on his heels twenty feet from Bony, and Bony continued with his artistic efforts for a full three minutes. Then he asked, casually:

"What do you in the Land of Burning Water, you men of the Illprinka?"

"We were hunting kangaroos, and so keen was the chase that we forgot we had passed out of our own land."

From a similarity of several words with those of the Worcair dialect Bonaparte understood this statement. Without heat, he said:

"One needs to be clever to tell lies with success."

The Illprinka man was ill-formed for an aborigine, but there was power in his wide brow, evil in his black eyes, deepset beneath the frontal bone.

"We saw the white man's horse-car burning in the gully and came to look-see," he said, sullenly. "We saw the burned man inside. We saw your tracks down there. We saw where you picked up something fallen from the white man's horse-car. You givit that thing, eh?"

Slowly Bony shook his head.

"You would be wise to depart to your own country, and go soon and fast," he said. "What I find I keep. It isn't yours. What I have seen I talk about. Who was the white feller in the great bird?"

"I do not know. I saw no great bird."

"Liar! The white man in the great bird came from your country. He told you to watch for white man's horse-car. He told you he would burn it. You all come look-see to pick anything you find, eh? The big bird can't set down white man around here. You see, man of Illprinka, I know. Now go back to your own country."

"You shall come with us," the fellow said

"I should not be happy with you," Bony told him calmly.

"You will come with us, or you will be killed."

Bony laughed.

"You talk like a lubra. I shall remember you."

The Illprinka man stood up, distorting his face to an even further degree of ugliness. He had walked to the camp in sprightly defiance. Now he went back to his companions running, yelling to them, and they brandished their weapons and came to meet him. Bony stood up.

"Carry my swag, Burning Water," he cried. "I wish to fire without hindrance, and we must be on our way to the McPherson Station. Walk behind me, and keep your eyes on these gentlemen."

Almost at casual pace Bony left the camp and took the road to the plain. The aborigines on seeing him advancing towards them irresolutely packed together, harangued by the leader. Bony fired, and the bullet kicked dust close to their feet. They retreated down the road. Bony, with Burning Water walking behind him, continued. The small crowd ahead appeared not to walk fast enough to please, and another bullet whined uncomfortably over-head and scattered them. With the enemy wide on both flanks, Bony advised the chief of the Wantella Nation who was not too proud to carry a swag. "It was the secret of my illustrious name-sake's great military success. Had we attempted to escape from those people they would have attacked."

Not a little to Bony's surprise, Burning Water chuckled.

"They will be able to choose their battleground before we reach the homestead of The McPherson," he said. "Half way across the plain they will be favoured with plenty of cover. What will you do then?"

"I will decide when we reach the cover you speak of. Mean-while . . . Ah, not quite so close." In excellent imitation of a tram conductor, he added: "Hurry along, please!"

Again he fired and the man who had edged close skipped out of range without loss of time.

In this somewhat unorthodox manner the unusual pair of strangely met men moved out of the foothills and began crossing the plain. As they progressed so the vegetation covering the land changed. At first the road crossed exceptionally wide clay-pans which if joined together would have provided a super speed-track for racing cars. Once across the pans the road "flowed" over slight undulation covered with annual saltbush. The mirage lay heavily, and presently the hills became vast mountains, with water stretching far back along their valleys.

The Illprinka men appeared to be walking on stilts, and the occasional old-man saltbush, ten feet high, seemed to be fifty feet in height. Now and then the road passed close to one of these giant shrubs, forcing Bony and his companion on the march to make a detour of it.

What further astonished Bonaparte this astonishing day was the persistency of the Illprinka men. Their purpose was appar-ently to obtain possession of the attache case, and although only nine in number they showed no nervousness of being attacked by the people of the Wantella. Chief Burning Water walked beside him, carrying the swag as though it were a feather. His eyes were shining and his full lips were expanded in a broad smile. He knew at any given second the approximate position of every Illprinka man, and sometimes he advised that a bullet be "pumped" into this or that bush.

"Are those trees ahead?" Bony asked.

"Yes, oaks. But farther on is a belt of old-man saltbush we'll have to pass through because there is no way round."

"Then let us reach and pass through the belt as soon as possible. Come on, the sun's westering."

They presently entered small and separate belts of oak, and, leaving the road, were able to proceed by skirting these belts. Beyond them the road crossed a further vast area of annual saltbush, and an hour later there grew above the mirage what looked like stately blood-woods a hundred feet high, but which were the old-man saltbush. Into this belt the forms of nine naked black men dissolved.

"There we shall meet their spears," predicted Burning Water. He was quite placid. He seemed to be waiting for Bony to reveal signs of nervousness, or even plain funk.

"How far are we from the homestead?" inquired Bony.

"Two miles."

"And how far through is this belt of old-man saltbush?"

"About half a mile. We must pass through it."

"You appear to be amused at something," Bony softly said, yet abruptly stiff.

"I am waiting to see how wise was Chief Illawalli when he made you one of the great ones among us."

"You are in no position to doubt Illawalli's wisdom," Bony said, icily. "Remember, you advised retreat back in the cabbage-tree camp."

Burning Water became instantly contrite. Bonaparte's blue eyes gleamed and his lips pressed into a thin straight line. Without speaking further, he walked on, Burning Water stalking at his rear a smile once again in his eyes.

Five minutes later they entered the belt of giant shrubs, growing atop small mounds of red sand each had collected. They could provide shelter for an army, yet so spaced were they that a truck could be driven among them without touching a leaf.

"Come on!" Bony cried.

He broke into a steady trotting run, heading to the west for a quarter of a mile, then turning northward and zig-zagging. Following as though he were a trailer attached to a truck, Burning Water ran close and constantly looked back.

Came the first spear. Burning Water shouted: "Look left!" Bony saw the sunlight reflected by the facets of quartz with which the spear was tipped. He saw the weapon turning on its long axis whilst in flight and speeding towards him to intercept him. He checked and the spear passed within a foot of his chest.

He saw the second spear before Burning Water, and the man who launched it from his spear thrower. Bony fired as he ran, but missed: excessive practice is necessary to hit a target with a pistol whilst running. Continuing to zig-zag, sometimes running back over his own tracks, at times making circles, he led Burning Water ever nearer McPherson's Station homestead.

"Down!" shouted Burning Water.

Bony instantly fell forward on his hands, and a spear silently passed over his prostrate body. Up again, he turned and ran fast in the direction from which the weapon had been thrown. His nostrils were quivering. His blood glowed with exquisite fire, for circumstances had temporarily removed the chains of civilized restraint from a nature in which hereditary influences constantly stirred.

He came upon the man who had thrown the last spear in the act of fitting the haft of another into the socket of his wooden thrower. He came upon him suddenly, and so uppermost in him now was his aborigine ancestry, that he forgot the correct use of his automatic pistol. With his left hand he grasped the man's spear, and with the pistol in his right hand smashed the spearman into soggy unconsciousness.

Now with the spear in his free hand, he ran on. It was, perhaps, as well that he did not observe the grin of approbation in the face of the regal man who followed him, like a father following a loved son on a first hunting trip.

Twice Bony fired at vanishing forms. He reloaded the pistol even as he ran, the spear tucked under an arm-pit. His blood was tingling although his breathing rasped from the unaccustomed exertion. No longer was he the hunted; and not long after the first personal encounter he came face to face with the fat and skinny-legged leader.

They almost collided. Bony yelled. The leader shouted. His spear was raised and hurled in action almost as quick as a lightning stroke. Bony thrust his spear as he leaped aside to avoid the other. He yelled again as Skinny-legs took the weapon in his chest.

Suddenly there arose shouts and yells, and sounds of a general conflict all about them. Aborigines appeared on all sides. Nine! They appeared to number ninety, and Bony rushed at the nearest. Then a big hand reached across his right shoulder and bore down the pistol. Another hand reached round his waist and the arm to which it was attached became a gripping vice. There was laughter in the voice of Chief Burning Water when he shouted:

"It is finished. These are my people. They were coming to

see what had made the big smoke from the burning car. Oh, my brother, my son, and my father! You are now to me like The McPherson himself."

The rage went from Bonaparte like water leaking from a cracked glass.

"Old Illawalli was wise, wasn't he?" he asked.

CHAPTER 3

"THE McPHERSON"

THE homestead of McPherson's Station was situated on a shoulder of the higher land bordering the northern edge of the plain on which Bonaparte and his aboriginal companion had met such serious obstruction. Between it and another shoulder westward of it flood-water from the high land had gouged a steep-sided gully, and this deep gully provided an excellent foundation for the massive concrete wall, damming back a practically inexhaustible supply of water.

The homestead itself presented a picture of rugged solidity seldom found in the Interior. The house, surrounded by exceptionally wide verandas, was the centre of a veritable oasis of citrus-trees, grass lawns, rose beds, and a sub-tropical vegetable garden, proving the astounding fertility of the soil—given an abundance of water. The men's quarters, the outhouses and the stockyards, in combination with the house, gave a clear impression of thoroughness in construction.

Sitting at his table desk placed before the window of the station office, the man himself exuded solidity. Seated, he could be mistaken for a big man, for his head was big, his shoulders were thick, and his hands were short-fingered and powerful. Slightly more than fifty years old, his hair was grey as was his moustache. His eyes, made small by fierce sunlight, were grey, too, strength lurking in their depths. The heraldry of his caste lay exhibited on a plain-backed chair—a felt hat with a five-inch brim and a stock-whip having a silver-mounted handle.

Engaged with writing letters, a distant murmur of voices distracted his attention, directed his gaze through the fly-netted window, across the garden of lawn and rose beds, past the old man who was attending to the sprinklers, beyond the fence and downward to the plain where the road disappeared among a growth of tobacco bush. With impatience he clicked his tongue, attempted to continue his writing, failed, and again gazed with greater interest at the large party of aborigines advancing up the road to the homestead.

They were still half a mile away, and again clicking his tongue McPherson used long-distance spectacles the better to understand the unusual excitement. Now he could distinguish individuals, could see walking in front of the crowd Chief Burning Water and beside him a smaller man who was wearing stockmen's clothes.

This man the squatter did not know. He observed that an aborigine following the stranger carried the stranger's swag, and so unusual was a stranger on foot in this Land of Burning Water that he replaced the spectacles in the case and with a cutter proceeded to slice from a plug sufficient tobacco to fill a pipe.

Thereafter he waited, obtaining satisfaction from the speculation the rare advent of a stranger provided. Now he could see the stranger's features with the naked eye, and abruptly he frowned so that his face wore a scowl. Quite still in his chair, he watched the entire party skirt the garden fence and so pass beyond his radius of vision to the clear space eastward of the house.

The scowl vanished when the stranger passed the window on the office veranda, from which he called in soft tones:

"Is anyone there?"

"Come in!" McPherson snapped.

Bony entered the office, to stand just within the fly-netted door. McPherson swung his body in the swivel chair quarter-circle to stare at the stranger. His grey eyes never once blinked as they took in every detail of Bonaparte's dress, every feature of his face.

"Good day!" he said.

"Good day! Mr McPherson?"

"Yes."

The affirmation was more than acknowledgment. There was stiff inquiry in it, the uncompromising attitude of the powerful towards the unknown.

"My name is Napoleon Bonaparte," he explained. Deliberately he made the ensuing pause. Then, as though it were an afterthought barely worthy of mention, he added: "I am a detective-inspector of the Queensland Criminal Investigation Branch."

The statement was sufficiently startling to make the grey eyes blink. It did not, however, affect the voice.

"Oh! You don't look like a police inspector."

"A detective-inspector," Bony corrected. "May I sit down?"

"Eh . . . what!"

"I suggest that you invite me to be seated."

"Oh—ah—yes, certainly. Take that chair. Put the hat and whip on the desk."

"Thank you."

A rising tide of red blood deepened the tanned complexion of the squatter. He felt he had been reproved for lack of manners, and this he did not like. A detective-inspector indeed! Silently, he watched Bonaparte manufacture a cigarette and light it; watched the spent match being placed in the neatly halved and beautifully carved emu egg-shell which served as an ash tray. And then the stranger's clear blue eyes were regarding him.

"I have been in the Queensland Police Force for twenty-two years, Mr McPherson," Bony said, calmly. "I have ranked as inspector for twelve years. Having been asked to conduct an investigation into matters unusual in the Land of Burning Water, matters such as the murder of two stockmen, it was my intention to arrive incognito. Events which have occurred today, however, have resulted in a change of mind."

"Looks as though Sergeant Errey is too damned interfering," McPherson said, harshly. "I can myself deal with the stockmen affair and other annoyances."

"Quite so," Bony agreed. "Annoyances, yes. The killing of aboriginal stockmen is more serious than an annoyance. The somewhat prolonged hostility between the Wantella tribe and the wilder Illprinka blacks has become more than an annoyance to certain public bodies."

"Well, I wish the societies and the police would leave me and my blacks alone to deal with what are our affairs and what I have said are annoyances. My father dealt with many in his time. We are not here living in a flash city, or even within reasonable distance of any police controlled township. My station nowhere joins settled country, as you probably know. Out here a squatter has to be a law to himself. He finds yelling for a policeman is useless, when the nearest policeman is almost a hundred miles away and worked to the bone doing things which are not true police work."

"Still, the times are different from those of, say, twenty years ago," argued Bonaparte.

"The times here are no different from what they were when by father settled here eighty years ago," flashed McPherson. "The trouble among the blacks is their affair, and they can look after it. The theft of my cattle is my affair, and I can attend to that. When the wild blacks who killed my two stockmen are caught they can be handed over to Sergeant Errey. There is no cause for a detective-inspector to come out here to investigate what's plain and above-board."

"Still, those public bodies I mentioned are persistent," Bony pointed out, smiling slightly. "I have here an official communication addressed to Sergeant A. V. Errey, and others whom it may concern. In the circumstances I will open it. It introduces me to Sergeant Errey and others. It gives specific instructions, and it is signed by the Chief Commissioner of Police for South Australia, who has borrowed my services."

The letter was accepted and read by McPherson. He appeared to take longer than was necessary, but other than anger no emotion was betrayed by him. Without comment the letter was passed back to Bonaparte.

"You must have met Sergeant Errey on the road."

"Was that him driving the coupé car?"

"Yes. He left here about twelve, taking with him a black to Shaw's Lagoon for further questioning."

"Indeed! Any other passenger?"

"Only Mit-ji, a Wantella man."

"Sergeant Errey had been out here several days, had he not?"

"Yes, ten days to be accurate. He's a keen man, and he came to go into the matter of the murdered stockmen. Drove the car to a hut forty miles out on the run and from there took to horses."

Bonaparte lit his third cigarette. Then:

"Did he say if he was at all successful in his investigation?"

"I think he had hope that way, but he was fairly close-mouthed. How did you come to miss him on the road?"

Almost unconsciously McPherson's attitude was changing. He was beginning to recognize in Napoleon Bonaparte those qualities Bony had in a flash of time recognized in Chief Burning Water. There was growing in the squatter's mind a conviction that the stranger was all he said he was, and all that was said of him in the undoubtedly genuine letter signed by a Chief Commissioner of Police.

The change was evident not only in McPherson's voice. It was revealed by changing poise. He was becoming cautious.

"I will come back to Errey in a moment," Bony said, quickly, and added with notable deliberateness: "Who out here owns an aeroplane?"

"Who——"

McPherson paused to stare at the stranger to the Land of Burning Water; then his gaze passed to beyond the window.

"An aeroplane! Why, I know of no one who owns an aeroplane. Why?"

Bony's agile mind sought for truth, and found it. This man did not know who owned an aeroplane, but the question created the belief that some particular person could own an aeroplane.

"I have become interested in an aeroplane; fast, a monoplane, painted a uniform silver-grey, and flown by an expert. It came from the west; it returned to the west. What stations are in that direction?"

"None for four hundred and fifty miles. Beyond my western boundary the country is unfenced, virgin. It's all poorish country, able to carry stock only after a winter like we've had this year. It's inhabited only by those Illprinka blacks, and they have caused the trouble here in recent years."

"Well it's most curious," Bony said, lighting yet another cigarette and dropping the burned match into the emu-shell tray. "You know, of course, those cabbage-trees growing beside the road on those hills yonder?"

McPherson nodded.

"I was camped in their shade at noon today eating my lunch, and this is what happened."

Slowly, precisely, Bonaparte related the extraordinary incidents culminating in his meeting with Chief Burning Water. He spoke like an expert police witness although he had never entered a witness-stand since he had risen to the rank of inspector. But while he was speaking he watched the reactions of the man listening to him. These neither pleased nor disappointed; they were the normal reactions of any decent man to a story so terrible.

"So you see," Bony concluded, "while you have a right to regard the theft of your cattle as an annoyance, and, considering the circumstances of your isolation here, can even be permitted to regard the murder of two of your aboriginal stockmen as a matter for your personal attention, this murder of Sergeant Errey falls into a much more serious category, one which rightfully requires the services of a detective-inspector. Who do you think, *might* be flying that machine?"

Bony fancied that McPherson's lips were less coloured with blood, a little grey; but the grey eyes were steady and hard and the voice was brittle.

"I don't know who *might* own such an aeroplane, and if I thought of any who *might* own an aeroplane I would not name him. It would not be just."

Bony bowed his head, and he said:

"I deserve that reproof, Mr McPherson. To resume. Two points regarding the murderous attack on Sergeant Errey are obvious. First: the pilot knew that Errey was leaving today for Shaw's Lagoon. Second: he was sufficiently well practised in dropping bombs to hit two targets in succession—the trees beneath which I was camped, and Errey's car which was moving. There are, too, excellent grounds for a supposition."

Here Bony swiftly related the arrival of the Illprinka men and their subsequent attack on him and Burning Water.

"It looks as though those Illprinka men were purposely camped not far from the gully into which the burning car rolled; that they were detailed, as it were, to be in readiness to remove anything which escaped destruction. The leader betrayed as much when he insisted that I gave him Errey's attache case. If this is all true, then the pilot is in league with the Illprinka tribe. Do you know of any white man living away out in that open country?"

"No, I do not," instantly came the reply, and Bony was satisfied. "Those blacks are getting beyond endurance. Did my people capture any of them?"

"One, I think. I clubbed him with my pistol. Another, the leader, was killed, if memory serves me. He was an evil fellow, anyway, and he tried hard to kill me."

A gong at the rear of the house was struck, evidently announcing dinner. McPherson rose to his feet as though he had been impatiently waiting to hear it. He stood staring down at the still-seated Bonaparte who again observed that occasionally the squatter could not mask his thinking. His problem was how to place as a guest a half-caste detective-inspector—accept him into his house, or have him conducted to the men's quarters. Quite clearly Bony saw it: saw, too, the decision when it was made.

McPherson on his feet was less physically imposing. His legs were short and bowed by much riding. He said briskly:

"You had better come and be introduced to my niece who has

run the place since my mother died. Where did you leave your swag?"

"Out at the back of the office."

"It'll be all right there. I'll have it taken to your room later on. Any luggage at Shaw's Lagoon?"

"Two suitcases. I left them at the police-station. I see you have a telephone, but I saw no line along the road. Are you in touch with Shaw's Lagoon?"

"Yes, the wire is laid more direct. Want to ring now?"

"Please, I must communicate with the police-station."

CHAPTER 4

THE McPHERSON'S JUSTICE

McPHERSON conducted Bony from the office to the south veranda of the big bungalow-style house, and through what evidently was the main door into the hall. This hall amazed Bonaparte. Never in any station homesteads had he seen a hall so richly furnished —not even in those mansions, designated homesteads, he had visited on the sheep farms near Sydney and Melbourne. Tapestries illustrating Scottish battles hung from the walls. A grandfather clock lorded it in a corner. Broadswords and claymores rested on the arms of a teak rack. Jacobean settees and chairs and small tables flanked the gleaming parquet floor of darkened mulga.

From a passage at the end of the hall appeared a girl whose coiled hair was as black as his own, whose eyes were as blue as his own, whose skin was the texture of the white roses decorating the lawn outside. She was of medium height, under thirty years old, and wore a plain black dress the severe cut of which appeared to enhance her striking charm of face and figure. A further surprise was given by McPherson:

"Flora, allow me to present to you Detective-Inspector Bonaparte. Inspector, my niece, Miss McPherson."

Bony bowed in grand manner. The somewhat stilted form of introduction was made quite naturally, and his mind remarked it.

"I ask your pardon for my somewhat war-worn appearance,

Miss McPherson," he said, gravely, but with a distinct twinkle in his eyes. "I left Shaw's Lagoon as a stockman seeking employment. Circumstances, and the kindness of your uncle, have transformed me to a senior police officer. I possess a braided uniform, a pair of beautiful gloves, a walking stick, and a peaked hat; but alas, my wife has never permitted the regalia to leave the tissue paper in which it was received from the tailors and outfitters."

He was not sure, but he suspected a responding twinkle in her eyes. She did not smile when she said:

"I am happy to meet you, Inspector Bonaparte. I saw you arrive with Burning Water. Your coming has caused much excitement."

"I was almost overwhelmed by the welcome extended to me," Bony stated, the twinkle still evident to her.

Now she smiled, saying:

"The blacks are like children—in many things."

"The Inspector will be staying for a few days, dear," McPherson cut in. "His luggage is being brought in by Price who is leaving at once. Should be here by half-past eight. I suggest that dinner be delayed."

"As you wish, uncle. I will see that Ella prepares the room next the bathroom for Mr Bonaparte. Oh, and perhaps, Mr Bonaparte you would like a cup of tea?"

"It would be a really valuable gift—after a shower."

"Of course, and a drink before the shower would be another," she said, laughing at him. "Uncle, attend to our guest and be your charmingest. We have so few guests, Mr Bonaparte, that we cannot afford to neglect them."

Bony bowed again, less grandly, and McPherson led the way to the dining-room, and yet again Bony was astonished and betrayed it only with a narrowing of the eyelids.

He followed his host to a massive Jacobean sideboard which must have weighed a ton. Only with effort did he prevent his interest becoming vulgar. The long table was set for two, tall hard-wax candles set in silver sconces were ready to shed soft light on silver and cut glass. Full-length portraits in oils of men dressed in tartan and kilt were suspended from the walls, iron-faced men with prominent jaws and small blue or grey eyes, men with faces reddened, not by the sun of Central Australia, but by the keen winds of the Scottish Highlands.

Bony surveyed them above the rim of his glass.

"Your ancestors?" he inquired.

McPherson nodded, saying

"Everything here was brought from Scotland by my father and mother. That is he above the fireplace. I had it done by a man in Melbourne from one of those old daguerrotype pictures. They were all a tough crowd, the McPhersons. Just fancy a man, with his wife, coming right out here when the advance of settlement was only just this side of the Diamantina. They brought all their possessions on three bullock wagons. You know anything about furniture?"

"Next to nothing. Jacobean, isn't it?"

"So they told me. I don't know anything about furniture, except what I've seen in the homesteads on the way to the railway. We still use the iron kettles and pans and things the old people brought with them. Tough. Humph! I often wish I was a quarter as tough. Well, I'll show you to your room and the bathroom, and leave you, as I've work to do before dinner. There's what we call the library if you're interested in books."

The bedroom was in keeping with the hall and the dining-room. Towels lay over a brass handrail. The narrow bed was monastic. There was no floor covering. There was one strikingly discordant note—a gaudy dressing-gown and a pair of blue leather slippers waiting on a chair and the floor. The squatter noticed these articles, and grunted.

"That gown and the slippers were left here by a visitor," he explained, irritably. "Don't think I'd select such colours for my-self. I'll leave you. You know where to find things, and the maid will bring tea—if she hasn't discarded her clothes and gone back to her tribe. And don't worry about your clothes at dinner. I've never dressed for dinner since my mother passed on."

"I have a reasonably respectable coat in my swag which will conceal my working shirt," Bony said, adding: "Above table I will appear, well, not naked. I am going to thank you now for the hospitality you have extended to me, and express the wish that I shall have your assistance in my work."

"I will do what I can." McPherson was facing the window and Bony observed the smallness of his eyes. "Why did you tell Price just now that Errey had met with an accident?"

"Because the town exchange is not in an official Post Office, and the manner in which poor Errey met his death cannot be made public for the present. I had another reason. I never tolerate interference with an investigation I have begun, and you can imagine the result of the destruction of Errey and his car did it become public. There would be a half-squadron of Air Force machines sent to find that mysterious plane, and then you and I and the blacks would have to go and find the Air Force pilots forced down in that open country."

"You intend to keep it dark, even from Price?"

"I intend to keep the matter dark from the outside public until I can say: "Sergeant Errey was murdered in such and such a manner and this is the man who killed him and his aboriginal passenger."

"You first have to arrest the killer."

Bony's eyes widened, and the squatter winced as though the light in the blue eyes gazing at him was a weapon. Bony's voice was metallic when he boasted:

"I shall not fail to bring Errey's murderer to justice."

"You will if the Wantella justice reaches him first. The crime was committed on Wantella land, and the Wantella blacks thought highly of Sergeant Errey."

Left to himself, Bony passed to the window from which a sectional view of the dam wall could be seen. He was not interested in the view, however. His brain demanded opportunity to think, to adjust thought to the unusual. For the first time in his career Bonaparte was thrown off his balance.

He surveyed the incidents of this day, the people he had met. Only the girl appeared normal. Burning Water was slightly abnormal. More so was this Donald McPherson. They would have to be pinned for close examination, like butterflies pinned as to a board and examined through a glass by a naturalist. There would be time later for that—after his body was refreshed.

Turning away from the window, he picked up the dressing-gown. The trace of bewilderment in his eyes gave place to an expression of pleasure, for one carefully restrained inhibition had been admiration for colours in clothes. Ah! Those beautiful ties and socks he had put away in favour of more conservative colours!

The shafts of the setting sun slanting through the open French windows rested on the gown, illuminated its glories. In such a room and in such a house, it was a sheer monstrosity. Its basic colour was a bright yellow and on the base were laid bars of purple and squares of Cambridge blue. What kind of guest had he been who selected such a combination of colours even in a dressing-gown? And the slippers! They were of soft doeskin leather. They had long pointed Eastern toes. Their colour was sky-blue.

Slippers and gown he carried to the bathroom: when he returned he was wearing both and carrying his clothes.

His swag had been placed on a chair, and on a small table were tea and cakes. He now felt refreshed both physically and mentally, and, with a sigh of contentment, he sat in a chair beside the table he placed in front of the long dressing-mirror. And in that mirror, which, too, was slightly out of place, he surveyed himself, admired himself in Joseph's coat, and ate and drank.

What a gown! What slippers! What a room! What a house! What an investigation awaited him! He could not command his mind whilst encompassed by those alluring colours.

On the floor he unrolled his swag and took from it clean underwear and shaving tools. Again he went to the bathroom, and afterwards dressed, putting on a neat dark-grey serge coat over the clean khaki shirt. Now he felt better, and the clamour in his mind insisted that he hide the dressing-gown beneath the bed pillows and the slippers beneath the bed. He sat down again on the chair to begin the manufacture of a cigarette. Began, for not then did he complete the task. In a flash he was on his hands and knees beside the unrolled swag.

Sergeant Errey's small attache case he had so carefully rolled in the swag before leaving the camp of the cabbage-trees, had vanished.

The shock succeeded, when past efforts had failed, in restoring his mind to calm normality. He recalled clearly that minute of time in which he had placed the attache case on top of the unrolled blankets and then carefully had rolled and strapped the swag without possibility of case, or any other article, falling from it.

Beyond this fine homestead, beyond the painted Land of Burning Water, lay a shadow as black as night, a shadow in which flickered the flame of human emotions and passions. Flame in the shadow! It was there, all right. He could feel the heat of the flame in the chill of the shadow.

What had Chief Burning Water said? Why, he had said: "We have seen what we ought not to have seen." Why did he say that, if he did not know that those Illprinka blacks were present to remove anything not destroyed by the fire: if he did not at least suspect they were acting on the orders of the pilot? That would more than hint he knew, or suspected, a particular man to be the pilot of the aeroplane.

Then McPherson had said just before he had left' that very room: "You will (fail) if the Wantella justice reaches him first. The crime was committed on Wantella land, and the Wantella blacks thought highly of Sergeant Errey." What lay behind that? Was it not the betrayal of knowledge, or suspicion, coinciding with that contained in Chief Burning Water's statement? If those two men did not know the pilot of the aeroplane, then both of them based on other facts a good guess.

The house and its owner were not normal here on the edge of Central Australia. Chief Burning Water was abnormal, because of his long and close association with the McPhersons. McPherson was a travesty, a problem. He offered hospitality like a man not wanting to but unable to refuse. There was no warmth in him. Even his temper was not warm. He did not speak with the easy freedom of the bushman, and that seemed to be natural in him and not the evidence of fear. Only the girl was warm and human and open; but even she presented a problem.

Without the slightest hesitation she had accepted him as her uncle's guest, when he had appeared to her travel-stained, escorted by aborigines to the homestead instead of arriving on horseback or by car. She had evinced no hostility towards his mid-race; had accepted him without question.

Bony's subsequent actions might have led an observer to form the opinion that his mentality was not normal. His eyes became brilliant orbs of blue radiating light. On his dark face was a smile more of gloating than amusement.

Snatching the dressing-gown from under the pillow he held it to his faintly quivering nostrils. Then he donned the garment, stood before the mirror, and turned himself to view the picture from every angle.

"Let me tabulate my emotions," he murmured to the reflection in the mirror. "My brain feels stimulated. My spirit seems to be something light within me, something I can feel. It is as though I were intoxicated, and I'm sure this particular reaction is not due to the glass of lager I drank in the dining-room. Nor is it due to the prospect of solving a profound mystery. No. No! It is due to the gown itself. It is the kind of gown I would buy for myself—if I were not university educated, if I were not an inspector of detectives."

Sighing, he removed the garment and again hid it beneath the pillow. Although certain the missing attache case was not among the articles of his swag he removed them all, before rolling up the swag and pushing it under the bed.

He was still on his knees when, through the open windows, came a human cry of distress. It was like a spring lifting him to his feet. Tensed, he listened. He heard now the sound like a man's face being slapped, and this sound was instantly followed by another cry of distress. Out on the veranda, he again listened.

For the third time the cry was uttered; and now he knew it came from the stockyards beyond the men's quarters.

His room faced west. He stepped off the veranda, followed a garden path made of termite nests, skirted the detached kitchen and wash-house, and passed through a gate, to cross the open sandy ground to the long building, in the door frame of which was standing a white man dressed as a cook.

Beyond the men's quarters, Bony saw over against the rails of the stockyard, a crowd of aborigines. Their backs were towards him. Among them was he whose cries answered the sound of face slapping. Then the group abruptly split asunder and Bony saw the duck-clad figure of the squatter. Then, like Jonah being spewed from the mouth of the whale, there shot from the centre a naked figure, who raced with astonishing speed along the northern fence of the garden, over the concrete wall of the dam, to disappear among the bloodwoods.

Towards Bonaparte came Chief Burning Water and Mr Donald McPherson, coiling his stockwhip. He said:

"There goes one of your late enemies, Inspector. I have been administering the McPherson justice. It is always better to flog than to hang. Hanging doesn't hurt."

CHAPTER 5

THE THREAT

MR DONALD MCPHERSON and his guest sat in cane chairs on the south veranda. The sunset colours had drained from the plain, lying two hundred feet below the house, and from the sky which now was a uniform pall relieved by the stars. Save for the croaking of bullfrogs by the dam it was very quiet.

"The blacks have buried the body of that Illprinka man killed this afternoon," the squatter said.

"I know nothing about any body that required to be buried," Bony lied, calmly. "Do you often flog an aborigine?"

"Very, very seldom. Chief Burning Water takes care of minor delinquents. He can hit hard. I taught him to box."

"He's an unusual man."

"He's outstanding among an unusual race. We grew up together. My father would not send me to a city school. He brought out tutors, three of them. They were all Scotch. Every one of them could recite all the poems of Burns, and they knew everything there is to be known about the tartans. They brought me up on Sir Walter Scott and the tenets of the kirk, and having made me an expert with the three R's, my father took me in hand with the rules of business and keeping books. In many ways my father was shrewd and long-sighted—if he hadn't been, he wouldn't have survived here—but on one point he was not just to his only son.

"By keeping me back from school down in a city where I would have rubbed shoulders with other boys and have gained a balanced outlook on life, he didn't serve me too well. I never went off the place till I was twenty-two, and then it was to accompany the overseer and half a dozen blacks with cattle to what used to be called Hergott Springs, and from there down to Port Augusta.

"The only friend I had in my youth, in fact the only friend I've ever had is Burning Water. He's three years my junior. My mother, who saw the want of a companion for her son, interested herself in Burning Water, and he proved worthy of her interest. What the tutors taught me I handed on to Burning Water. What I did, he had to do. My father took a great liking to him, and eventually he lived here as one of the family."

"And yet he went back to his own people," Bony said.

"He did, and he went back for a particular reason. When I became a man I was sealed into the tribe, and after Burning Water was made a man by his people we used to talk about the blacks a great deal. You see, I was, to all intents and purposes, brought up with them. I understood them, and through me Burning Water came to recognize what was good in our civilization and what was bad.

"Under the last head man, the tribe became loose and slovenly in obedience to its own laws and customs, and when he died, Burning Water decided to make himself head man and pull the tribe together. He and I both knew that the road to extinction was sign-posted by disregard for customs and contempt for laws. Burning Water felt he had a mission. Come to think of it, it is a damned fine mission."

Bony rolled a cigarette. "And he has succeeded?"

"There's no doubt about it. He pulled the tribe together in less than six months. He modelled himself on my father, for whom he had great affection and respect. He said to me one day: 'What is the secret of life? The answer is, discipline. You white folk are strong because you know discipline. My people have become like a mob of steers because they have lost the discipline imposed by the laws and customs created for them in the Alchuringa. I must force them to respect the laws and follow the customs, so that they will become men and women and not just eating beasts.' That he has done."

Bony said. "Do you think it possible he had fore-knowledge of the attack on Errey's car."

"Of course not." McPherson spoke angrily. "Burning Water thought a lot of Errey, and Errey considered him a personal friend. Used to talk to Burning Water for hours about the aboriginal beliefs and customs. Burning Water often goes off alone. You see, it's part of his job to visit the tribe's sacred storehouses, and to keep an eye generally on the tribe's land."

"And has he had much trouble with the Illprinka tribe?"

"Not till recently. They became troublesome about six years ago. You know much about the blacks?"

Bony laughed, saying, as he stared at the void masking the fragrant garden and the plain beyond it:

"Enough to be convinced of how little I do know. Ah—there's Price's car!"

"Yes. He's about where those cabbage-trees are. It'll be too dark for him to see the wreckage of Errey's car. . . . Oh yes, the blacks are a damn sight wiser than we are. My father liked them, but he took a strong line with them. He had his troubles, you know. There were mother and my sister and me, the baby, and only two other white men and the wife of one of them. They were all here for years.

"The old man had a triangle put up. He didn't shoot the blacks when they got out of hand. He didn't poison them or hang them. He flogged them. Always said flogging hurt more than hanging. and that a live black was more useful than a dead one. I've never had to flog one since Burning Water became chief. The fellow today doesn't count. He was an Illprinka man."

"Do you use them as stockmen much?"

"A great deal. I employ a white overseer who lives with his wife and family at the out-station, a white men's cook, and the old fellow you probably saw tending to the sprinklers. Other than those three all the work is done by the blacks. My mother used to train the young lubras to housemaid and cook, and my niece carries on with breaking them into house service." McPherson sighed. "But you know how it is. Without warning a girl will vanish leaving her clothes behind, to be seen next day with the tribe. You can't manage these people."

"What about Burning Water?"

"Yes, perhaps I was too sweeping. Nevertheless, there is a part of them you can't change. It might be because they're too human. Well, Price ought to be here in twenty minutes."

"How long has Price been stationed at Shaw's Lagoon?"

"Two years. He's a good man, intelligent. How do you intend to work with him?"

"With reserve—until I am sure of him. This is my investigation and I will not let up on it until I have put a rope round the neck of that pilot. I will not brook interference from Price, or from anyone else. I shall tell Price that the steering gear of Errey's car failed when it was rounding a bend, that it crashed against the hillside, caught fire, and then rolled down into the gully. By the way, is there a tracker attached to the police station?"

"No," replied McPherson. "When the police want a tracker they ring me. Burning Water won't permit any of his men to stay in Shaw's Lagoon. I wish that blasted pilot would crash somewhere out in the open country."

"Oh, why?" mildly inquired Bony.

"Because I don't want publicity outside, you understand. It wouldn't do me or the station or the blacks an iota of good. The annoyances to which they and I have been subjected are our affair, and we always have been capable of settling our own affairs without fuss."

There were grounds for the squatter's objection to the publicity such a murder of a police officer would obtain, because Bony was confident that the pilot of the airplane was behind the theft of McPherson's cattle, the murder of two Wantella blacks, and other crimes. He now understood, a little more clearly, the mind of this man sitting with him.

That insistence on being able to look after "their" own affairs; that insistence that even the crime of killing was an annoyance, more than hinted that McPherson was jealous of the police and of police protection. Bony thought he could now understand the cause of McPherson's hostility to any restrictions imposed from outside his own land save only those imposed by financial institutions. The man had been born of people still imbued with the idea of feudal rights and obligations, and all his life he had been cut off from advancing thought. He had stayed still, locked away out here; perhaps had never been to a city.

"I suppose you go occasionally down to one of the cities for a holiday?" he asked the squatter.

"Only once. I went to Sydney. Had a headache all the time I was there. Couldn't sleep. Couldn't even think properly. I came home again after a week. To me it was like being in a madhouse."

"But Miss McPherson——"

"Flora goes to Melbourne for the first three months of every year. She's different. She was brought up in a city, but she likes being here with us, all the same. Here's Price."

Bony accompanied the squatter to welcome the constable, and the three proceeded at once to the office, where Price asked:

"Sergeant Errey—how is he, sir?"

This policeman was a man. He possessed McPherson's jaw, but he was bigger, quicker in movement. His mind worked more swiftly as could be seen in his tanned clean-shaven face and keen hazel eyes. He was dynamic and efficient. His manner of addressing Bony obviously impressed the squatter.

"First, here are my credentials." Bony murmured.

Price's fleeting smile was a shade grim.

"Following what you stated at the station four days ago, sir, I checked up through divisional headquarters. I shall be glad to render any assistance I can. But Sergeant Errey——"

"I greatly regret, Price, to say that Sergeant Errey is dead," Bony cut in. Swiftly he told the story of the "accident." "He had with him a passenger, a Wantella black named Mit-ji, who also perished."

Price's lean face revealed his horror.

"It doesn't seem possible," he slowly said.

"I know," Bony almost whispered. "Still, that's how it is. It appears that Errey was taking the black, Mit-ji, to Shaw's Lagoon, for further questioning concerning the murder of two aboriginal stockmen. I will continue, not from where Errey left off but from where he began. You will have the sad duty of dealing with the wreckage and the bodies."

"Were you the only witness?" Price asked.

"Yes. I will write my statement before you leave. I would like you to defer the inquest as long as you possibly can. I have several reasons for asking that. Er—I will be making my report to your Chief Commissioner, which you might post for me on your return to the township."

"Very well sir."

"I have a favour to ask of you, too. I don't like to be addressed as 'sir,' 'Inspector'—if you like, but I prefer merely the abbreviated name 'Bony.' You see, Price, I'm not a real policeman."

"Tell me," Bony proceeded, "is there a squatter inside your district, or outside it, who flies an aeroplane?"

"An aeroplane! No. We have a visit from the Flying Doctor sometimes. His headquarters are at Birdsville, three hundred miles away."

"Indeed! What kind of a machine is it?"

"Monoplane. A new one. Had it only six months."

"What is its colour?"

Price frowned. Then:

"Light grey, I think. Yes, light grey."

"Not a silver-grey. Kindly be definite on the point of colour —if you are able."

The constable pondered, again frowned.

"No, I don't think it's silver-grey. I saw the machine only once—two months ago. Why, Mr McPherson, probably you can answer the Inspector. Dr Whyte visited you that time."

Bony glanced at the squatter. McPherson had been standing in the door frame, his back to them. Now he turned to answer Price.

"Dr Whyte's machine is a light grey in colour," he said. "Yes, he was here two months ago. Came to see my niece, not me. They met in Melbourne last year. If you're ready we'd better go over for dinner. It's getting late."

On the way across to the house, Bony said to Price:

"Is this Doctor Whyte a good pilot?"

"Yes, Inspector, and a good doctor, too."

Flora McPherson warmly welcomed the constable, and Bony instantly saw another facet of her character in this meeting of youth with youth. This evening she was wearing a semi-evening gown of French-grey ninon and her hair was done in a style less severe. She smiled at him; but it was to the policeman she offered her arm.

Bonaparte was destined never to forget that meal, served by efficient aboriginal girls, smartly dressed even to silk stockings and shoes. There were two serving direct from the kitchen; and although in the morning they might be missing and found in the camp as the good Lord made them, they disproved the lie that these people cannot be trained.

Bony was not displeased that Price and their hostess conducted the conversation and that McPherson was taciturn and answered questions monosyllabically. He was still feeling like a man bushed and the gleaming table and soft light, the smooth service and the atmosphere of solidity and security, failed to banish from his mind the array of grim men who watched from the canvassed walls.

Flame in the shadow!

On what was McPherson pondering? His replies to questions were abrupt; once he made an affirmative answer by mistake. Had *he* taken Errey's attache case from the swag, to destroy the dead sergeant's notes on the murder of the two stockmen? Both he and Burning Water must be held suspect of knowing who *might* be the murderous pilot. Well, after preliminary probings here at the homestead, he would have to go out to that hut and endeavour to follow Errey's trail. Yes, up to the point when Errey decided to take Mit-ji to Shaw's Lagoon.

Mit-ji—ah—yes, Mit-ji. Mit-ji knew something about those murders; otherwise Errey wouldn't have arrested him. Mit-ji was probably in league with the Illprinka men, because the stockmen had been murdered during the theft of a large number of McPherson's cattle. Supposing the theft of cattle was connected in some way with the pilot of the aeroplane, as seemed likely since the machine had come from, and returned to, the country of the Illprinka. Then supposing that the pilot had destroyed Errey's car, not for the purpose of killing the sergeant but for the purpose of silencing Mit-ji?

The theft of the cattle and the killing of the aborigines who guarded them at first appeared all black. The murder of Sergeant Errey by a man flying an aeroplane appeared all white. Yet the last might have been dependent on the first, and the two together partly white and partly black.

It was going to be a really good investigation, he was sure. He was pleased now that he had decided not to present Price with the real facts of the death of Errey and Mit-ji. Price appeared in an excellent light; a man eminently suited to his particular job which was much nearer the administrative side of police government, than "pinching drunks."

Then, of course he, Bonaparte, had as usual his old ally, time. There was plenty of time to conduct the investigation, which would have to include two separate cases of crime appearing to have a joint origin. . . .

Probably because of his non-participation in the conversation, Bony was the first to hear the sound of a distant aeroplane engine. One of the two aboriginal maids was standing at his side, offering a dish when he heard the faint and somehow sinister sound. He turned slightly sideways, the better to look up into her face to ascertain if she, too, had heard this sound.

None of the others saw the quick clash of gaze, the swift understanding of a man and a woman. Bony knew then that the lubra knew the truth concerning Mit-ji's death with Errey, as did probably every aborigine within hundreds of miles. He saw in the big black eyes naked fear.

Flora McPherson was speaking to Price and her uncle of the possible assistance which might be rendered the widowed woman in Shaw's Lagoon. McPherson was saying he would do anything suggested.

"Pardon me, everyone," Bony said, his voice clear and quick. "Mr McPherson, I hear the approach of an aeroplane. I suggest that all lights are extinguished."

"Why on earth——?" began the girl.

"Yes," snapped the squatter. "Out with those lights."

Bony bent over the table and blew out the candles in the sconces. McPherson jumped to his feet and strode to the lamp on the sideboard.

The room now was illuminated only by the reflection of a light in the passage without, and Bony saw the tall figure of the squatter for a moment. Then that light vanished, and McPherson could be heard shouting for all lights to be put out.

Price was demanding to know this and that, supported by Flora McPherson. Bony moved to the open French windows, through which quite plainly came the noise of the oncoming machine. Through the windows passed the half-caste, across the wide veranda and down the steps of the rose-bedded lawn. The stars were bright. The night air was soft, warm and laden with rose scent. The croaking of the frogs by the great dam of water was banished by the rising roar of engine exhausts. Bony went on between the small beds of standard roses, managed to escape the arms of the sprinklers, and stopped when he reached the bottom fence. There he stared into the night.

Presently he saw it. It had no navigation lights. It was flying at a great height beyond the dam, and when it began to turn in a giant circle Bony knew that the pilot had sighted the dull star-reflecting sheen of the water and had picked up his land-mark.

He was coming down. The sudden decrease of engine power told that. The plane became a shadow passing across the faces of the stars, and because it appeared lower than it actually was, it seemed to Bonaparte that its descent in giant circles was much prolonged. It drifted out over the plain, vanished, reappeared, coming to pass directly over the house. But no, it passed over the dam, its engine breaking into periodic bursts of power which finally became sustained.

Now the plane was away to the north, beyond the sky-cutting edge of the house roof. That the pilot had nerve to fly at night was proved. That he had complete confidence in his engine and his instruments was proved, too. The roar swiftly increased. It was approaching the house. Bony waited, no fear in his heart, only a fierce desire in his mind to identify the machine with that from which Errey's car had been bombed.

Then the roof edge, silhouetted against the sky, was abruptly blurred by the shape of wings and dragon-fly body. The plane was a bare five hundred feet from the ground, and the thunderous song of its engine deafened the staring Bony, who was confident it was the same machine he had seen at noon. His feet registered a slight shock. A missile had struck the ground close to him. He knew its position, and he flung himself down and waited. No explosion came.

Possibly it was not a bomb, but a message! If it should be a message of some kind, then Bony simply had to have it. On his hands and knees he moved forward to the approximate position of the missile, fear now a stabbing torment. The arrival of McPherson on the veranda drove him on. The squatter was asking for him. Price was wanting to know why the lights had been put out, and the girl was saying that perhaps the pilot of the machine was urgently looking for a landing place.

Then Bony's hand came in contact with the "bomb." It was a treacle tin with an air-tight lid. The force of the concussion with the ground had forced off the lid, and from the tin opening lay a ridge of fine sand. It had been filled with sand—and a sheet of paper.

Bony pocketed the paper. The tin he emptied of the remaining sand, and hastily buried it, with the lid, in a rose bed. Then he strolled towards the house, murmuring:

"All things are for the brave—even a big slice of luck."

But his heart was a thudding hammer in his chest.

CHAPTER 6

BONY IS PERSISTENT

IT was after midnight when the squatter and Bony said goodnight to Price on the road above the gully, in which lay the remains of a modern car and two men. Price drove on to Shaw's Lagoon: Bony and his host returned to the homestead, which they reached shortly before one o'clock.

"Well, I suggest a peg, and then bed," McPherson said.

"I find that suggestion good," Bony agreed quietly. "I too will make one: that we have the peg in the office. There are a number of questions I would like settled before I go to bed. Otherwise I will probably not sleep for worrying about them."

"Hope they won't be many," the squatter objected, almost rudely. "I'm tired—and sick."

"So am I—which is another reason why I don't wish to go to bed yet. Memory is the devil at times."

"Humph! . . . All right. You go into the office and light the lamp. I'll get the drinks."

McPherson found Bony making cigarettes, the number of which did not appear to indicate an early retirement. There were four cigarettes already made, each with the "hump" in the middle, all lying in a row. Bony did not look up until he had rolled the fifth cigarette and placed it beside the fourth. Near to the cigarettes McPherson set down the tray.

"Just help yourself," he said. "I feel like a good stiffener."

"So do I, although I seldom drink," Bony confessed. "I find alcohol blurs my mind, not exhilarates it. Ah—well! I think we both have an excellent excuse tonight. That pilot did his foul work efficiently. I can hardly think he is that Dr Whyte who visited here two months ago. Is there a romance, do you know?"

"Er—Yes, I believe so. Whyte seems a decent man, but not good enough for Flora. No man would be."

Bony drank and then lit his first cigarette. There was no hint of levity when he said:

"On several occasions I have been sentimental to the extent of defying red tape and regulations and that kind of thing. I have a failing for match-making—or I ought to say clinching a match I have asked Price to get in touch with Dr Whyte. I want the doctor to pay a visit here in the near future."

"Oh!" McPherson slowly exclaimed.

"Yes. You see, I hope to persuade him to take me up in his machine. I'd like much to have a look over all that open country to the west. Somewhere in that open country that renegade pilot must have his headquarters—a shed for his plane, petrol supply, which is doubtless replenished by a truck transporting the oil. And a truck leaves tracks to be seen easily from the air. Price spoke highly of Sergeant Errey. I have a duty towards the sergeant's widow and son."

"And that is?"

"To set that pilot on the road which ends at an open trapdoor. You know, there are killers and killers. I could discourse on them for an hour. All fall, roughly, into three classes, the worst by far being that claiming the cold, clever, deliberate murderer. Cold, clever and deliberate is that pilot. He killed Errey because Errey had found out too much. Or he killed Mit-ji because he feared Mit-ji would betray him. He couldn't kill either without the other; and it made no difference to him how many he killed. How old was Mit-ji?"

"Six years older than Burning Water."

"Did Errey bring him in from the camp of the murdered stockmen?"

"Yes. There were the three of them. He managed to escape when the Illprinka blacks raided the camp and speared the others."

"The two killed—were they old men, too?"

"Oh no; both were young. The lubra of one told Errey, so Burning Water tells me, that Mit-ji was an accomplice of the raiders, that she often had seen him sitting alone by a little fire sending messages, and that the night the attack was made he was not in the camp. Can't blame the lubra for talking to Errey. A black girl can love as passionately as a white woman."

"Yes, that is so," Bony agreed slowly, staring hard at the squatter. "What you say of Mit-ji indicates that he was disloyal to his own tribe. There may be other traitors. You really have no idea who that airman might be?"

McPherson answered in the negative by shaking his head. He did not look at the questioner.

"Forgive me for being a bore so late at night, but I have so much to accomplish before next week," Bony continued. There were now four cigarettes remaining on the table. "Forgive me, too, for being unpardonably inquisitive. The vice is born early in all journalists—and detectives. Now we know one facet of the character of the man who killed Errey and Mit-ji. He is an expert pilot and, too, an expert bomber. I understand that this Doctor Whyte was in the Royal Air Force during the latter portion of the Great War. That's by the way, however.

"A man doesn't take grave risks without just cause. This unknown pilot took risks when he attacked the car, and he took risks when he flew over this house earlier this evening. Although he did everything he could to make himself sure there would be no witnesses of his destruction of Errey and the black, he certainly accepted the risk of being observed. Therefore, his motive for killing those two in the car was powerful. If it were not then the fellow must be a lunatic.

"What was his motive for the double murder? I believe this to be a question easily answered. His motive was to destroy evidence against himself for complicity in another crime—that resulting in the killing of your two stockmen. He knew that Errey had obtained evidence, or he feared that Errey would obtain evidence through the mind of Mit-ji.

"I find support for this theory in the fact that Australian aborigines do not run off with cattle in the mass. I know of only one instance in history when an aborigine stole stock wholesale, and, like Burning Water, he was outstanding. I refer, of course, to the Black Squatter, a Victorian native who, in the early days of settlement, compelled his tribe to drove off mobs of sheep to stock a portion of tribal land still left from the robbing white men.

"That the pilot of the aeroplane is directly connected with the murder of your stockmen, the theft of your cattle, totalling some three thousand, the unrest of the Wantella tribe and boldness of the wilder blacks, the Illprinka, is a theory one can be pardoned for believing to be a fact."

There now were but three cigarettes lying on the table. Bony, unusually indulgent, helped himself to whisky and water.

"I am, Mr McPherson, conscious of your difficulty in accepting me for an inspector attached to the Criminal Investigation Branch of the Queensland Police Department. Price is experiencing the same difficulty. However, I can assure you that I was not raised to my present rank through political or social influence. My birth was a serious bar, and, to achieve eminence in my profession, I had to prove myself not only worthy of it, but doubly so. This is a democratic country—I don't think!

"As a policeman I am a fearful failure; but as an investigator

I am a success. I fail as a policeman because my mind refuses to be confined within prison bars of red tape. But I am what I am because—well, because I am Napoleon Bonaparte.

"Now, at the beginning of my investigation here, I find that the murder of Sergeant Errey and Mit-ji is the culmination of a series of outrages committed against you. I mean, the culmination of the series to date; for that air pilot will strike again and again until I finalize his career of crime.

"From what you have told me of your history, and from what I have learned through preliminary inquiries, together with the result of study of your circumstances, I can well understand your attitude of hostility to what you regard as outside interference. Such hostility, however, cannot prevent me from finalizing my investigation. Please tell me, who is that airman?"

There followed a profound silence. McPherson's gaze was directed to the remaining cigarettes on the table. There were but two. His face angled upward and his cold grey eyes stared at the slighter man lounging easily in his chair. The full grey moustache actually bristled, whilst rising blood reddened still deeper the sun-reddened complexion of his face. Then with swift violence his hand rose, and the clenched fist crashed upon the table. His head was thrust towards Bonaparte like that of a mongoose attacking a snake. His voice, when he spoke, was low, but vibrating with passion.

"I tell you I don't know," he said. "If you call me a liar, I'll fetch my people to tie you, and I'll flog you as I flogged that Illprinka man. When I say a thing I'm finished with saying it."

"Well, then, let us pass to another subject," Bony compromised, but with an icy gleam in his eyes. "Tell me about Miss Flora McPherson and this Doctor Whyte."

"I know next to nothing about Whyte. Flora is my sister's only child and she came here after my mother died. Do you want to know how much money I've got in the bank?"

"I wouldn't ask you that," Bony said, quietly. "If it were necessary for me to know, I would find out—through other channels. No, I don't wish to know how much money you have in the bank. I would, however, like to know why you find yourself unable to be frank with me."

"Blast you! I'm being as frank as I intend to be with a damned, interfering, half-caste detective. And now I'm going to bed."

"Very well, then," Bony said quickly, and McPherson made no move to retire to bed. "Tell me why you refused to launch a prosecution six years ago, against the person who forged your signature to cheques amounting to close upon three thousand pounds."

"I refuse to say. It's my business. It was my money. I'm going to bed."

The squatter now stood up. Bony remained seated. His right hand went out to take the fourth cigarette of the five he had made. He found this one to have a hole in the paper and so discarded it for the last.

"I must point out that the murder of Sergeant Errey falls into a different category to those misdemeanours you name annoyances," Bony proceeded, whilst steadily regarding the standing squatter. "By the way, Sergeant Errey's small attache case was stolen from my swag."

"When?" barked McPherson.

"After my arrival here, I think."

"Rot! Who would take anything from your swag?" McPherson demanded—and sat down.

"I placed the attache case inside the swag, before Burning Water and I left the cabbage-tree camp. I made it quite secure. When I unrolled the swag in my room this evening it was not there, but all my other possessions, such small objects as shaving brush, hairbrush and comb, were exactly as I had placed them. Burning Water carried the swag down from the hills and across the plain, as I required freedom to use my pistol arm. After his people met us one of them carried it and left it propped against the rear wall of this building. Who brought it to my room, d'you know?"

"I don't. The groom, a black, took it to the kitchen. One of the two maids would certainly take it to your room. I didn't steal the damn thing—if it were stolen and didn't fall from the swag."

"I am not accusing you, my host. Its theft is not so very important, for after all I like to gather my own evidence in my own way. You mentioned that Mit-ji was an old man suspected of communicating with the Illprinka blacks. Are there any other Wantella men so suspected?"

"I've had my eye on a fellow named Itcheroo."

"Ah! Perhaps it can be accounted to Itcheroo that the pilot knew of Mit-ji's arrest, and now would know I witnessed his bombing of the car, that I retrieved a flat object belonging to Errey, and that I was here when he flew over the house this evening. I must interview this dangerous Itcheroo, and then we'll go off to bed."

Bonaparte had done all he could to obtain the confidence and the assistance of the man still angrily glaring at him; and now had arrived his predetermined time to break McPherson's opposition.

"I understand that you never married," he said. "I understand, too, that Miss McPherson is the only living relative. Your opinion of her sterling qualities is warmly supported by me. Who was the visitor here who left that extraordinarily vivid dressing-grown and the blue doeskin slippers?"

McPherson's face became as grey as his moustache. Bony saw panic leap into his eyes, noted how the hand holding the pipe was faintly trembling. But the squatter's voice was wonderfully controlled.

"He was a man who came up from Melbourne to write a book," the harsh voice barked. "I tell you I'm sick of this conversation, this cross-examination. I'm going to bed."

"In normal circumstances I would not be so persistent," Bony said, and there was no buoyancy in his voice. "I am a man hating always to be hurried. I like to proceed with an investigation in my own plodding manner, declining assistance from anyone, resenting assistance if offered. I know this much, already. The man you say came here from Melbourne to write a book was a half-caste like me.

"In normal circumstances, I would regard the theft of Errey's attache case from my swag as in no way annoying. But, Mr McPherson, the present circumstances are not normal. No, not when a man drops bombs from an aeroplane and flies over a house at night to drop a treacle tin containing a threatening message. Here it is."

With his right hand Bony pressed the end of the fifth cigarette into the emu-egg ash tray, and with the left proffered the squatter the piece of paper he had found among the sand inside the treacle tin.

McPherson's face became grey. He stared into Bony's eyes, and automatically his right hand accepted the paper. He read aloud the message, written in a small and neat hand.

"You had better give in and retire. I am becoming impatient. If you don't surrender I shall strike again and again, and I shall strike harder.' "

The paper planed down to the surface of the table desk, and Bony picked it up and placed it inside a slim pocket-book. For twenty seconds McPherson stared at him before saying:

"You win. The aeroplane pilot is my natural son."

CHAPTER 7

CHAPTER 7

PAGES OF HISTORY

THE McPherson—so referred to by Chief Burning Water and by all the aborigines on the station—helped himself liberally and pushed the decanter and water jug towards Bony.

"I don't like being beaten," he said thickly.

"Defeat is a school in which truth always grows strong," Bony told him. "I cannot recall who wrote that, but it is apt. Believe me, I don't regard myself as a victor. I held a fifth ace in that message, and another good ace in the dressing-gown and slippers. You see, I know myself, and I know my kind. This airman says he will strike again and again, and I suppose he will. What d'you think about him?"

"Yes, Rex will carry out his threats," replied McPherson. "I fail to understand him, and yet somehow I do understand him a little. Like to hear about him?"

"Naturally."

The squatter gulped his drink, and with the tobacco cutter began to prepare loading for his pipe. He was calm now after a period of mental crisis. His arrogance had vanished. His body had lost its former stiffness in action. He seemed smaller than he actually was. Bony rolled his sixth cigarette.

"I must be just to myself before I tell you about Rex," McPherson stated in preface. "I want you to understand me, so if you find me abnormal I can be more just to my lad. You see, I have never had the opportunities of gaining the outlook to life possessed by you, and by men who have had the sharp edges rubbed off them by association with competitors. Even that idea I have got from a book.

"I blame my mother for a little and my father for a lot. He was, like his forebears, though but just in all things. She was virile and courageous, self-dependent and frugal. I think I know more about their early background than I know of my own, through the books they brought with them.

"They were of the same age, and were I to speak to you in their tongue you probably wouldn't understand me. They were young, both well under thirty, when they came here, having pushed on ahead of the settlement extending westward to the Diamantina. How they ever stuck it I don't know; and how my father came to leave me close on a hundred thousand pounds beside this property I fail to understand. They don't breed men and women like them nowadays.

"Picture them! They came with all their possessions loaded on to three bullock wagons, one of which was driven by that old man you saw tending to the lawn sprinklers. It happened to be a good season but that was the only thing in their favour. My sister was a baby in arms, and my mother was carrying me. When the baby was sick she doctored her; when I was born the lubras tended my mother.

"My father always got on fairly well with the blacks, and I think that was because of his sense of justice. He compensated them for the use of their land, as, he told me, Batman did down in Victoria. My mother found no difficulty in making friends with the lubras, and so, despite setbacks, they and those with them became established, the others who came with them being the three bullock drivers.

"It naturally followed that my sister and I grew up in close contact with the aborigines, especially with the children of our own generation. But the time came when my sister began to crave for a wider world, the outside world of men and women of our own race. Our father and mother encouraged us to read the books they had brought from the homeland, little understanding that those very books pictured a wonderful world beyond the vast and empty one in which we lived.

"So my sister fled with a surveyor. He was a good man and married her as quickly as was possible. Flora was their only child. I did not leave here. Flora got to hate the place and the country. The older I became, so the greater became my love for the country and those who inhabited it.

"'I was considered headstrong, and my parents imagined that I would quickly fly to the devil if they sent me down to a city school, far from their watchful protection. My father had been tutor-taught, and was hostile to schools. That was why he had sent up here a succession of three Scotch tutors. Not until I was turned twenty-two was I permitted to journey away down to Port Augusta."

McPherson paused to refill his glass and to relight his pipe.

"The only youthful friend I ever had was Burning Water. You

and I agree that he still is a fine looking man. In those days he was a kind of deity to me. He had a sister named Tarlalin, meaning water lying at the feet of bloodwood-trees, and after my lessons had been learned for the day we three would race away to our bush humpy and there I would teach them what I had learned. Tarlalin was a dunce, but her brother sopped it up easier than I did. And the blacks married me to Tarlalin without my knowing it.

"Came the time when the blacks took me away to the bush and proceeded to seal me into the tribe. My father and mother raised no objections on the score that being thus allied to them, I would not in the future have any trouble with them, or from them. Shortly afterwards Burning Water was sealed into the tribe. Now as warriors we were permitted to join in with the secret ceremonies.

"Then I fell in love with Tarlalin. Why does a man fall in love with a particular woman? Why should a white man fall in love with a black woman—or vice versa like Othello and Desdemona? The good Lord probably knows—we don't. Tarlalin had always been good looking for an aborigine, and when I fell in love with her she was the sweetest thing that breathed.

"We went bush. The chief and Burning Water and almost the entire tribe approved. It might all have been otherwise had I known white women, but I have never regretted having known Tarlalin. I was as close to this land of sand and scrub and burning water as she was, as all her race are.

"My mother was shocked and then indignant, but my father didn't raise a rumpus. He said the boy must have his fling; that later on I would marry a white woman and settle down and have an heir to carry on the line. Extraordinary man, he once knocked me down for saying damn, and in this instance he was wrong, for I have remained true to Tarlalin.

"I am certainly not going to offer excuses for myself. You can have but little idea of the young man I was grown to, the isolation to which I was born and reared, the cast-iron rules imposed by my father and endorsed by my mother. They seldom differed, but my mother wanted a parson brought out to marry us white fashion, and my father scoffed at the idea and made up his mind that it was but a youthful fancy.

"He had a house built for us up along the reservoir gully, and there Rex was born. Rex became the cause of the only serious quarrel I had with my father. He wanted the boy to live with him and mother. Tarlalin objected to her son being taken from her, and I wouldn't have her living here because my mother could never approve of her.

"The years passed and Tarlalin died, died before she became old. My father then had his way with the boy, and my mother came to dote on him as well. Still more years passed. My father died. My sister died. Then my mother died, after Rex had been sent to a college in Adelaide, a course I determinedly insisted upon. The last word she uttered was the boy's name."

Bony was making his seventh cigarette, his gaze directed at his task; and the squatter paused to reload his pipe. Bony was not a little interested to note that this unburdening was making McPherson actually appear young.

"I suppose it's because I'm a dunce at the science of living that on some counts I cannot understand my father and mother," McPherson continued. "With me they had been strict, as though I were a young animal that must be trained. Their attitude to Rex was exactly the opposite. He could do no wrong. He had to have this and that, and whatever he wanted to do he could do. When my father died, he left the boy at school an income of two thousand a year without any qualifications or conditions whatever, other than that he was unable to touch the capital.

"When he returned from college for the last time Rex was flash. He was no good. Whatever he wanted he must have. He even regarded me as a semi-idiot. He said I'd have to be modern, have to have aeroplanes on the station to overlook the cattle instead of wasting time sending stockmen out. I refused, and he went down to Adelaide for two years and got himself taught to fly aeroplanes.

"News came that the trustees who managed his capital had dissipated it. Rex's income stopped. I thought it a damn good thing it had stopped. Rex came home, and all the money he had was left over from the sale of an aeroplane and a car.

"I gave him all the chances, for he was my son; and when he laughed I gazed on the face of his mother. But he was finished. He debauched the blacks. He would clear out with those of his own kidney, go bush in the open country, hunting women of the Illprinka tribe.

"He was away on one of those expeditions when Flora came to manage the homestead, her father having followed her mother to the grave. She'd been here two months, and the place and life had become orderly and peaceful when Rex returned from the open country.

"You can imagine what followed. Rex wanted Flora, seemed

to have the idea that Flora hadn't a say in the matter. He swore
he'd become reformed when she turned down his—well, unorthodox advances. He spurned his companions. He asked to be made
my overseer, and I assented. He asked for a comfortable salary
and I gave it to him. He swore he would be worthy of his name:
he lasted five months.

"He offered Flora marriage, and Flora as kindly as possible told
him she couldn't marry him because she didn't love him. So what
did he do then? Why, he persuaded four of the blacks to join him,
and they abducted Flora and ran off with her, headed for the open
country. Burning Water and I caught up with them in time.

"The limit had been reached. I sacked Rex. Gave him a cheque
for a thousand and told him if ever he showed his face here again
I'd give him in charge for a dozen crimes we'd kept dark. Burning
Water and his father dealt with the four blacks who had assisted
in the abduction.

"Then followed the affair of the forged cheques. How could I
prosecute a man who reminded me of Tarlalin every time he
laughed: a man whom I would try to please just to see him laugh?
After that there followed a period of peace, broken by the first
theft of my cattle and a letter Rex wrote. He said I was getting too
old to manage a station, and that I would have to retire to live
comfortably in a city. He would take over the station, and if I
refused to accept this idea he'd ruin me by stealing all my cattle
and running them in the open country, where he'd form a temporary station of his own.

"I took no notice of his absurd ideas and his threat. Then he and
the Illprinka blacks made the second raid, and another letter came
from Rex demanding that I retire and hand the station over to
him. I was to signal my surrender by making an oil smoke. Instead,
Burning Water and I took a party of blacks into the open country
and tried to locate the cattle. We found none and lost two of the
blacks in a fight.

"Constant trouble became rife among the Wantella aborigines,
lasting until Burning Water was made chief after his father died.
There's still trouble simmering, because there's still hostility
towards Burning Water and me, kept alive by Rex. I understand
from Burning Water, who in turn gets to know things, that Rex
has built himself a homestead, has broken down the sectional mode
of living of the Illprinka blacks, and has drawn them into one big
mob.

"He's an Ishmael: always was. The final shove that pushed him
over the edge was the money my father left him which was taken

away by those dishonest trustees. Where he got his vices, I don't know. I've never been really bad, and there was no hint of vice in Tarlalin. But he's my son, and it's my place to deal with him. It has been my money and my cattle he's stolen, but he has stolen other things as well—the lives of Errey and Mit-ji and those two stockmen.

"And now, Inspector, you have come. D'you know, I'd determined to be my lad's judge and executioner. I thought it would be best—in fact, I still think so—for all concerned, to take all my bucks and go after Rex and deliver justice. You can, perhaps, now understand why I don't want you or any other policeman interfering. I'm the last male McPherson, for Rex cannot be counted; the last representative of all those men in the dining-room. It is my duty to obliterate the stain I have created on the honoured name. I have let loose on the world a human devil, a monster who has been a torment to me, who had put an awful fear into the heart of a good woman, the agony of grief into the heart of another; and has brought ruin to a tribe of blacks who, no matter how wild, were at least morally decent."

Abruptly flinging backward his chair, McPherson stood up.

"I'll see you in the morning," he shouted. "I can't stand any more tonight. When you've finished with the whisky, turn out the light. You know the way to your room."

CHAPTER 8

FACETS

I

WHEN the sun was gliding the tops of the bloodwoods bordering the gully between the land shoulders, Bonaparte was standing on the dam wall, watching the fish jumping for flies. The cement-faced barrier was all of two hundred yards in length, and was at least a hundred feet high from the bed of the gully. Wide enough on the top to permit a wagon to be driven across it, it barred back a reserve of precious water sufficient to defy the worst of droughts.

Smoke was rising from the house kitchen, and from the kitchen-dining-room beyond at the men's quarters. The white-clad figure of the men's cook appeared from a cane-grass meat house carrying a tray of beef steaks. For a moment Bony turned to gaze out over the golden pavement of the plain to the distant hills, softly blue-grey and mysterious, an inviting picture hiding its hideous tragedy.

Crows cawed and galahs shrieked. Calves bellowed for their yarded mothers, awaiting the milking. And Napoleon Bonaparte began another day's work by seeking an interview with the men's cook. Just inside the kitchen doorway he greeted the tall white figure standing before the stove with its back to him.

The cook twisted his body, and then continued to twist his neck until he was able to look back over a narrow shoulder. He was an elderly man, and was engaged in transferring the beef steaks to a large iron grill.

"Good day!" he said, his voice thin and piping. "How's things up your street?"

"Fairly quiet, I think," he said, finding himself in the usual interior of a kitchen-dining-room. "Have you many to cook for?"

"No—oh, no! Only me and old Jack and half a dozen nigs. I bake the bread and cake for the big house, but that ain't much. I can do the flamin' lot standin' on me head. It ain't a bad job, as far as it goes. We all has to work under the ruddy capitalist system, but the time ain't far off when us workers will break our chains."

"You think they ever will?" inquired the interested Bony.

"Too right they will," asserted the cook, and with a crash he tossed the empty tray to a nearby bench. "The day's gonna come when us slaves will take over the means of production, distribution and consumption, and then there's gonna be no more unemployment and starvation and wars and things. I tell you——"

"Stow your noise!" commanded a deep and full voice from without. Following the voice, entered the old man whom, late the previous afternoon, Bony had seen attending to the garden. He wore long white side-whiskers like the Emperor Franz Joseph, and when he removed his old felt hat he revealed a cranium completely bare of hair.

"You and your revolutions and slaves and up-and-at-'em workers," he scoffed. "Why, you touch your forelock to the boss every time you see him, fearing you'd lose your poisoning job." Then to Bony: "Good day to you, mister! Has this gallows bird made a drink of tea yet?"

"Well, I was hoping so," Bony ventured.

"Coo!" snorted the cook. "Can't you wait for breakfast? Think a man's a slave to be makin' tea all day and all night?"

"Stow your noise, and let me at the tea billy," said the ancient, and strode towards the kitchen range whereupon stood a steaming billycan. As he passed Bony, he winked one eye. Taking two bright tin pannikins from a row hanging on wall hooks, he filled them and returned to the table. "Here you are, mister! Help yourself to milk and sugar, and don't take any notice of our local poisoner. He's not too bad."

Having well laced his tea with milk, he removed the square board, covering a seven-pound jam tin serving as a sugar basin, and proceeded to help himself to spoonful after spoonful.

"Hey!" cried the cook. "You go easy on the sugar."

Again the lid closed over one bright eye, whilst the other sparkled at Bony.

"Stow your noise," again came the command. "First you're a slave and then you're not. First you blackguards the boss and then yell because he might go bankrupt. You are the most cussedest poisoner I've ever come in contact with."

The cook grabbed a pennikin from the wall, filled it, and stalked to the table. If anything, his mood was a little lighter. He indicated the ancient with a motion of his long head.

"He thinks hisself smart," he said to Bony, adding directly to the allegedly smart one: "Anyhow how's things up your street?"

They sat on the form flanking the long table, and the cook began the loading of a black pipe with jet-black tobacco.

"Not too good, Alf," the old man replied, his bright eyes clouding. "Something's 'appened what I can't make out. You know that bed in front where them Madam Leroy standards is growing?"

"Yes. Didn't you show 'em to me that day you swore you'd ask for your cheque if the hoppers came again. They come the next week, but you're still 'ere."

"That's the bed," asserted the old man, triumphantly. "Well, on the grass near that bed, what d'you think I found?"

"Dunno. Not a quid note, I'll bet. I'll bet there ain't one on the flamin' station. What did you find?"

Bony, seeing that he was supposed to ask the same question, asked it.

"I found a dent deep enough to put me hand in."

"A dent!" exclaimed the cook. "What kind of a dent?"

"Just a dent, Alf, just a dent. And in that dent was a lot of dry sand. Now—you tell me how dry sand got into that dent; and how the dent got into the lawn when last evening there wasn't no dent, and the lawn was wet from watering and there wasn't any sand, wet or dry. on the lawn at all."

"Well, I suppose the flamin' wind blow'd the sand into that dent, you old fool," growled the cook.

"Stow your noise!" snarled the ancient, and gulped loudly at his tea. "I tell you there wasn't no dent there last evening, and no sand, wet or dry, in the dent last evening. What I'm asking you is to tell me how that dent got there."

"How the hell do I know how the dent got into your lawn?" asked the cook.

"Well, as your mind's a bit weak, Alf, I tell you something else what I can't make out."

The cook rose to his feet, stalked to one of the open windows and expectorated a stream of diluted nicotine.

"There's lots of things you ain't making' out this mornin'. What's this new one?"

The old man stood up, seemingly the better to make his remarks clearer by means of sauce bottles, milk jug and sugar tin.

"Now, this here's the bed of them Madam Leroys," he began. "This here is the dent on the lawn. Now here, in this part of the Madam Leroy rose bed, is where I seen a disturbance of the ground, and under the disturbance I finds a treacle tin. It's been buried there."

"One of the dorgs, I suppose."

"Dorg me eye. In that treacle tin was a lot of dry sand, the same as the dry sand in the dent. Now why should anyone bury a treacle tin with sand in it, in my best rose bed?"

"Yes," Bony said in support. "Why should anyone bury a treacle tin in that rose bed?"

"How do I know?" demanded the cook. "Why do dorgs bark? Why do men work like slaves? Why do motor steerin' gears go bung at the wrong time? Why do airplanes fly around after dark? Why do nigs walk about carryin' suitcases?"

"Suitcases!" exclaimed Bony.

"That's what I said," stoutly maintained the cook. "Early this mornin' I seen Itcheroo walkin' away from the stockyards, carryin' a suitcase. All he wanted to complete the pitchur was a top 'at."

"Was it a large suitcase?" pressed Bony.

"Large! It wasn't much larger than a fair sized damper. What with the nigs carryin' suitcases around before breakfast, and dents and dry sand and airplanes and things, the world's comin' to a pretty fine pitch."

"The world!" sneered the old man. "What d'you know about the world?"

"More'n you do, anyhow. You ain't seen the flamin' world for the last seventy years," replied the cook.

II

Bony was admiring the roses when the breakfast gong was struck and Flora McPherson emerged from the house.

"Good morning, Inspector! Don't you think old Jack is wonderful, growing these roses in the middle of Australia?"

"I am uncertain which is the more wonderful—the garden or the gardener," Bony smilingly said. "Good morning!"

She caught his mood, standing with black hair teased by the breeze and gazing southward over the plain into which already was creeping the mirage, the burning water. She was thinking that to rely on first, or even second, impressions is an error. Bony said:

"I met the gardener only an hour ago. How old is he, do you know?"

"Well, Jack says he's only seventy-one, but uncle knows he must be over ninety."

"Ninety! Then he will not be old until he's past a hundred and twenty."

"He's one of the great originals," she said, as they walked slowly to the house. "Old Jack came here with grandfather; drove one of the bullock wagons. It was grandmother and he who first started the garden here. The locusts came and destroyed it time and again, but Jack now defies them by protecting all the garden with sheets of hessian. Have you seen the cemetery?"

"No."

"It's over there beyond those sugar gums. You should visit it sometime. It's a shrine. Ah, here's uncle looking for his breakfast. Morning, uncle!"

"Morning dear! Morning, Inspector!"

McPherson's bearing was again erect, defiant of the world.

"I have been admiring the garden," Bony said when he had followed the girl up to the veranda. And there he sighed loudly, adding: "I do wish you people would call me merely Bony. My wife does. So do my three boys. So does my Chief Commissioner and my department chief. It's Bony, lend me a quid—meaning a pound. It's Bony, give us a tray-bit—meaning give me a three-penny piece. It's Bony, do this or go there. No one ever thinks of me as a detective."

He said this with such gravity that both the girl and the squatter were nonplussed.

"I seldom think of myself as a detective," he went on. "My Chief Commissioner is a violent man destined to die with his boots firmly laced to his feet. He damns and blasts me. My wife calls me from my study (where I may be reading of the latest method of bringing out finger-prints on clothes), to cut the wood or fire the chimney, she being a firm believer in the superiority of fire over a brush to effect the removal of soot. So, you see, when I am addressed as Inspector I look around for this strange fellow."

He followed the girl to the breakfast-room where covered dishes on a side table awaited them.

"I am so used to being called Bony that were you to call me Bony it would be a distinct pleasure."

"Goes with me," assented McPherson.

"And I will call you Bony, too, if you will forget to be a detective and hide nothing from me," supplemented the girl.

Bony's brows rose a fraction.

"Hide anything from you, Miss McPherson!"

"Yes—Bony. I want to know just what did happen to Sergeant Errey. I want to know why you ordered the lights to be put out when that aeroplane was coming last night. I want to know why uncle was shouting at you last night when you were in the office. I'm not a fool flapper, you know."

Bony flashed a glance at his host, to see him staring down at his plate. Then, steadily, he regarded the girl opposite him at table. He noted again her wide brow, her clear blue eyes, her firm chin—the McPherson chin, the mould of chin possessed by all those tough men in kilt and colourful jacket who glared from the walls of the dining-room. In her face was something greater than mere beauty. He said, quietly:

"No, you are not a fool flapper, Miss McPherson. However, the information you seek will occupy time in the giving, and I'm a hungry man. They say that when men are hungry they are bad tempered. I would hate to reveal my bad temper to you. After breakfast we will talk about things. Toast?"

The meal proceeded, and Bony drew McPherson to talk about the dam wall which the squatter, assisted by the blacks, had built. McPherson was the first to rise from the table.

"I have a job of work to do on the run this morning. I'll be home for lunch, dear."

When he had gone, Flora and her guest rose and, at Bony's suggestion, they passed out to the veranda where the girl was made comfortable in a lounge chair and provided with a cigarette. She had taken two whiffs of the cigarette before Bony began the story about the destruction of Errey's car. After that she forgot it, till it burned her fingers and she tossed it impatiently aside. From the crime of murder committed from an aeroplane, Bony told of the skirmish on the plain with the Illprinka blacks, and the dropping of the message in the treacle tin by the pilot of the plane that flew over the house the evening before.

"He's mad," she whispered. "I think Rex has always been mad, but uncle wouldn't, or couldn't, ever see it. Poor uncle! He used to be so—so different, before Rex came home from school."

"You know about Tarlalin?"

"Yes, I know. And I understand, too. A love story is always —a love story. I told you about the cemetery—the shrine—you must go and see. What are you going to do about Rex?"

"That is a question I have been asking myself," Bony replied. "You see, I am less concerned with the catching of criminals than with the investigation into the crime. It is the building of a case for presentment to the actual police, who act accordingly, which appeals to my somewhat peculiar mind. I came here, hoping to be confronted with an outstanding mystery that would tax all my powers. Shortly after arrival I was made happy by the prospect of an outstanding investigation. And now . . . And now . . . I feel that the investigation has taken charge of the investigator.

"You ask me what I am going to do about Rex? Normally I would doubtless retire from the case and leave the police, and possibly the military, to hunt this madman in the open country and effect either his arrest or destruction. I am beginning to think I ought to do otherwise; that I ought to be a real policeman for once, and go after Rex myself. The police—and no doubt there are many excellent bushmen among them—may well fail to arrest Rex McPherson, because he is living in open country, hundreds and hundreds of square miles of it, protected by wild blacks who, with their cunning bushcraft, would certainly be able to prevent his capture.

"Of course, Rex McPherson would be captured in the end, but before his capture was effected it is probable that more lives would be taken by him and his blacks, and some taken by the bush itself. Which is why I think I ought, this once, to be a policeman. Burning Water and I could do more than all the outside men, and do it more swiftly."

The girl sighed audibly. Then:

"It is going to break uncle's heart. It's breaking now, I think. It would be a mercy if a star fell on Rex. I wonder what he'll do next?"

"I would like to know what he's contemplating," Bony said, his smooth brow unusually furrowed. "We'll have to take precautions. You need not be nervous of a repetition of that early adventure, for I am seeing to it that you will be guarded."

"Thank you—Bony." They were silent for a space, and then she said: "I'm not nervous, but I'm terribly, terribly afraid of him. Rex is tall and handsome and his eyes flame at one. In them there's something which terrifies me."

"You know," Bony said, lightly but with conviction, "I can be an excellent policeman when I like. I have told your uncle already today that my Chief says I am a wretchedly poor policeman. I use my adjective, not his. You need not fear Rex McPherson because I am going to arrest him, and hand him to a judge and jury. Meanwhile, you would make my mind easy if you did not go out riding, or leave the homestead. Will you grant me that request?"

She nodded her raven head and raised her eyes to him.

"I expect you have wondered how I, a half-caste, have risen to the rank of inspector in the police force," he went on, and she knew he was talking to give her time to regain composure. He told her of his mission-rearing, his passage through High School and the University, of the early love affair that went wrong and drove him back to the bush, and of his long career as an investigator.

"Eventually I married a wonderful woman who, too, is a half-caste," he said in conclusion. "We have three boys, the eldest of whom is attending my old University and who is going to be a doctor-missionary. So you see, Miss McPherson, what a jolly fine fellow I am."

That made her laugh, and partly defeated the depression visible in her eyes.

"I would like to ask you a question," he said.

Again she nodded her head.

"Are you in love with Doctor Whyte?"

Now her eyes became big. A blush swiftly covered her cheeks.

"Thank you, Miss McPherson," he said. gravely. "I am glad to know it because I have, in your uncle's name, asked Doctor Whyte to pay us a visit. Now I must hurry away, and hope you will excuse me. I'll listen for the morning tea call. I like strong tea, and have observed that you do, too. *Au revoir!*"

Bony bowed and left her; left her to listen to the dwindling sound of his footsteps on the termite-nest garden path. Another half-caste! It was singular how she feared one half-caste, and now was so sure she liked this one. Why, he was almost the nicest man she ever had met.

An offshoot of the great Worcair Nation, the Wantella Tribe had never been as numerically strong as the Illprinka Tribe which was an offshoot of the Illiaura Nation. The beginning of the original homestead, and the construction of the first wall across the gully to the west of the house, at once provided for the members of the Wantella Tribe additional supplies of food and water: and it was to prevent a continuance of the pollution of this water supply by the wild blacks that the first McPherson constructed a low wall across a gully to the east of the house to supply what became a permanent camp drawing to the vicinity of the homestead the many groups of individuals comprising the tribe. Each of these groups was governed by the old men whose word was the law; and when the groups came together to perform some important series of ceremonies, or by reason of the reduction of waterholes, caused by drought, there was much quarrelling and fighting and killing, resulting in the splitting again of the tribe into the respective groups.

For twelve years the united tribe remained in a ferment of quarrelling and killing, caused chiefly by the intrigues conducted by the leaders of the groups who struggled for the leadership of the tribe. Then there emerged a man strong enough to unite the groups, subdue the warring elements, remove the more persistent opposition, and gather into a Council of Old Men those who would support him. He was the father of Chief Burning Water.

The son of one of the malcontents was Itcheroo, now elderly and bitter, a man suspected of magic, communicating with the spirits of the Alchuringa, pointing the bone and other nasty practices. He, with others of his ilk, were ready companions for such as Rex McPherson, and only by chance had Itcheroo not been one of the party assisting Rex McPherson in the abduction of Flora. Which is why he was still walking the stage of life.

Itcheroo had often accompanied Rex McPherson on women-hunting expeditions into the country of the Illprinka Tribe, and he was the first to ally himself with Rex McPherson on the return from his exile to take up residence in the land of the Illprinka.

Itcheroo was a traitor to his tribe, and to the man who wisely governed it through Chief Burning Water. For his services Itcheroo expected no reward; his hatred of Chief Burning Water and his intense admiration for the evil Rex McPherson were more than sufficient. He liked to practise magic, not because of any desire to use it for acquiring property, but because of a desire to be feared.

With these two spurs to drive him, he had become proficient in the black art of pointing the bone and, among other things, in the less sinister practice of mental telepathy. He was able to project through space mental pictures to be received by minds open to receive them; and he was able to clean his mind, like a slate is cleaned of writing by a sponge, and so receive thought-pictures projected by a distant mind.

And now Itcheroo squatted on his heels, close to what had become a little, almost smokeless fire. His crossed forearms rested on his knees, and his forehead was resting on his magic churinga stone (which no other human eyes ever had seen) that now was resting on the upper of his crossed arms.

His disciplined mind was astonishingly controlled. Normally it was like that of the white man, or any other man, open to receive impressions and ideas and thoughts, passing in procession so swiftly that much was waste material. Now there was but one thought occupying his mind, one impression, one mental picture, the picture of a small attache case being consumed by the flames of a fire.

Although the actual fire was dying, although his eyes were registering no visual scene, his mind continuously and clearly saw a bright fire consuming a small leather case. The fire in the mental picture did not die down, neither did the leather case progress into ashes. It was a mind picture stilled, like one of ten thousand pictures comprising a film fixed upon the screen because the projector had ceased to function. And away beyond the horizon of mirage and sand-dune and scrub sat another man, in similar pose, seeing with the eyes of his mind the same, stilled picture.

Presently Itcheroo found his mind rebelling against the iron discipline placed over it. He found it increasingly difficult to maintain the picture of the leather case being burned by the fire, and ultimately it faded, flickered and vanished, to be replaced by images of crows and the branches of the scrub trees vibrating in the wind. Now he could hear the crows and the wind in the scrub; and, too, he could smell tobacco smoke.

First he moved his arms so that his eyes might become used to the daylight by gazing at the earth beneath his legs. Then his right hand slid up and over the forearm to take the precious churinga stone and slip it into the dillybag suspended from his neck. That accomplished, he raised his head, to see, squatted opposite him beyon dthe fire, the stranger half-caste in the very act of blowing cigarette smoke towards him. For a full second of time he looked into the cold eyes of Napoleon Bonaparte, and then his gaze was directed by the gaze of the cold blue eyes to the fire, in which still remained charred portions of the leather case and the charred leaves of several notebooks.

"So! You big feller magic feller, eh?" observed Bony. "You stealum sergeant's dillybag from my swag, eh? You sendum mulga wire to Illprinka feller, and Illprinka feller he run and tell-it Rex McPherson. You fine blackfeller all right."

CHAPTER 9

THE ENIGMA

THE gully eastward of the McPherson homestead was far less steep-sloped than that dammed by the great concrete-faced wall. The floor of the eastward gully was wide and comparatively flat, providing an excellent ground in the shade of the bloodwoods for an aboriginal camp. Through the camp lay the long sheet of almost permanent water created by a low barrier composed of firmly cemented boulders; and on either side of the water were built the humpies of tree-boughs and bags and bark, small humpies sheltering families and large humpies sheltering the unmarried bucks and the widows.

This morning the entire camp exuded an atmosphere of domesticity. Below the dam wall lubras were engaged washing dungaree trousers and the shirts used by bucks, reecntly employed as stockmen, who now had rejoined the tribe, these garments having to be returned to store. About the large communal fires lubras were baking iron-hard flap-jacks of flour as the nardoo seeds were scarce, and men were fire-hardening spear points or carving spear throwers, or making head and arm bands and dilly-bags. The birds maintained an incessant tumult, to which were added the barking of dogs and the excited yells of a ring of young men surrounding two who were fighting with bare hands with reasonable conformity to the boxing rules as laid down by the Marquess of Queensberry and introduced by the second McPherson through Chief Burning Water.

At the upper end of the sheet of water was situated the chief's humpy. He was now lying outside it, on the broad of his back, with a small girl on one side of him and his younger wife, and the mother of the child, on the other.

The child, pot-bellied and straight-legged and in the toddling stage, was engaged in constructing, with the contents of a box of matches, what was supposed to represent a fowl-house. The site of the building was on the chief's naked stomach.

"It's not high enough yet," he observed in the Wantella dialect. "Chook-chook will fly out if you're not quick."

With the enviable concentration of small children, Burning Water's youngest child continued to build the walls of the "chook house" until the mother said she thought they were high enough. Across the walls were laid matches to support pieces of leopard-wood bark, representing the white man's iron roof sheets. Eventually the house was finished, and with a swiftly changing countenance the child regarded her prostrate father with laughter-lit eyes.

"Willi-willi no blow down chook house this time," she taunted, and the man and the woman joined in admiration of the building. "You wait till a willi-willi comes along," Burning Water said.

"It won't blow my chook house down this time," predicted the small girl, and then fell into a pose still and expectant.

Chief Burning Water had to obey certain rules in this game. He was not to sit up. He was not to shake the house down with the muscles of his stomach. He was to lie perfectly flat and try to blow down the house by blowing across his chest. As he took air into his lungs, the child and its mother alternately watched the man's expanding chest, to be sure that an upheaval of its foundations would not be the cause of the house's collapse. Pop was likely not to play the game fairly, if given the chance.

Burning Water expelled air in the direction of the house, but it defied the attack, and the child and its mother shrieked with joy. Again Burning Water blew and again failed.

"I'll do it this time," he boasted. "You watch."

For the third time he drew air into his lungs, and then with mighty effort he blew downward along his great chest towards the house on his stomach. Purposely he contracted his stomach muscles and the house fell in ruins.

The toddler and her mother shrieked with glee, the little girl chanting:

"Ya ya! You moved your tummy! You moved your tummy!"

"I didn't," Burning Water indignantly denied.

"You did! You did! You did!" chanted the victor.

Burning Water pretended to be crestfallen and exhausted with effort, and then the child jumped upon his stomach and danced until he rolled his body and she fell to the ground. All were laughing when the elderly wife working over the "private" fire called that the strange half-caste was approaching the camp.

At once the younger woman ran into the humpy and the child ran to join her. The older woman went on with her work as she was supposed to be past the period of being attractive to any man. Burning Water stood up, dusted himself by shaking his body much like an animal, and then called for his pipe and tobacco.

The older woman trotted to the humpy to take the pipe and tobacco plug from the younger who remained within its shelter. Burning Water saw Bony halt when fifty yards from the camp and sit on his heels in conformity with aboriginal etiquette. The tobacco and pipe were brought to the chief, and he left camp to welcome the visitor.

"Good day!" he said, his black eyes beaming, and on his face a smile.

The now standing Bony repeated the greeting, adding:

"I've come to talk of men and matters, and I suggest we make a little fire up the gully where we can draw maps."

Burning Water nodded assent, and together they walked from the camp to a bend in the gully where flood-water had scooped a great hole in the right bank. Here they made a fire and, like men down the ages, sat on their heels one either side of the rising blue smoke.

"Did you see the aeroplane last night?" inquired Bony.

"Yes. Its coming alarmed the tribe, for even the children knew that Sergeant Errey and Mit-ji died because of the aeroplane."

"You kept silent on that point?"

"Yes. But—well, you know how news cannot be hidden."

"I suppose Itcheroo was the newspaper?"

"You know about Itcheroo?"

"More than a little. The aeroplane pilot dropped a message when he flew over last night. Here it is."

The small sheet of paper was passed through the fire smoke to Burning Water who read the neat writing on it, and afterwards stared at his visitor with eyes empty of expression.

Bony stood up, waited for the chief to stand. He then gave the sign seen by Sturt when that explorer met aborigines beyond the north-west corner of New South Wales. Solemnly he said:

"We stand on the square of squares, and within the circle where we face the moon rising in the east. Who wrote that message?"

"Rex McPherson wrote it."

Again Bony made the sign and then sat down on his heels. Burning Water followed his action.

"We talk in confidence," Bony said slowly. "I am glad you recognized me, and I appreciate your reluctance to reveal what The McPherson might not like. Let your mind be easy. The McPherson has told me everything: about Tarlalin, about Rex their son, about the troubles Rex created, about the abduction of Miss McPherson. What do you think—about Rex?"

"When the brat was born its head should have been dashed against a tree. It became a man with a mind more evil than a world filled with Itcheroos. If The McPherson had but granted my request."

"Oh! That was——?"

"I wanted him to let me and my bucks go into the Illprinka country and there exact justice for the crimes done against us. But The McPherson would not. He might have let us go if Rex McPherson had harmed Miss McPherson that time he abducted her."

"I suppose it is that The McPherson still loves his son," Bony suggested, and was surprised that he was wrong.

"No. The other thing is greater."

"The other thing!"

"Justice."

"I still don't understand."

"Then listen. The McPherson is like Pitti-pitti who lived in the Land of Burning Water in the days of the Alchuringa. Pitti-pitti was half kangaroo, half snake. He made the eagles, the doves, the emus and the kangaroos, but he would not make snakes because he knew they were bad.

"One day a blackfellow went to him and asked him to make great trees to provide good shade from the sun as the scrub tree gave only poor shade. And so Pitti-pitti began to walk about over the Land of Burning Water making bloodwood-trees. But all the walking about made him tired, and he made two sons to help him with the work. One son was evil and the other was good: the good son loving the kangaroo part of his father, and the evil son admiring the snake part of him.

"The evil son went away behind a river of burning water, and there he laboured to make a snake. Not being as good as his father at making things, the evil son could only make a small snake, a little grey snake the colour of the saltbush. The little grey snake ran about all over the country dropping baby snakes, and presently many of the poor blackfellows were bitten and died very quickly. When the kangaroo-snake man found out what his evil son had done, he said:

" 'I loosed the snake in me when I made my evil son who made the little grey snake that ran about dropping little baby snakes that grew up to bite the poor blackfellows and make them die. It is all my fault that poor blackfellows are lying dead in the Land. of Burning Water. What can I do to atone?'

"A willy wagtail who heard him say that said to him:

" 'A great evil has been done. You first created the evil. You must finish the evil. If you don't, the little grey snakes will kill all the poor blackfellows and none will be left to sit in the shade of the bloodwood-trees.'

"And so the kangaroo-snake man took his evil son to the top of a high hill, and there he bound his evil son to him and he jumped from the top of the high hill and both were killed. But the evil lived after him and his sacrifice was in vain."

Burning Water, having finished his story which he and all his tribe believed to be pure history of those fabulous days of the Alchuringa, proceeded silently to smoke his pipe. The head band of white down, glued to a base of human hair, forced his grey hair upward to a waving plume. Even in the inelegant posture of sitting on his heels his bearing was graceful. Bony saw its intended allusion to McPherson.

"The McPherson has more than hinted to me his dislike of my coming to investigate the crimes which have been committed in the Land of Burning Water," he said, quietly. "What you have said concerning Pitti-pitti and his evil son applies, of course, to The McPherson and his son, and The McPherson's thoughts about his son. The McPherson must not be permitted to judge, sentence and put the sentence into effect."

"It would be a thing greater than I could do," asserted the alleged savage man. "But The McPherson is a great man. Sometimes I have thought him a greater man than his father. After he and I and some of the bucks had stopped Rex from carrying off Miss McPherson, he said to me he would punish Rex by banishing him from the Land of Burning Water. Yesterday he came to me. He said: 'It is enough, Burning Water. Tomorrow—meaning today— I will call all the bucks from the run, and you and I will lead them into the land of the Illprinka and find Rex, and I will hang him as I was responsible for his birth.' "

It was as though a blind had been drawn upward to reveal another McPherson to Bony. He saw a man as near to the aborigines and their philosophy as Burning Water was to the white race and its philosophy. He saw a man steeped from early childhood in aboriginal thought; and, as he, Bony, had put on the veneer of white civilization, so McPherson had put on the veneer of the aborigines' mentality.

"It would be a bad thing for him to do," Bony told Burning Water.

"It would be a foolish thing for him to do, for, like Pitti-pitti he would not right the wrong done by his son," Burning Water said, surprisingly. "What does a blackfellow do when he sees a dangerous fire?"

"He calls on the lubras to put it out," Bony replied.

"Therefore," continued the chief, "it is not The McPherson's task to put out a fire which threatens to burn us all. All my life, The McPherson has been my friend and I have been his friend. This dangerous fire, called Rex, has put a barrier between us. In this matter of the dangerous fire, he is the man and I am the lubra."

They fell silent, the chief smoking his pipe, Bony his eternal cigarettes. Then:

"Do the Illprinka men trespass on your land much?"

"More and more. I have urged The McPherson to let the Wantella teach them a lesson, and he says always that the time is not yet. We have gone often into the Illprinka country to get back stolen cattle, but we never found them."

Another period of silence held them smoking thoughtfully.

"Do you think it's likely that The McPherson would surrender to his son's demands?" asked Bony.

"No. He couldn't do it now, when he knows we know how the sergeant and Mit-ji died. No, not that. He decided to act like Pitti-pitti did, back in the Alchuringa days."

"Would you assist him to attempt to do that?"

Burning Water moved the direction of his gaze away from the questioner. He hesitated before saying:

"If the McPherson asked me to go with him to take and hang his son, I would plead with him not to go. But if The McPherson ordered me to accompany him I would obey. He is my chief. As I have told you, he is my friend."

"Well, then, let us pass to another subject—Itcheroo," Bony proceeded. "You remember that I put Sergeant Errey's attache case in the swag before we left the camp of the cabbage-trees? Well, when I unrolled the swag in my room after having bathed yesterday evening, the case was not there. This morning I found Itcheroo squatted before a little fire and sending or receiving a mulga wire.

In the ashes of his fire were the charred remains of the case and the sergeant's notebooks.

"We need not bother ourselves at this time with the hows and whys of that theft, for overshadowing them is the fact that Itcheroo is in Rex McPherson's service."

"I have suspected it for some time," replied Burning Water. "Mit-ji was another magic man, and I am glad Mit-ji is dead. Were Itcheroo to die we would be happier. Perhaps The McPherson will give his assent. There are those who wouldn't miss with a spear once The McPherson said it was to be so."

"Oh! Well, we'll leave Itcheroo for the time being. Did you see Doctor Whyte when he was here two months ago?"

"Yes." Burning Water chuckled. "I found Doctor Whyte kissing Miss McPherson in the garden."

"Did you like him?"

"He is a brave man. He flew his aeroplane upside-down, and he made it fall like a leaf falling from a gum-tree. He took me for a ride one day he was here. I liked it."

"Where did he land his machine?"

"On the edge of the plain beyond the great dam. The McPherson had all my people removing the sand walls between the claypans to make a landing ground."

"I have sent for Doctor Whyte," Bony told Burning Water. "I would like him to take me out over the country of the Illprinka. Meanwhile I want you to call on two or three of your reliable bucks to maintain guard round the house at night, for in my mind is the possibility that when next Rex McPherson strikes he will try again to abduct Flora McPherson. The message indicates that he is still determined to force his father to retire and hand the station over to him. That would presuppose he thinks no one saw him kill the sergeant and Mit-ji; or he is mentally deranged and cannot view the inevitable consequences of that act. Do you think he is mad?"

"No. He's like the white man's devil. He thinks he is the greatest man in the world who need fear no other man."

Bony stood up, and Burning Water rose to stand facing him.

"Would you," began Bony, "would you accompany me into the land of the Illprinka to take Rex McPherson and bring him back to be handed over to the police for trial and judgment?"

"If The McPherson said——"

"Never mind The McPherson in this matter. It is between you and me."

For half a minute the chief of the Wantella did not reply.

"I would. It would be a good thing for us to go into the land of the Illprinka and take Rex McPherson. That would bring peace to The McPherson and to Miss McPherson and to all my people."

Bony smiled and held out both his hands. They were gripped in black ones.

"We may go tomorrow, or the day after tomorrow. Now draw for me a map of the tribal lands."

Chief Burning Water took up a stout twig and, selecting sand which was level, he drew a large-scale diagram of McPherson's Station and the land westward and north-westward of it, filling in with ranges of sand-dunes, creeks and watercourses, and vast areas of cane-grass swamps.

"This last winter has been the best season for some years," Bony reminded Burning Water. "When Rex came to live in the open country, and afterward till this last winter, the seasons were dry, almost droughty. Now—can you mark, on the map, waterholes in which water would be almost permanent?"

Burning Water marked three positions on the sand-map: one at the western extremity of the plan lying through McPherson's Station, another a little to the north of west of the McPherson homestead, and the third farther to the north.

For several minutes Bony studied the plan. Then he looked up into the watching eyes of Burning Water, saying:

"I will think of these matters, and we will talk of them again. Do you know what an enigma is?"

"Yes. It is a riddle," instantly replied the chief.

Bony smiled, and gave the sign Sturt had seen.

"You are an enigma," he said, laughingly.

CHAPTER 10

MORE FACETS

AFTER lunch, taken with Flora McPherson *tête à tête* as McPherson had not returned from his business on the run, Bony lounged on the cool south veranda. The morning had passed without certain watchers having seen a column of black, oily smoke signalling surrender to Rex McPherson's astounding demands; and in Bony's mind was speculation regarding the manner and the time young McPherson would execute the threat dropped from his plane.

Bony would have liked much to know the purpose of his host's trip outback because, according to Chief Burning Water, the squatter's decision the previous day had been to call all the aborigines to the homestead. Today, McPherson might well be taking measures to safeguard his cattle from another attack by the Illprinka blacks.

The feeling was gaining strength that the investigation was taking charge of him, that forces were moving which would ultimately nullify his efforts to finalize work he had been sent to do. Himself always master of an investigation, he now suspected that, were he not particularly "alive," he would become but a minor participant in it, in which case a blow might be given his vanity, with dire results to those dependent on him, as well as himself. Like the illustrious man whose name he bore, his first failure would mark the beginning of the end of Detective-Inspector Napoleon Bonaparte and the emergence from that personality of a half-caste nomad of the bush. Success had become a drug: failure of the supply would spell the end of a brilliant career.

Two roads were open to him. He could retire along that road leading to security in the success he had already achieved of unmasking the man who had committed the crimes tabulated for his investigation. He was able to prove that one particular man had instigated the theft of McPherson's cattle, had been thus directly implicated in the murder of two aboriginal stockmen, and was responsible for much inter-tribal unrest. His allotted part had been accomplished; the remainder was the concern of the ordinary police who would without doubt charge the criminal with the murder of Sergeant Errey.

The other road, however, beckoned him with imperative gestures. But this road was fogged by McPherson's attitude of quiet hostility, by his determination to tread a path of his own, and by the inaccessibility of the criminal so early unmasked. To follow this road meant undertaking strenuous hardship and facing grave danger to achieve in success nothing more than already achieved, save an additional supply of that drug on which he so much depended.

To follow the second road was to travel far into the "open" country inhabited by a tribe of fierce and relentless aborigines, and there apprehend a wily half-caste armed with the latest weapons provided by science and aided by a people who are past masters in the art of concealment and evasion. Locating and arresting a criminal in a large city would be child's play in comparison, for Rex McPherson could move at will over a hundred and fifty thousand square miles of semi-desert country. It would mean undertaking the work of a large body of police and aircraft.

Such a force might well demand a year to achieve the arrest or destruction of Rex McPherson. McPherson's idea of taking a party of the Wantella blacks into the open country to exact justice was more likely to succeed and in a much shorter period of time. More likely to succeed but not likely to succeed, wherein lay a subtle difference.

He was still pondering this matter when Flora McPherson stepped out to the veranda, where she was received by a suavely polite man who arranged for her a chair and offered her a tailor-made. cigarette from the silver box he had brought from the lounge.

"Now tell me what deep schemes you are trying to hatch," she said, seriously.

"They are about you and Doctor Whyte," he told her as though to lie was an impossibility. "I have been expecting to hear that the flying doctor has left Birdsville to visit us, and I have been hoping to hear of his departure because I rather want him to show me from the air as much of the Illprinka country as possible. Then, too, I have been thinking of Burning Water. What a travesty he must have appeared in clothes."

"Indeed, he wasn't," came the instant defence. "He wore clothes as naturally as you do—as uncle does. I came here first on a Sunday, and I was introduced to a tall attractive black man wearing a suit of spotless duck and white tennis shoes. I had never imagined an aborigine wearing anything but dirty rags and speaking in a kind of guttural broken English. You see, the only aborigines I'd ever seen were those haunting the stations of the Transcontinental Railway."

"What an introduction to the race!" exclaimed Bony.

"I was to be further astonished by him when he played me at tennis at which I thought I was passably good," she went on. "You ought to see him and uncle as captains of matched cricket teams." Flora laughed. "And you ought to see the blacks playing cricket, too. Oh no! Burning Water was never a travesty in clothes. Why, he is the McPhersons' greatest achievement in Australia, and if the blacks had been given the chances the Maoris got in New Zealand they would today have been as cultured and as good citizens."

"I see that you have a deep admiration for their qualities," Bony murmured, charmed by the forthrightness with which this girl expressed herself.

"I have. What is it that makes the world go round?"

"Money."

"No."

"Love."

"No. I'll tell you. It's loyalty. Only the basest of us are not actuated by loyalty: loyalty to one's class, to one's people, to one's ideals. The blacks are as loyal as the best of us. Here they are loyal to their rites and beliefs and customs, to Burning Water and to uncle. They call him not the boss but *The* McPherson. I'll own they were drifting when Burning Water and uncle pulled the tribe together, but that was no fault of theirs. They have helped to make McPherson's Station. Burning Water helped Uncle with the dam wall. Uncle has achieved much, but his greatest achievement is Burning Water."

"You get along very well with your uncle?"

"Of course. Uncle appeals to my mothering instinct."

"And do you like living here so far from the cities?"

"Again of course. In the city I am a mere cipher. Here I am able to give full scope to a gift for organization. I am a somebody. Besides, I am a throw-back."

"Indeed!" Bony said, with well simulated incredulity.

"Yes, it's the truth. Both my mother and father hated the bush. I'm like my grandmother and the wives of all those men pictured in the dining-room. I'm more loyal to the clan than my mother was, but don't think I'm not being loyal to her, will you?"

"Certainly not; and that is the truth, because I want especially to please you this afternoon. I have a favour to ask. I am going to ask you to go away from McPherson's Station until this Rex McPherson affair is wound up."

"Oh, but that would be silly," she countered. "Where's the necessity?"

"The necessity lies in your uncle and myself having complete freedom from concern for your safety. Rex threatens to strike again and harder still. He might destroy this house, and everyone in it, with his bombs. He might even attempt to abduct you again. I have the feeling that his next attack will be even more spectacular than what has already happened."

"Was this why you asked Doctor Whyte to visit us?" she asked.

"No. I spoke the truth when I said I wanted him to take me up to see a portion of the Illprinka country. However, if you did consent to take a holiday in one of the cities you would be rendering both your uncle and me a service. Doctor Whyte could fly you as far as Broken Hill and the railway."

"I'm not going."

"The situation here may develop in such a manner that your presence would create fatal restrictions. You see, we'll have to act against Rex McPherson. He cannot be permitted to continue. It will mean going away into the open country after him, and if you are still here either your uncle or Burning Water, with the majority of the bucks, will have to stay to guard you."

"I can look after myself."

"It is probable that you will be confronted by a personal danger from a bad half-caste, and when a half-caste is bad—well, he is so. He has already proved in a shocking manner how ruthless he is. I fear I will have to press the urgency of your taking a holiday."

"Why be annoying?" Flora demanded, her eyes afire.

"Not annoying, surely, Miss McPherson. Possibly persistent."

"Then don't be persistent. When you are persistent I can't help thinking you are a detective."

"But really, all joking aside——"

"I am not joking. I am not leaving McPherson Station. I'm not running away from a bad half-caste. Grandmother never ran away when the homestead was threatened by the blacks. If Rex threatens me I shall kill him. See. . ."

Her hand went swiftly to the neck of her low-cut blouse to appear again holding a small automatic pistol. The swiftness of the action aroused Bony's admiration, and silently he watched her return the weapon to the soft-leather holster strapped beneath her left armpit.

"I know how to use it, too," she said, firmly and a little pale. "Burning Water coached me."

"Burning Water appears to be proficient in many branches of sport," Bony surmised.

"Now you're being sarcastic," she flamed at him.

"I am sorry, Miss McPherson. I should not have made that remark," he told her contritely. "I fear it's a bad habit I've got from my Chief Commissioner, who in condemnation of anyone asserts they must be sickening for something. But really I am a little uneasy about you, and that is my excuse. If you promise me not to hesitate to use that weapon if you are ever threatened by danger I would be less uneasy about you."

"It will not be necessary for me to make the promise. But I'm not going away and you mustn't make me."

"Make you!" he echoed. "How could I make you?"

"You could make me go all right. I know that, and so do you. But please don't insist. I'd feel cowardly if I ran away—even when you had made me."

Bony sighed loudly, with pretended pain.

"To hear you speak one would think I was a real policeman," he said, and laughed. "What I said was only a suggestion."

Bony stepped off the veranda into the hot sunlight and, with his hands clasped behind his back, trod the yielding paspalum grass lawn to arrive at the bottom fence and there lean against one of the squared and white-painted posts.

Beyond this fence the ground sloped sharply downwards to the mile-wide verge of claypans two to three hundred feet below the higher ground. Vast sheets of burning water covered the table-flat verge of the plain so that the low tobacco-bush and acacias beyond were raised to tall masts, waving palms and fantastic shapes to be likened to nothing on earth. Effectively hidden was that wide belt of old-man saltbush in which Bony and Chief Burning Water had skirmished with the Illprinka blacks.

The land shoulders, west and east of the homestead jutting farther into the lower land, shortened the view of the plain's extent. The road to Shaw's Lagoon slipped furtively down the slope where it furtively entered the stream of burning water. Thence it undulated over the plain, crossed the far verge of claypans and rose upward to twist among the distant hills and flow for mile upon desolate mile towards the farthest west outpost of civilization and white law.

It was no wonder that McPherson considered himself, as his father had done, to be a kind of dictator who made laws, who exacted obedience to his laws and punished disobedience. Like his father, he would not long survive if he ever became timid enough to rely on a yell for a policeman to acquit himself of "an annoyance."

Bonaparte was not yet used to this garden which in itself was a monument to human courage and tenacity and dauntless effort to create and maintain beauty. Here and there the sprinklers shed their rainbow hued showers upon the gleaming grass. There grew two fine lily-of-the-valley gums, casting broadbased spear-heads of inviting shade. Over there, roses climbed an arch of trellis and made a sanctuary of the seat below them. To the west and the north an eight-feet-high wall of cane-grass protected the garden from the withering hot winds.

In the eastward wall was a door, and beyond this part of the wall a line of graceful sugar gums bore aloft jade bracelets to catch the rays of the brilliant sun.

A famous English novelist wrote a story about a door in a wall beyond which lay—— And through this door in a wall of cane-grass Bonaparte passed to enter—a shrine. It was all a shrine, a place of quiet beauty, for cemetery, which hints at cement and coldness, is not the right word for this place of the sleepers.

The shrine was square-shaped and walled with cane-grass, and in extent was approximately half an acre. In the centre was a white marble fountain—a woman holding aloft the torch of truth from which a thin column of water rose and plumed into spray which descended into the shell-like basin. The entire floor of this place was a lawn in which small circular beds of roses seemed like incense bowls. Against the north wall lay two massive slabs of red granite: three similar slabs were over against the south wall. And over all, roses and grass, fountain and red granite slabs, danced the shadows of the sugar-gum leaves.

Bony slowly passed to the twin slabs of red granite where he read the names chiselled deep and wide. Angus McPherson appeared on the one, and Flora McPherson appeared on the other. There were no dates and no epitaphs.

A little awed, conscious of standing on hallowed ground, Bonaparte turned to skirt the fountain and to stand before the three slabs resting side by side. Names were chiselled on all three, but those on the outside had been obliterated with cement which easily could be removed when the vault beneath had received its casket. The name on the centre one contained but the one word—Tarlalin—pronounced by McPherson, "Tar-lay-lin."

Tarlalin! The name itself was poetry. Tarlalin! An Australian aborigine was lying beneath that magnificent slab of red granite brought all the way from Scotland. Tarlalin!

The bodies of Australian aborigines had rotted to dry dust in the hot sands of the deserts: had slowly perished in creeks and waterholes: had swelled with the effect of the white man's poison: and festered with the effects of the white man's bullets. They had been flogged at Sydney, hanged at Brisbane, loaded with chains at Adelaide and at Perth: had sunk into the ferntree gullies of Tasmania. The aborigines had been debased, outraged, jibed at and made the butt of both coarse and refined wit. They had been drawn into the shadow of a civilization which, compared with theirs, was a riot of criminal lunacy. And here in this beautiful shrine one man of all the thousands who had sinned consciously and unconsciously against a race had made atonement when reverently he had laid to rest one aboriginal woman in a mausoleum of imperishable granite, protected from the withering wind by the wall, from the hot sun by the branches of the sugar gums, perfumed by flowers, cooled by luscious, vivid, green grass.

Tarlalin! One aboriginal woman of all the countless women who, down through the ages, had been little better than beasts of burden, been used carelessly and cruelly by men; regarded without honour, without value, save the questionable value of producing children that were seldom wanted because of the hard-won food they would eat and the precious water they would drink. Of all those numberless women but one had been loved greatly in life and greatly honoured in death.

Bony breathed her name again and again. It stirred him in a manner never before experienced. What had the white girl said ruled the world, when he had answered money? Why, loyalty! Of course, she was right. Loyalty was actuating McPherson now —loyalty to his own name, his own people, his own clan. He was now fighting for what? To preserve his name from being soiled and Tarlalin's memory from scorn and derision. He was fighting an evil spirit, threatening Tarlalin's memory and his own name.

And McPherson should win his fight. Oh yes, he should win it. Bony would ensure victory, ensure security for a woman's memory and a man's name. No hint of public derision should reach the man who so signally had honoured a woman of Bony's own mother's race. Here in this shrine was the die cast for him. Here began the road he would take. Tarlalin! She could have been the mother he had never known, the unfortunate who laid herself down to die in the shade of a sandalwood-tree, holding in her arms a sleeping babe that grew up to become Detective-Inspector Bonaparte.

Old Jack spoke twice before Bony became aware of his presence.

"She's a pretty little graveyard, ain't she, mister?" remarked the little old man who looked so like the Emperor Franz Joseph when his old felt hat hid his bald cranium.

"Oh, hullo, Jack. Where did you come from?"

The ancient chuckled, and Bony could hear no irreverence in it.

"I was a-lying down over there having forty winks," explained Old Jack. "It's nice and peaceful in here, ain't it?"

"Yes, it is. And very beautiful. Tell me, who is that stone to cover—presently?"

"That one! That's the boss's resting-place-to-be."

"Ah! And the other?"

"That's the resting-place-to-be of the young master that went away years back."

"Rex McPherson, eh?"

"That be him, mister. You know about him?"

"Yes. He hasn't done much good has he?"

"Well, no," slowly agreed the old man, to add: "But he's only a bit wild. He wasn't handled right, to my way of thinking. Aye, he were a bonnie boy, and he grow'd up to a fine looking man, too. Full of spirit, you know. Devilment more'n anything. The boss was a bit severe like with him after he came from school."

Bony regarded the little old man standing peering up at him with bright eyes. Old Jack went on:

"Yes, mister, this here's a beautiful place. The woman lying yonder thought of it first before it ever happened. She loved flowers, you know. So do I. Y'see over there at the feet of them two slabs of Angus and Flora McPherson? That's where I'm going to take my last long sleep. The boss has promised me that, and he'll keep his promise, never fear."

Bony's gaze wandered from the bright eyes. Loyalty! The girl was right.

After discussing cabbages and kings over the tea cups, Bony visited the office where he remained for twenty minutes before walking thoughtfully to the blacks' camp.

At fifty yards the scene he gazed upon was indolent and peaceful. Chief Burning Water was lying in the shade and again permitting a "chook house" to be erected on his stomach, and it was this that brought the heavy frown to Bonaparte's forehead, for here he was confronted by that facet of the aborigine's character which is the fatal bar to his advancement in step with other races. Educate him as you will, influence him as you may, you cannot eradicate his supreme indifference to tomorrow.

"The McPherson is not yet home," Bony informed Burning Water.

"There is nothing unusual about that," the chief asserted. "The McPherson no doubt has found other work to do from that he set out to do. I have known him go away for the day and stay away for a week."

"But other circumstances in conjunction with his absence give ground for worry," Bony pointed out. "Constable Price says there is no word from Doctor Whyte in reply to the telegram asking him to pay The McPherson a visit. Also, I am unable to get through to the out-station. The line is dead. There is a white man out there, isn't there? Married, too."

"Yes. Tom Nevin is at the out-station with his wife and two babies. A tree branch must have fallen across the line, because Mrs Nevin would be there to answer a ring."

"There has been no wind for a week to break a tree branch to fall on the telephone line," Bony pointed out. Then he added a question that in view of Burning Water's physique, was strange. "How do you feel?"

For a full two seconds Burning Water stared into the blue eyes of the lesser man, and then he repeated the question. Bony said: "I feel like a dingo when danger threatens from down wind, a danger he can't smell or see. I am uneasy. It is like the quiet of evening when the thunder clouds are gathering in the west."

Only now did the black eyes of the chief reveal concern now that possible danger was communicated to him by another. Bony could see his mind at work searching for this possible danger as the dingo's nose will work in similar effort.

"Tell me," Bony said, quietly, "what view can be gained from the tank stands?"

"Only the plain to the south. They are not high enough to let a man see over the scrub on the high land. But there's a tree at the head of this gully which gives a view all round. It's less than half a mile away."

"Ah! Let us walk to that tree and see how the world looks."

Together they walked along the gully bed to avoid the deep water gutters bringing flood-water into the main stream.

"Is Itcheroo in camp?" asked Bony.

"Yes."

"He will bear watching. However, we may find a use for him in certain eventualities. During the Great War, so I understand, the British authorities purposely left spies at large so that the spies could transmit false information. No doubt shortly after The McPherson left the homestead in his car this morning Itcheroo conveyed the fact to an Illprinka man who, in turn conveyed it to Rex McPherson waiting for news of the smoke signal, announcing his father's capitulation. That we have not a spy in Rex McPherson's camp is a distinct disadvantage, isn't it?"

Burning Water grunted assent, and, when he offered no comment, Bony spoke again.

"A living Itcheroo would be of greater value to us than a dead Itcheroo. Therefore, because The McPherson is absent, kindly refrain from sending him back into a tree or a stone or whatever it was he came from. Whilst you have been lying down in the shade and thinking of pleasant things, I have been thinking of nasty things and of nasty men whom you and I together will have to fight."

"Without The McPherson I am like a man bushed," growled Chief Burning Water. "He is my chief and him only do I obey. I wait for him to say: Do this or do that. I suppose it has become a habit, like the bad habits the old McPherson's wife used to tell about."

"I understand," Bony said. "Is this the tree?"

This tree, a magnificent white gum, had long been used as a lookout by the Wantella tribe. Steps had been cut into trunk and branches where difficulty in climbing had been met, whilst in the fork of the topmost branch a platform had been constructed, looking like an eagle hawk's nest.

Bony first gazed to the west and the north, and there was no need to look elsewhere. Beyond the edge of the carpet of scrub extending to the horizon rose columns of dark-brown smoke, columns separated into sections, section following section upward to merge into mushroom-shaped clouds tinted with gold by the westering sun.

"Now, what do you make of that?" asked Bony, a hint of triumph in his voice, that hint betrayed in the voice of those who delight in saying 'I told you so.' "I can make nothing of them. Can you?"

"Yes. I can read," replied Burning Water. "You see that signal far beyond the others to the north-west? That says come to big corroboree. All the others are saying they will."

"Oh, is that so? When there are men like Itcheroo over there one would think that sending up smoke signals was unnecessary."

"There are few Itcheroo," Burning Water pointed out, truthfully. "The number of answering signals would say that the Illprinka tribe is much scattered."

"So they would," agreed Bony. "So they would. On the sand map you drew for me you placed a waterhole far to the north-west. That sending smoke would be in line with that waterhole, eh?"

"Yes. It's probably a pick-up signal from the one at the waterhole which is a hundred and forty miles from here."

"Oh! What's the waterhole like, the country round it?"

"It's a small lake filled quickly by two creeks, and when it is full it is very deep. It's a place for water-birds and all round it lie big sand-dunes. The waterhole southward of it on my map is a hundred miles farther to the west and not so good. There is a chain of deep holes on a creek which begins and ends in about six miles."

"Ah! And the waterhole at the westward end of the plain?"

"That is closer to us—about a hundred miles away. Water lies in deep channels along the edge of a big cane-grass swamp. I have been to that waterhole. The cane-grass swamp—dry, of course in ordinary seasons—covers land almost as much as McPherson's Station."

"Good hiding place, evidently."

"All the people in the world could walk into that cane-grass swamp and be hidden for ever," answered Burning Water, whose knowledge of the world's population could be nothing but vague.

Standing on the swaying platform of boughs and supporting himself by holding to one of the two natural supports, Bony turned to gaze eastward, when he saw almost below the tree a large clearing in the scrub, in the middle of which tiny black figures moved about a low bush humpy.

"That is the Wantella ceremonial ground," Burning Water explained. "Those down there are of the White-ant Totem. They are going to have the ceremony of the White-ant tomorrow. I am glad it is the White-ant ceremony, because it will not take longer than a few hours. The ceremonies in series taking days and nights to perform often weary me."

Bony's interest in those about the humpy in the clearing swiftly passed, and returned to the smoke signals, which portended a period of quiet in the Illprinka country. The Wantella man waited on him, alert now like a most suspicious dingo, apt to see danger where danger did not actually exist.

"Can The McPherson read those smoke signals?" Bony asked.

"As I can," came the answer.

"Tell me. Before those raids on The McPherson's cattle, Rex McPherson sent a letter to his father telling him to retire and give the station to him, or he would steal the cattle. Do you remember how long after the letters were received that Rex McPherson did steal the cattle?"

"Three or four days at the longest. The McPherson told me that it appeared Rex McPherson made all his plans before writing the letters."

"And don't *you* think that having sent The McPherson a letter last night he will strike again in a day or two?"

"Yes. The McPherson swears he won't hand the station over to his son. I expect it is why The McPherson hasn't come home yet. He's planning to keep his cattle from being stolen."

"You may be right—that the cattle will again be Rex McPherson's objective, Burning Water, but it may not be this time. It may be some other: for instance, it may be the abduction of Miss McPherson."

Burning Water caught Bony by an arm, pulled him so that he came to stand chest to chest and looked up into black eyes now large and angry.

"I had not thought of that," he said. "I see now why you feel like a dingo in danger from down wind. You are like The McPherson. You look into the days that are to come and plan for them."

"And I try to look into the minds of distant men and read them as you read those smoke signals," Bony added. "Listen. The McPherson goes outback in his car after breakfast this morning. Itcheroo sees him go and he sends a mulga wire to an Illprinka man, who tells Rex McPherson that, instead of sending up the smoke signal saying he will give his son the station, The McPherson has gone outback in his car. This afternoon the leaders of the Illprinka tribe send up smoke signals calling all the tribe to a waterhole a hundred and forty miles away. They wouldn't be doing that if Rex was going to make another raid on The McPherson's cattle, would they?"

"You reason like The McPherson, my brother."

"I reason better if he, reading those smoke signals, thinks all the Illprinka men are retiring to that distant waterhole to hold a corroboree. The situation, my brother, is certainly not clear, but it makes me glad I reached a particular decision when gazing on the tomb of your sister, Tarlalin."

CHAPTER 11

McPHERSON MOVES

As Burning Water had said, a squatter seldom can be sure, on leaving his homstead, when he will return to it. So many problems arise without warning to demand instant attention that a projected absence of a few hours may extend into several days.

When McPherson left his homestead, the morning following the visit of the aeroplane, his intention was to run out to Watson's

Bore, where there were a dozen male aborigines working as stock-men. There was no telephone at this hut situated midway between homestead and out-station on country appearing to the uninitiated as semi-desert despite the growth of buckbush, cotton· and flannel-bush, and the green-sprouting tussock-grass.

The bore itself was half a mile from the hut on lower ground denuded for miles of scrub by the cattle. Situated on the north-western edge of the Great Artesian Basin, from its inverted L-shaped above-ground iron casing flowed every twenty-four hours half a million gallons of steaming water, forming the genesis of a creek which in turn had created a lake amid distant sand-dunes.

McPherson reached the hut a few minutes before eleven o'clock to find a solitary aborigine to greet him—one named Titchalimbji, shortened to Tich to save breath. Tich was rotund and oily but clean. Ever cheerful, he was a man who, grown up with McPherson, had evinced a keener interest in cattle than his fellows, and finally had been promoted to boss musterer.

"Good day!" he shouted, hurrying from the hut to the car.

"Good day, Tich! All the boys away?"

"Too right!" exclaimed the boss musterer with immense satisfac-tion. "I push four of the loafers across to the Basin to have a look over them breeding cows. The others I tell go away out to Hell's Drift. I bin there yestiddy. Ground bog enough to trap a rabbit. You come in have a drink of tea?"

McPherson nodded and followed the fellow into the hut, at one end of which was the open hearth and a few blackened cooking utensils. In the middle was the long table flanked by forms, and at the other end on the floor was a toss of blankets left by the occupiers of the communal bed they had slept in.

Tich made tea in a blackened billy and McPherson filled a tele-scopic cup he took from a pocket. Seated on a form, he helped himself to sugar and then proceeded to cut chips from a tobacco plug, the cold and empty pipe dangling from his lips against the full grey moustache. Seated opposite him was Tich, waiting for gossip, wondering, hoping. His eyes were big as he stared at the ignited match held to the pipe bowl, and they became still bigger when McPherson's hand slid into a waistcoat pocket and brought out a cigar.

"You like cigars," stated the squatter as though there could be no argument about it.

"Too right, boss! You give-it that one, eh?"

McPherson proffered the cigar and a fat hand reached forward

and accepted it. The round face was expanded in a grin of anticipated pleasure, and into the wide mouth went half the cigar, to
be masticated by strong but tobacco-stained teeth. Presently Tich
swallowed, like a camel, and said:

"You fetch out tucker, boss?"

"Yes. You bin hear about Sergeant Errey and Mit-ji?"

"No. What about?"

The squatter related the grim details as given him by Bonaparte,
and during the recital the expression of good cheer never once left
the round black face or the round black eyes. When he had done,
Tich said cheerfully:

"Who you think that plane feller, boss? Rex?"

"Yes, Tich, it was Rex," McPherson admitted, sadly and des-
perately. "He's put himself beyond the pale. He flew over the
house last night and dropped a letter in a treacle tin. He wrote in
the letter he was going to hit me again and hit hard this time.
There's another policeman at the homestead now, a big feller half-
caste policeman who is going to catch Rex—or thinks he is. He
won't, because we're going to catch Rex ourselves."

"Too right we catch Rex you say so, boss," eagerly asserted
the aborigine. "We cunning fellers all right. You bring here Jack
Johnson and Iting from out-station. Ole Jack he cunning feller.
Best feller in Wantella mob, any'ow."

The fat face continued to bear the expression of cheer, but in
the voice now was definite entreaty. McPherson smoked for
several seconds without speaking. Then:

"All right, Tich. I'll go on out for Jack Johnson and Iting. I'll
have to fetch extra saddles and bridles. You can come out for the
rations, and then you can go after the spare horses and yard
them. We can ride to the boundary and let the horses go there.
They'll be a drag on us in the Illprinka country."

Tich, having taken the rations into the hut, walked out into the
night paddock after the night horse, and on it rode away into the
horse paddock accompanied by his excited dogs and yelling himself with excitement. McPherson drove away and covered the fifty
miles to the out-station in an hour and a half, to be welcomed by
Mrs Nevin and her two children, and by the blacks who were
camped above a water-hole farther down the creek.

"Tom out, Mrs Nevin?"

"Yes, Mr McPherson. They're moving cattle from the north-
west corner, as you said to do last night. You'll stay for lunch?"

"Thank you. But I can't stop long. Tell Tom I'm taking a
couple of saddles and bridles, and Jack Johnson and Iting back

with me. Meanwhile I'll write him a note and leave it on the office table for him."

The woman suspected the strain, seeing it in his eyes, hearing it in his grim voice, but wisely she refrained from inquiry and bustled away to prepare the meal. The two small girls accompanied the squatter to the office at the end of the veranda, unafraid of him, babbling gossip about a calf they were rearing and about a newly-robbed galah's nest.

The great McPherson spent a minute chatting with them, and then asked for silence while he wrote a letter to "dad." They stood beside his chair, silent and tense, waiting for him to finish the letter before continuing their chatter. He wrote:

DEAR TOM.

Stay at home till you hear from me. Shift the blacks into the sheds and keep them from going away. I am expecting trouble from the Illprinka. Rex has threatened again, and we know what he is. I don't think he and the wild blacks will come here, but you can't take chances. I am leaving five hundred cartridges for the rifles on the shelf above the door. If Jack Johnson and Iting are not away I'll be taking them with me. Flora will be all right at the homestead. That inspector will be there and he's no fool, but I've got to beat him and deal with Rex myself. You know how it is. So long!

The letter, sealed into an envelope, he left on the writing table and, talking about calves and young galahs, he was accompanied by the children to the car from which he took the boxes of cartridges and returned with them to the office. From the veranda he shouted for Jack Johnson and Iting.

A black urchin told him Iting was away with the men, and a chain of voices extending down the creek took up the cry for Jack Johnson. Presently he appeared, a man as tall as Burning Water but walking with a slouching gait. Over-long arms dangled from massive shoulders. A prognathous jaw, a pimple of a nose, a protruding frontal bone and deep-set eyes, combined to make a face truly ape-like. A thin piece of bone was thrust through his nose, and from the forehead-band of red birds' down dangled five gum leaves.

Jack Johnson, one-time sparring partner to the young McPherson: now the Wantella medicine man. Jack Johnson, the most horrific looking aborigine in the back country: yet famed for his patient good humour and skill in healing. His voice was gruff:

"Good day, boss!" he greeted the squatter.

"Good day, Jack. I want you and Iting to come with me to Watson's Bore, but they say Iting is away after the cattle. You come all right?"

The deference to the aborigine's wishes was significant. It indicated an understanding of aboriginal affairs which to the aborigines are of as great importance as affairs are to white people. That Jack Johnson wore only the pubic tassel announced his non-employment by the station, and, his freedom of action. Yet there was no hesitation in his voice—or in his mind. The McPherson wanted him. That was enough.

"Too right, boss! What we do, eh? Cattle ride?"

"No, Jack. I want you to come with Tich and me and the others. We're going out into the Illprinka country."

Now the black eyes gleamed and the lips parted to reveal grinning teeth.

"You go without me, boss, and I kick up a hell of a row," the fellow said, clenching his enormous hands.

"I wouldn't go without you, Jack Johnson," McPherson said softly, affected by the man's loyalty of which he had never felt doubt. "But not a word to any one, understand? Fetch a couple of saddles and bridles from the harness shed, and put them in the car."

Again, quite willingly, he talked of birds and animals with the two little girls who clung to his rough hands. They passed into the house where he chatted to the lonely woman of things he thought would interest, but when she looked at him he sensed the uneasy fear in her mind concerning the renegade son.

The woman and her two children emerged with him from the house half an hour later and accompanied him to the car about which was gathered that portion of the Wantella tribe temporarily camped here. In the back seat of the car sat Jack Johnson, bolt upright, solemnly important, proud of the distinction.

There followed a scene illustrative of McPherson's closeness to these allegedly primitive people. From the car he took a five-pound box of plug tobacco and presented each lubra and each buck with a gift. He knew them all, their names and their totem and their relationships; his knowledge of the last was extraordinary. He asked one old woman how her rheumatism was, and another how her burned leg was getting on; if this young man had taken that young woman to wife; and another when he was going to be sealed into the tribe. And the while he spoke to them the two white children clung to the hem of his old coat and the white woman chatted and laughed with her black sisters. When he drove away it was to the accompaniment of men's shouts and women's shrill cries of farewell.

It was half-past two o'clock when he reached Watson's Bore.

Tich, obviously untroubled by the consumption of the cigar, welcomed them with broad smiles and the intelligence that the spare horses were yarded. The inevitable tea had to be sipped scalding hot and the five minutes spent in smoking and gossip. After that McPherson brought into the hut a part-bolt of unbleached calico and needles and thread, and started the two aborigines at the task of making small ration bags. On such an expedition as he was about to lead there would be no time for hunting food.

They were thus engaged when the absent stockmen returned, to pour like black water into the hut with the intelligence about the Illprinka smoke signals. The black water then had to pour out again, carrying McPherson with it, and, to obtain a better view, he and Jack Johnson climbed to the hut roof and sat astride the apex.

"Looks like they're going to hold a corroboree away over at Duck Lake," he shouted down to those on the ground. "What d'you think?"

"Too right, boss," they and Johnson agreed, the latter adding: "All them Illprinka men go away back from our boundary."

The squatter reached the ground before he spoke again.

"It'll give us a chance to move a long way into the Illprinka country in quick time," he said. "It lets us in through an open gate. They'll be at the corroboree for days, but we must give them a chance to get away back. I'll go to the homestead for Burning Water and one or two more, and we'll wait till near sundown before leaving."

The squatter saw the significance of those signals but he failed to look into the mind directing them. He saw only the surface, the fact that the withdrawal of the Illprinka men to Duck Lake would mean the removal of the human screen protecting his son's headquarters. He was governed by the thought of exacting the McPherson justice, of dealing with an "annoyance" in the established McPherson manner.

An expeditionary force numbering no more than twenty would have distinct advantages over a more numerous enemy. Such a force would be able to move more swiftly and secretly than a large body of men. The horses would have to be discarded to reduce the chances of discovery before the moment of attack. His force would be partly armed with rifles to blast a way to Rex, the fountain-head of dishonour and disaster out there in country inhabited only by wild aborigines, in country beyond the law's normal reach and authority. If it could possibly be prevented there would be no outside publicity.

These thought occupied his mind whilst he drove his car along the road to the homestead, a mere track crossing undulating country belted with low scrub, paved with clay-pans, ridged by sand-dunes and graded by strips of plain.

The telephone posts carrying the single wire to the outermost post of white civilization came westward to flank the winding road when the road crossed a wide area of wind-scoured land dotted with fantastically shaped cores of sand still to be removed by the wind and the rain and the sun's heat. The track wound in and out among these sand-cores, passing sometimes under the telephone wire, and presently McPherson saw ahead the wire lying across the road.

A break! It had not been broken when he passed a few hours before on the outward journey, but it is the last straw presented here by the alighting of a bird or the buffeting of a willi-willi that finally parts rusting wire.

He stopped the car to effect repairs, having the leg irons and body harness of the linesman on the car's floor, and by chance he stopped the car beside a sand-core shaped not unlike a small cathedral. And he was standing on the running board with head and shoulders over the side whilst "fossicking" for the tools when he heard from behind him the voice which always had been clipped, concise and unemotional.

"Come backward with your hands empty, father."

He knew the voice only too well, the flat tones beneath which lurked the cultural training, and even before he obeyed the command and stepped down to the ground the fire of anger burned into his neck and face. His actions, however, were deliberate, unhurried. The unknown depths of his son's character he suspected.

And so he turned to look upon Tarlalin's son, in his heart the desire that he would not witness the man's smile. About Rex McPherson were five Illprinka men, desert blacks, three wearing not even the public tassel, their bodies caked with grime, their hair and beards rolled into tassels of filthy fat and grit. Rex was dressed in khaki drill shirt and trousers. He was shaved and clean and spruce, and despite his rage McPherson felt a degree of pride.

"Come forward, father, away from the car," Rex ordered.

There was a vast difference between this half-caste and Napoleon Bonaparte. Bonaparte's skin was a medium brown: this man's skin was almost black, prevented from being black by a reddish tinge. He was six feet tall, fairly proportioned but not big. His features were devoid of the aborigine's cast, strikingly handsome. His teeth were clean and perfect in formation. His eyes were small and black and steady in action.

"You dirty renegade!" shouted the squatter. "You rotten murderer! What are you doing on my land? Are there no limits to your effrontery, you blackguard? You yourself murdered Sergeant Errey, if you didn't actually kill my stockmen. Why, you——"

"Now, now, father, calm yourself," Rex urged, suavely polite, a smile on his face, cold hate in his eyes. "Did you get my note in the treacle tin? I aimed to drop it on the front lawn, but it was dark, you remember."

"I got it all right," ground out McPherson. "What of it?"

"What of it, my ancient parent? Why I expected to see your surrender smoke this morning. Did you forget about it?"

"You know I didn't forget about it," shouted McPherson. "You must be mad if you've any hope of getting my property. I may be ancient, but, by heck, I'm still a man. And anyway, you fool, you wouldn't have the station five minutes before you'd be hauled off for trial and execution."

"Tut tut, father!" Rex implored, and there was insult in the word father. "I will have to continue the campaign I see. You haven't tasted sufficiently my growing power. When I have the station, as well as the Illprinka country, and then all the blacks at my call, I'll defy a regiment of soldiers to capture me. I know what I'm doing, and what I am going to do. Age is always so stubborn, father, and you are growing old."

Before McPherson could again shout his rage, his son spoke an order and the Illprinka men rushed the squatter and proceeded, despite his struggles, to bind his arms to his sides with common white man's rope. Panting from exertion, McPherson saw Rex vanish beyond the sand-core, to reappear a moment later carrying a portable telephone. He was pushed towards the half-caste who sat on the ground with the machine by his legs, and he was cuffed behind the knees to force him to sit beside the machine.

Then one of the blacks brought to Rex the homestead end of the severed line and this end was attached to the portable telephone.

"Now, father, I am going to call up Flora for you. You are going to tell her that your car has broken down and you want her to drive out here for you."

"Oh quit your father-ing, you mealy-mouthed devil. What's your idea? Tell me that. Talk like a man—if you can."

"Now now, father, don't be impatient. All in good time. The idea, as you call it, is this. I ring the telephone. You call for Flora. You tell Flora your car has broken down and to come out here for you. You see, you are so stubborn. I want you to retire from business and hand the station over to me. All you have to do is to arrange about the deed of gift and sign it. In the present circumstances, of course, you could not do that, but you will transact the business if you know Flora is with me and will become my er—wife if you unduly delay in the transfer of the property."

"Bah, you rat! I'll call Flora all right."

"Should you alarm her, should you raise her suspicions that all is not quite as it should be, I shall deal with you severely. Such hostile action taken by you won't stop me eventually getting my own way."

McPherson's mind raced.

"Of course, father," continued Rex inexorably, "that detective you have staying with you might want to accompany Flora, but he won't really be in the way. However, you could tell Flora in a casual tone that you think the little trip would do her good, and that you are not keen for the detective to accompany her as you don't like the fellow."

McPherson glowered and his lips creased in contempt.

"Go to the devil," he said wearily.

CHAPTER 12

CANE-GRASS SPLINTERS

FLORA met Bony on the veranda after his visit to the blacks' camp, and she was quick to note the frown of perplexity furrowing his brow.

"Hullo!" she cried, cheerfully. "I've been waiting for you. Dinner will be ready almost at once, and I do like a tiny cocktail before dinner. Where have you been with your magnifying glass and litmus papers?"

"I have been looking at smoke signals sent up by the Illprinka people. They are going to hold a corroboree at a place called Duck Lake. Your uncle has not yet returned?"

"No. He'll be home some time, though. Now please come along and join me at the bar."

"Indeed! But what of all these ancestors? Are they not sufficiently convivial for bar company?"

It was his pretended *naïveté* that delighted her most in him.

"Uncle says they look terribly jealous and spoil the drink," she explained. "I agree with him. Just imagine the situation they are in, frozen there on the canvas and unable to step down and taste good 'wuskey'. The poor dears can't even smell it. Now please make me a corpse reviver."

"Ah—alas!" murmured Bony. "How constantly am I reminded of the deficiencies in my education! How does one make a corpse reviver?"

"Don't you know? I'll show you. Will you have one, too?"

"I beg to be excused. You see, I suffer from an awkward social disability. Spirits—and spirits appear to be the ingredients of a corpse reviver—have on me an effect of deep depression. Perhaps, in the circumstances, you will not mind if I choose a small glass of lager. Shall I do the shaking for you? Yes, I fear I'm a common man having common tastes."

"Now you are being sarcastic," she told him, brightly.

"I deny it. Has any one called up from Shaw's Lagoon?"

"No. Were you expecting a call?"

"From Doctor Whyte."

"Oh!"

"Is your uncle often detained out on the run? He said this morning he would be home for lunch."

"Yes, quite often," she replied. "You see, uncle never goes away without food and camp gear in case he is forced to stay out. Generally, however, if he's staying on at the out-station he rings and tells me so. You're not worrying about him?"

"No—oh no, Miss McPherson. An hour or so ago I tried to get through to the out-station on the telephone, but the line was dead. I wanted to get in touch with your uncle."

"Did you try again before you came in?"

"No."

"It's annoying, isn't it? Something often happens to the line, even to the line to Shaw's Lagoon. A tree branch will break and fall on it, or a mob of galahs will perch on it and break it—why, there's the telephone bell ringing now!"

"It is probably the reply telegram from Doctor Whyte," Bony surmised. "Excuse me."

"Certainly. I must see about dinner. Come and tell me at once if it is about Doctor Whyte."

"I will—with all speed."

A minute later Bony was hearing a strange voice.

"Hullo! That you, Mr McPherson?"

"Mr McPherson has not yet returned home," Bony said. "I am a guest staying here. Who are you?"

"I'm Nevin, the overseer at the out-station. I've been trying to raise the homestead for the last couple of hours. D'you know when the boss is expected home?"

"Haven't you seen him today?"

"No. I've been away. But he's been here. He had lunch with the wife and he left about one o'clock for Watson's Bore. Are you the detective the boss was telling me about?"

"I am. Why?"

"Blast! I don't know what to say or do," said the gruff voice. "The telephone going bung and then coming right again makes me think things."

"When did you last ring up?" asked Bony.

"Half an hour ago."

"Then Mr McPherson must have discovered and mended the break during the last thirty minutes. Why are you so uneasy about him?"

Nevin did not reply and Bony waited before saying:

"If you are doubtful about anything, if you think anything is wrong, please tell me. Mr McPherson left this morning with the intention of returning at lunch time. He didn't say he was going as far as the out-station."

Still Nevin did not speak and Bony was beginning to believe he had broken the connection when he said:

"I'd rather not say anything. If the boss mended the wire he must have found the break between you and the hut at Watson's Bore. You ought to see him in less than an hour at longest."

"How is that?"

"The telephone line runs nowhere near the road this side of Watson's Bore. I'll ring up later. When the boss gets in ask him to call me at once, will you?"

"Hold on!" Bony urged. "Remember, an hour is quite a long time-period. Much may happen during such a period."

When Nevin again spoke his voice was sharp and his words hurriedly spoken, indicative of anxiety not to continue the conversation.

"Things will be all right, I expect. I'll ring later. So long!"

Thoughtfully, Bony walked back to the house. A glance at the sun told him the time was half past six. That Nevin was anxious was evidenced by his voice and determination not to say too much. For the second time Bony was met by Flora at the open door.

"Who was it?" she wanted to know.

"It was Nevin," he replied with a cheerfulness he did not feel. "Nevin says that your uncle had lunch with his wife, and that, as the broken telephone wire has been repaired during the last half-hour, we can expect him home within an hour."

"Nevin is right," she said, steadily regarding her guest. "Uncle would follow the line for only two or three miles on the whole journey. He mightn't have seen the break on his way out, or it could have happened when he was beyond that part of the line. Is there anything you haven't told me?"

"There are hundreds and thousands of things I haven't told you," he countered. "Why, if I told you everything I would be out of character. I wouldn't even be a detective."

"I suggest that we wait for uncle to have dinner with us," she said.

During the meal they fought a duel with the weapons Bonaparte could so expertly use. Thrice whilst they smoked a cigarette with the coffee she tried to trap him into confessing what was giving him concern, her defeat adding to her growing admiration of him. He could raise a wall, defying even her feminine wit, when her uncle would have failed to lay the foundation.

The glow of the sunset colours streamed into the room from the french windows, faintly tinting the silverware remaining on the table, seeming to pour colour into the roses comprising the table decorations.

"We'll have wind, I think, soon," predicted Bony.

"Yes, the sky promises wind," Flora agreed. "I hate windstorms. One gets so sticky when they blow."

Bony pressed the stub of his cigarette into the ash-tray and said, cheerfully:

"The weather signs urge me to offer a suggestion. In the motor shed I saw a smart single-seater. If your uncle doesn't turn up in ten minutes, what about taking a run out to meet him?"

"Excellent!" Flora cried, standing up. "I haven't been away from the house for days. It's my car you saw. May I drive?"

"Were it my car you could drive," Bony said, adding after a distinct pause: "I can drive but I much prefer to be a passenger so that I can admire the scenery. Shall we invite Burning Water and one other aborigine to come with us?"

"I'll run across to the camp and tell Burning Water," said Bony. "Shall we meet at the motor shed in ten minutes?"

The girl nodded her assent, and her eyes narrowed speculatively whilst watching him till he disappeared beyond the veranda. She was still standing thus when she heard him ringing the telephone in the office.

"Mr McPherson is not home yet, Nevin," Bony was saying while Flora was preparing for the drive. "I am going out to see what has delayed him. What is on your mind?"

He distinctly heard the overseer sigh.

"The boss came here for a couple of saddles and bridles," Nevin began. "He wanted two of the nigs, but one was out with me and he took only one, a buck named Jack Johnson. I asks myself why he wanted two nigs and two saddles and bridles when there's twelve nigs and twelve saddles and bridles at Watson's Bore, where there's not enough work for three nigs and saddles and bridles. D'you get me?

"Then the boss leaves a letter for me which says a lot and yet doesn't give much away. If I give much away to you he's going to give me hell later on. So you see where I stand. On the other hand, the Illprinka crowd have been sending up smoke signals which means one thing and might mean something quite different."

"Hum! I appreciate your position," Bony said, sympathetically. "What did Mr McPherson say in his letter to you?"

"It's the letter that's baling me up. Oh blast! I'll read it to you." Then, when he had read the letter, he asked: "What d'you think of it?"

"I think that, adding fact to fact, Mr McPherson left here this morning with the purpose of leading those blacks camped at Watson's Bore on an expedition into the Illprinka country," Bony answered. "When he arrived at Watson's Bore something happened causing him to decide to fetch two additional men from the out-station."

"Just so," Nevin cut in. "I reckon he intended starting off from Watson's Bore with the mob of blacks and horses. Then we come to the break in the telephone line your side of Watson's Bore by about thirty miles. That's what's upsetting me. I don't like things I can't understand."

"Nor I," swiftly added Bony. "I'm going straight away to find where the telephone line was interfered with, and I want to see it before it becomes too dark. I'll ring you immediately I get back. Yes. Not now. Time's valuable."

Bony hung up and ran to the blacks' camp, unmindful of his middle-aged dignity. He shouted to Burning Water and Itcheroo to come to him, and explained to them whilst they all returned to the homestead that he wanted their company. Arrived at the shed, Flora was found filling the tank of the single-seater. She asked for water for the radiator, and Itcheroo was told to fetch a bucket of water. Whispering, Bony said to the chief:

"I don't like the matter of that broken telephone line. More than an hour ago someone repaired the break. The McPherson was at the out-station for lunch. He went there for two aborigines and horse gear, and he left a letter saying he was going after Rex. I want you to come with me this evening to help protect Miss McPherson, if necessary. I am taking her because she'll be safer with us than over in the house, and I'm taking Itcheroo because I want to keep my eyes on him. You'll both ride in the dicky seat, and at the first sign of betrayal you smash him. Understand?"

Chief Burning Water smiled.

The car purred up the long gradient to the higher land beyond the yards, Flora driving, Bony seated beside her, the two aborigines sitting behind them. After the space of a few minutes, Bony said:

"The evening is quite warm, isn't it, Miss McPherson? Perhaps a little more speed would provide us with a cooler draught of air."

Flora's heart beat. She had set a trap with her slow driving and he appeared to have been caught by it. Now satisfied that he was truly anxious about her uncle, she pressed harder on the accelerator pedal, saying:

"If it's speed you'd like, watch me drive."

The speedometer needle rose to forty-five miles an hour, the car swaying as it followed the winding track.

"How far is it from the homestead to that part of the road where your uncle would first come to the telephone poles," Bony asked casually.

He glanced at the sun now three fingers above the scrubbed horizon, and she noted the action.

"About nine miles," she replied, braking the car to take deep sand-drifts lying over the track. Beyond the drifts she sent the needle up to forty miles an hour and kept it there, determined to make this man talk of what was in his mind. Presently he said:

"Is this car only a seven horse-power machine?"

Now Flora bit her lip and sent the needle to the fifty mark on the dial. The condition of the road made such speed positively dangerous.

"Ah, that's better," Bony cried. "The air at this speed is pleasantly cool. It is going to be a nasty day tomorrow, I fear. Dust and heat and sticky flies."

The sun had set. The shadows were barely distinguishable. The glory of the sky coloured the world, painting the leaves of the bushes with purple and the trunks of the trees with indigo blue, filling the dells between the ridges of wind-driven sand with quicksilver. The scrub passed by and they emerged into that strange country of sand pillars crowned with living grass. The telephone poles came from the east to cross this country in company with the road.

The men saw the sagging wire between two poles standing at either side of the track. At the lowest part it was a bare two feet above ground, but as the road passed near the right of the two poles the wire was not a danger. Flora stopped the machine.

"Please, all of you, stay here," commanded Bony.

He got out, flashed a meaning glance at Burning Water. Flora turned in her seat to watch him. Burning Water appeared restless. Itcheroo seemed intensely interested. They saw Bony walking to the lowest extremity of the sagging wire. They saw him examine the knot joining the evident break. They watched him trotting over the uneven ground, his head thrust forward. He stopped once to pick up something and examine his find before thrusting it into a pocket. Presently he returned to the car, and Flora searched his face for news. All he said was:

"Kindly drive fast to Watson's Bore."

CHAPTER 13

"ON THE EVIDENCE"

THE headlights illuminated the winding, uneven track, pencilling sharply the twin depressions made by car and truck wheels and along which Flora McPherson drove the single-seater. The lights

merged into a searchlight sweeping from side to side. Grey, formless things became stark tree trunks: formless mounds became
carved white sentinels, the old-man saltbush; declivities in the road
became chasms waiting to engulf the car until at the last moment
when their promise of destruction was changed into gentle invi-
tation to follow the road.

Flora had been driving for twenty minutes in a silence and
now she asked, imploringly:

"Well, what did you see? What did you find?"

"I read only the first chapters of a first-class story," he told her.
"Believe me, I have no wish to appear to be mysterious, but I
would like to read further, another instalment, before telling you
the story up to a point which could be said to conclude Book One.
How many books there are going to be written before the story
ends I am unable to state, even to guess."

"I am very curious—and anxious," Flora said.

"Of course! I can understand that," he said, quickly. "I will
tell you one thing now, and you must be satisfied with it. Your
uncle drove from Watson's bore to where we stopped the car just
now. He was there some time, probably mending the wire break,
and then he turned his car and drove like we are now doing
towards Watson's Bore. It is not unlikely that he will be there
when we arrive."

They talked of other matters, disjointedly and spaced by periods
of silence, for something like an hour when Flora said she thought
they were approaching the hut at Watson's Bore. Then they
appeared to be crossing a vast desert, and a moment later the beam
of the headlamps angled downward to reveal a belt of scrub
waiting to accept the car.

The bush rushed to meet them, and passed on either side like
white water passing a ship. It vanished, and again it seemed that
they were crossing a stony desert which actually was plain country
studded with annual saltbush. The air was cool but not cold.
The stars were unwinking and yet sleepy. Quite abruptly before
them was the ghostly hut silhouetted against black velvet.

No light gleamed through the single window. No spiralling
smoke rose from the round iron chimney. No dogs barked a
welcome. No one came from the doorway to shout a cheery
"good night" when the girl braked the car to a gentle stop.

Bony called:

"Hullo, there! Any one at home?"

His reward was the friendly mewing of a cat, and the cat stalked
with erect tail into the lamps' pathway.

"They've all gone away," said Flora.

"Every one is out, evidently," agreed Bony. "They haven't long been gone, however, for the cat is neither hungry nor thirsty and looks well fed and contented. Burning Water! Go into the hut, please, and light the slush-lamps. Itcheroo—stay where you are."

They saw Burning Water's tall body outlined in the door frame when he struck a match before entering. They saw him pass inside, and then interior light was born and grew to become strong as he applied fire to the fat-lamps.

"Itcheroo! Go now into the hut," ordered Bony.

"You sounded severe when you spoke to Itcheroo," Flora commented.

"Possibly. My impression of Itcheroo is not good. Ah! Is that not the front of a car peeping from round the corner of the hut?"

"I don't know. It may be. Your eyes are sharp, Bony. Let's see."

He was round to her side of the single-seater before she could open the door, and although self-dependent and liking independence, his gallantry pleased her. Together they walked to the hut corner.

"It's uncle's car all right."

Bony halted to look swiftly over its outlines and its position.

"Deliberately parked here without doubt," he said. "I'll examine it more closely later. Let us go inside."

They found Burning Water standing with his back to the large open fireplace. Itcheroo was sitting on an up-ended petrol case. The place shouted a hasty departure, for on the table were ration bags and tinned jam, packets of matches and even plugs of tobacco. Sugar was spilled and mixed with spilled tea. There was a wash basin containing traces of a dark green paste. Strips of unbleached calico lay on the floor, here and there on floor, table and forms were lengths of white thread some still passed through the eyes of needles.

"Sit down, please, for a moment, Miss McPherson," requested Bony.

She and the two aborigines watched him as though he were a conjurer about to exhibit a trick. With a boot toe he kicked at the blankets left in a mound on the floor. He picked up a cardboard carton and saw that it had contained one hundred soft-nosed, steel-jacketed bullets used in high-powered rifles. From the edges of the mound of still hot ashes in the fireplace he found pieces of three similar cartons and charred portions of the black oiled paper used in the interior wrapping. Lastly he picked up the basin containing the residue the dark-green paste which he touched and sniffed.

"I will not keep you long," he said, and passed outside where he remained for nearly ten minutes. On returning he sat down beside the girl and began rolling a cigarette.

"I hardly like to offer you one of my own made cigarettes, Miss McPherson," he said, calmly, giving no indication of what he had found or seen or done outside. "Would you like to try to make one for yourself?"

"No thanks. I don't want to smoke now. What have you——"

She felt his boot toe press gently on her foot and stopped what she was going to say. Just beyond the far side of the table sat Itcheroo, his eyes black discs encircled with white. Burning Water was about to speak when Bony cut in.

"You were camped here when the two stockmen were killed and the cattle stolen, eh Itcheroo?"

"No fear, boss," asserted Itcheroo, vigorously. "That time I camped back at station feller homestead."

"Oh yes, so you were. It was Mit-ji who was out here then, wasn't it, Itcheroo?"

"Too right, boss. Sergeant he took Mit-ji in his car to Shaw's Lagoon."

"And," Bony continued, "was killed when the sergeant was killed in his car. Mit-ji was all burned up, like the sergeant. Mit-ji he no more sit down along little fire and send mulga wire to Illprinka man who run and tell Rex McPherson. Mit-ji no more tell sergeant about Rex McPherson, eh? He cunning feller that Rex McPherson. He put fire to sergeant's car and burn Mit-ji all up 'cos he think Mit-ji tell-um sergeant all about him. What say I take you in car to lock-up feller in Shaw's Lagoon? Rex McPherson he come long quick and put fire to car, eh?"

Itcheroo blenched.

"You tell this feller boss where Rex McPherson camps all time, eh?" pressed Bony. "Then I not take you to lock-up at Shaw's Lagoon and then Rex McPherson he not put fire to car and burn you all up."

Itcheroo rose to his feet, and Burning Water tautened his leg muscles to spring. Itcheroo stood glaring down at Bony, and Bony stared steadily at him. The half-caste wished to travel only to a point along a particular road. He waited for Itcheroo to speak. And Itcheroo became sullen and sat down. He didn't laugh it off, as he would have laughed to turn aside an awkward question put to him by a tourist who then would have retired with the conviction that he was "very primitive." No. He stared with frightened eyes at a man he knew was as close to him mentally as was Burning Water.

"You cunning feller, eh?" Bony told him, and rose from the form.

He knew quite well it would be but waste of time to threaten or question further. It was more than likely that Itcheroo would not know where Rex McPherson had his headquarters, for that young man would prohibit his mental telegraphists from broadcasting the information. He had hardly hoped to obtain such valuable information so easily, and the purpose of his questioning was primarily to upset Itcheroo's mind and thus confuse it to the extent of failing to put two to two.

"Come! We'll go home," he said.

"But——" Flora began to object.

"The puzzle we can work out over a cup of coffee. Shall I drive?"

Offering no objection, the girl followed him out to the car into the passenger's seat to which he gallantly handed her. Itcheroo appeared with Burning Water after the fat-lamps had been puffed out.

"Not a word until the coffee is steaming fragrance before me," Bony said to Flora when the car had been parked in the shed. "I am tired with thinking but very much awake. I would like you to come with us, Burning Water. You can send Itcheroo back to camp."

"You shall have the coffee within ten minutes, Bony. The kitchen fire will still be in, but the cook will have gone to bed. What will you have, Burning Water? Coffee or tea?"

"As you will be making it, coffee certainly," was the answer. "It is now more than two years since you made coffee for me."

"Is it that long? It's your own fault, Burning Water. Where, are we going to have supper?"

"I suggest the office," Bony said. "I promised Nevin I would tell him the results of our trip." Flora went on towards the house, and Bony whispered to Burning Water: "Go with her. Never let her walk alone in the dark. Say you'd like to help her with the coffee and things. I still am like the dingo who feels danger from down wind."

He was slumped into the swivel chair beneath the hanging oil lamp in the office when Flora entered, followed by Burning Water carrying a large tray; and, on his feet in the instant, he made room on the table desk for the tray and stood waiting for the girl to be seated. He closed the door then, and asked Burning Water to shut the window.

Flora McPherson sat in her uncle's office chair set to the long side of the table desk, and proceeded to dispense coffee and sandwiches to a half-caste who sat at one end of the table and to a full-blooded aborigine chieftain who graced the other end.

Truly no Australian woman ever before served two such men. Glancing covertly at Bonaparte, she noted his neat appearance, his wavy hair ruffled by the wind, his slim body and hands having the fingers of the surgeon, fingers now so expertly busy rolling cigarettes, his keen-featured face tilted downwards towards his task. She glanced at Burning Water, Chief of the Wantella Tribe, noted his massive torso, ebony black in the light of the lamp, the arm bands of human hair, the dillybag slung from his neck with human hair and containing among other things a small automatic pistol which could leap into a hand at will. She noted the forehead band of white birds' down, and the tall tufted grey hair lifted high above it. Burning Water saw her looking at him and he smiled.

"The McPherson is a great man," he reminded her. "And Jack Johnson and Tich are good men, too."

"I know, I can't help worrying, and thinking that uncle is acting wrongly. I am just aching to know what happened."

"Ah!" sighed Bony, and setting down his cup he regarded Chief Burning Water. "I'll tell a story and when I have finished you can tell me where I told it wrongly. These sandwiches are delicious, Miss McPherson, and the merest dash of brandy in the coffee— Thank you.

"On the evidence found at the site of the telephone wire break, and from what we discovered at the hut at Watson's Bore added to the information Nevin has given us, the story runs something like this. I am sure of the general outline, but I may be in error regarding one or two of the details," Bony said in preface.

"The McPherson left here this morning intending to carry out a plan of action he had evolved against Rex. Rex had threatened to strike at him again, and he decided to get in the first blow.

"Arrived at the hut, something cropped up to cause him to go on to the out-station. It might have been that he wanted calico with which to make ration bags, or needles and thread he might have forgotten, for he had determined to carry out a raid into the Illprinka country, where his party would have to travel light and yet not be able to delay for the catching of food. Armed with rifles, they would not dare to fire them at game as secrecy of movement would be important. Even the horses would be left at the boundary of the Illprinka country, for horses require attention and a guard, and they make very plain tracks.

"Soon after The McPherson left here, Itcheroo lit a little fire and squatted beside it and flashed the news of the squatter's departure to his opposite number in the Illprinka country. Rex therefore quickly learned of his father's departure on what he would assume was a normal routine trip.

"Arrived at Watson's Bore The McPherson unloaded the rations if nothing else. As I have said, he may have forgotten calico or needles or thread, or he may have been persuaded to strengthen his party with the addition of two aborigines named Iting and Jack Johnson, both of whom are exceptionally clever in the bush. At the out-station he was told that Iting was away with Nevin who, with his men, was moving cattle away from the Illprinka country. So sure was he that Rex would strike again at the cattle, or even go to the length of attacking and destroying the homestead out there, he wrote a letter to Nevin and left five hundred cartridges for Nevin's rifles.

"And so, having warned Nevin of probable trouble, having told him to gather all the aborigines camped about the place to the outhouses and sheds about the house, he drove back to Watson's Bore, taking with him Jack Johnson and gear for two riding horses. On the way, he decided to slip back here and get Burning Water to go with them in the place of the absent Iting.

"You ask, perhaps, why he didn't take Burning Water with him this morning. There is, however, a slight barrier between him and his life-long friend, and only after consideration did he alter his first decision. Your uncle, Miss McPherson, has for some time been wanting to stamp out a dangerous fire, and Burning Water says it is not his place to do so. When a fire becomes dangerous an aborigine calls a lubra to put it out, and in this case Burning Water regards himself as the lubra.

"Meanwhile, Rex, knowing his father had gone outback in the car, and having failed to see any surrender signal, swiftly planned a counter move. With five of his bucks he travelled to the station road where it is crossed by the telephone line. The McPherson came along in his car, saw the break, and stopped to repair it, the wire having been cut, of course, by Rex.

"We know that Rex wants his father to retire from the station and hand the property over to him, and it seems probable that he saw the opportunity of personally persuading his father to accept the transfer. Mark you, I say it is probable, not certain. Rex had with him a portable telephone, and he might have had the intention of compelling his father to call up the homestead office and ask either Miss McPherson or myself to go out to him as his car had broken down.

"Anyway, whatever it was Rex wanted his father to do The McPherson refused to do it. I have the evidence to prove how determined is this young man. He obtained stalks of cane-grass and made fine splinters which he thrust under his father's finger-nails."

"Oh!" exclaimed Flora, her face white and anguished.

"This method of torture is never practised by the aborigines," Bony went on. "In fact, the aborigines are not given to torture of any kind. Rex, however, is allied to the white race which, with other races, has indulged with energy in the art of inflicting pain. We know how long it takes to breed vice out of animals, even to breed out physical defects, so that the strange personality called Rex McPherson cannot be attributed to his mother or his mother's people.

"His objective when forcing The McPherson to use the portable telephone was to get me into his power or, which seems more likely, to get Miss McPherson into his power when he could use her as a powerful lever for his blackmail."

"But——" interrupted Flora.

"One moment, please. The McPherson refused to accede to his son's demands and so submitted to torture. Blood drops on the ground and the cane-grass splinters illustrate the method of torture. Failing to achieve his desire, Rex and his blacks returned to their country.

"The McPherson revealed wonderful stoicism when he managed to mend the cut telephone wire, and then drove his car back to Watson's Bore, for there are blood stains on the wire and on the steering wheel of his car.

"At Watson's Bore the aborigines concocted a medicament for his wounded fingers by pulverizing gum leaves on a nardoo stone and mixing the paste with beef fat. Then, with his hands bandaged, The McPherson instructed each of them to take a quantity of flour in a calico bag, those of them best able to use a rifle were given a weapon and cartridges, and the expedition set out whilst we were examining the scene where the telephone wire was cut.

"The McPherson, to my way of reasoning, has gone off on a fruitless errand. He and the aborigines with him saw those Illprinka smoke signals and accepted their intelligence that a corroboree was to be held at Duck Lake and all Illprinka men were going back to Duck Lake. He probably has the idea of destroying Rex's headquarters which he believes are situated at Duck Lake, to destroy the aeroplane and then if Rex escapes to hunt him down and destroy him. I think that those smoke signals form a part of Rex McPherson's newest plan to obtain the station, and therefore should be disregarded. We must not forget that Duck Lake is far away and that the surrounding country does not offer the wonderful camouflage that that great area of cane-grass does at the western end of the plain.

"The McPherson may succeed. I doubt it. He sees no farther than visible smoke signals: I try to see into the mind of——"

Bony was stopped by the sharp ringing of the telephone bell. He rose without comment and placed the receiver to his ear. The others sat quite still, waiting, listening, trying to ascertain from Bony's replies who was calling. Whilst speaking he kept his back to them. Then he replaced the receiver and turned to them, eyes sparkling and face smiling.

"That was Constable Price," he said. "Doctor Whyte has just passed over the township. He dropped a message asking them to tell us to have the landing ground here illuminated for his landing. He'll be here in twenty minutes or half an hour. Burning Water! Race to the camp and bring all your people."

CHAPTER 14

A HAPPY LANDING

WHEN Henry Whyte emerged from protected adolescence to face the wide and very wicked world he was arrayed in the uniform of an officer of the Royal Air Force, and he was sent up into the blue to battle with his country's enemies. Fortunately for him, that was in the summer of 1918 when German air power was paralysed, and thus he received a sporting chance of survival.

Perhaps it was that he happened to be the seventh son of a seventh son, or it might have been that he was born in a year divisible by seven, but from the day of his first solo flight in training the history of his life was red-lettered with luck. At least this was said by his friends to account for his escapes from The Reaper.

In his somewhat unordinary character was a streak of cautiousness which really ought to erase many of the red letters, for many of his escapes from death were directly due to forethought and thoroughness in planning for the future. He was one of many sons of the rich who burn with ambition to do something.

After demobilization, Major Henry Whyte settled down to win his medical degree, and, having accomplished this, he was looking about for a practice when he happened to read an article describing the work of the first Flying Parson in Australia, whose headquarters were at Wilcannia, N.S.W., and whose parish was half the size of England. The corollary of the Flying Parson, of course, was the Flying Doctor.

Thus it was that Doctor Whyte came to Australia in 1927, then obtaining his transfer to the Australian register and taking a refresher course in aerial navigation. Ample means enabled him to begin his newly found career with means sufficient to stand the drain of two machines every year. They did not wear out, like motor cars.

Selecting Birdsville for his headquarters, Doctor Whyte never hesitated to fly anywhere in all weathers to succour men and women, even to transport them to the town hospital, to search for lost explorers, and to enhance the well being of a meagre population inhabiting a vast area of country.

He received Bony's telegram, dispatched by Constable Price and purporting to be sent by McPherson, when he arrived home at four o'clock in the afternoon from a long trip. Glancing through his case-book and finding himself comparatively free, he left Birdsville at six on the 400-mile journey to McPherson's Station where he had gazed into shy blue eyes and had felt tender red lips clinging to his own.

He ought to have arrived at the McPherson homestead when Flora and her small party were stopped at the break in the station telephone line, but then he was still engaged on the slight repairs to his engine the failure of which had caused a forced landing on a gibber plain one hundred miles south of Shaw's Lagoon. He got off the ground just before night took possession of it.

He ought then to have returned to Birdsville where his own landing ground would have been illuminated to receive him. What he did was to set off to locate a tiny outpost blanketed by night, unmarked by street lamps, an infinitesimal dot no larger than a pea on a football ground, trusting to his navigational skill to locate Shaw's Lagoon and so be able to reset the course to McPherson's Station.

He made an error of a sixty-ninth of a degree in his calculations worked out when his machine was high above the shrouded world and flying in the twilight of the sky. The error was small, but it might well have ended in a disastrous night landing. He passed Shaw's Lagoon fourteen miles to the west of the township, but quickly discovered his error and turned in an effort to find it —the pea lying on the football ground at night.

Quite a famous character at Shaw's Lagoon was one known to all and sundry as Beery Bill, an elderly alcoholic in monthly receipt of money from a trust fund sufficient to hire him a hut and to supply him with an almost unlimited number of schooners.

Beery Bill had been away all day with Constable Price and others on the dreadful business of the burned car in the gully bed. During the journey, of course, the supply of schooners of beer was non-existent, and it can be easily imagined with what avidity Beery Bill carried on when the supply was renewed. It soon became evident that the enforced abstention had put Beery Bill out of his stride, as it were, because he became unwell for the first time during his sojourn at Shaw's Lagoon and, to the amazement of the twenty inhabitants, he left the hotel to sit with his back against a pepper-tree in the street.

It was quite dark. The oil lamps in the few houses and the hotel sent only sickly gleams through the open windows. Beery Bill sat and wondered what on earth had gone wrong with him, and was thus dismally engaged with introspection when he heard the far distant hum of the aeroplane engine.

He was the only person in Shaw's Lagoon who did hear it, and knowing that his eyes could show him things unseen by ordinary mortals, he also knew that his ears could not play him such tricks. Ah! Here was a chance to entrench himself on the best side of Constable Price, and off he trotted—he was beyond walking— to the police-station with the news.

Out came Price to listen and to hear. Having expected to receive a telegram from the Flying Doctor it needed no inductive reasoning to arrive at the belief that he was hearing Doctor Whyte's machine, and that Doctor Whyte had missed Shaw's Lagoon and was returning in an effort to pick it out from the void beneath him.

Thus it was that shortly after Doctor Whyte realized his mistake in his calculations and turned his machine he saw far down ahead a pin-prick of red light magically grow to become a leaping fire. Down he went until his altimeter registered a thousand feet and he was passing above the fire to see people standing about it and gazing upward at his navigation lights, to see the firelight painting the sides of small houses and the hotel, for the bonfire had been lit in the centre of the one and only street.

Well, well! He'd always been lucky!

On his pad he wrote the instructions to be telephoned to McPherson's homestead. He wrote whilst the machine was climbing towards the lazy stars. He wrapped the paper about his pipe and tied it with fusing wire. Then he sent his ship down to within five hundred feet and dropped his message. Whilst circling the township, he saw a boy pick it up and race with it to Constable Price who had changed into uniform.

Now having his position, with only a hundred miles still to fly he reset his course and flew away into the unreal world of void and dim starshine, depending on his instruments for height and speed and wind slip. The bonfire at Shaw's Lagoon slid away beyond the tail, slid away to vanish beyond the rim of featureless void established only by the stars themselves. He sent the machine up four thousand feet and he had ample room to pass over the hill range whereon was that grove of six cabbage-trees.

Probably he was somewhere over those cabbage-trees when he saw a pin-prick of light on the invisible horizon ahead of the propeller. It was a white light and his guess was correct that it was made by a petrol lamp on the homestead veranda. Six minutes later he was flying over the homestead, looking down on the light which had dbeen moved on to the lawn, seeing the dim star light reflected by the water in the reservoir.

He had arrived but not landed. He circled twice, and then saw the red spark born westward of the homestead, saw it grow into a scarlet flame, watched it swiftly become a towering beacon, and sending the machine towards it, he saw about the beacon a crowd of naked aborigines, a man dressed and a woman arrayed in white.

Down he went in a giant spiral, noting the wind direction by the beacon's smoke. A hundred feet outward from it the ground was invisible to him. Ah! Outward from the beacon in opposite directions flowed a necklace of rubies, jewels which shone the brighter the farther they got away from the fire. He sent his ship up now whilst watching the ruby necklace begin to curve to the west, extend westward like the distant lights of a street, become stilled like jewelled arms extended to invite protection and safety.

Up and away towards the stars he climbed far to the west. Then he glided earthward with the engine just ticking over and the whine of the wind in the struts a new sound. He still could not see the ground, but down he went till the nose of the ship was directed to the open end of the avenue of torches, which excited aborigines whirled above their heads to keep them alight and burning fiercely. He felt the wheels touch ground, felt them touch again and then move over the slightly uneven surface. On went the brakes, gently at first, then harder to stop the ship from charging into the bonfire at the end of the fiery avenue.

The ruby necklaces broke into two fragments when the torch bearers raced with shouts and screams towards him. He could see and hear Burning Water bawling at them to keep back, but on they came, giving the impression that his ship was about to be engulfed by a sea of fire and flying sparks.

He watched impersonally the grey-haired chief and Bony race to the machine to keep back the excited aborigines, heard the chief's mighty voice threatening, commanding. The fiery tide halted, here and there ebbed, became stilled. He saw the woman in white running to the ship, behind her a line of fire, and he never was able to recall how he reached ground. Now he was holding her in his arms and feeling the press of warm lips on his own.

CHAPTER 15

A SPOKE IN BONY'S WHEEL

BREATHLESSLY, unwonted colour in her face, her blue eyes sparkling in the ruddy glare, Flora McPherson slipped from her lover's arms and turned to present the visitor to the patiently waiting Bonaparte and the Chief of the Wantella Tribe.

"Harry!" she cried, "this is Detective-Inspector Bonaparte."

Bony stepped forward and put out a hand. The doctor removed his gloves, ripped open the front of his flying suit, and fingered a monocle suspended by black cord. The monocle appeared to leap upward from the doctor's forefinger and thumb. It reflected the firelight. Then it was perfectly poised in the right eye.

"How d'you do, Inspector," he said, and there was neither drawl nor affectation in his voice. "Bony for short, eh?"

"All my friends call me Bony."

They shook hands.

"To use an Australianism: too right," the doctor agreed heartily.

He was no fool, this young-old man who began life as a destroyer and now was a mender. "Bony it is, comrade. And a smack on the jaw if you call me anything but Harry. And there's Chief Burning Water. How are you?"

Dr Whyte took three steps forward to meet the chief of an aboriginal tribe, and Burning Water shook hands delightedly.

"I am well, Harry," he said, compelled to gaze slightly downward because of his height. "I have thought of you, and I have looked forward to your next visit. I hope you will stay long."

"Leave it to me," and Dr Whyte brazenly winked. "How's the infant? D'you still let her build chook houses on your tummy?"

"I haven't yet been able to blow them down," Burning Water replied, laughing, and his people standing behind him joined in the chorus. The flying doctor stepped out of his suit, saying:

"You would be a marvel if you did. Well well! I'm damned glad to see you all. What a landing!"

"It was nice, wasn't it?" Flora agreed. "Now you must be tired and hungry. So late to arrive, too. What about your cases?"

"I'll get them out. Where are those trees we used to anchor the crate to, Burning Water?"

"They are back a little way, Harry. You could leave the aeroplane in my charge."

"Right oh! I'll get the cases first, though."

Willing hands took the two suitcases from him, and Burning Water began to call names and to shout orders. Almost as though they were professional groundsmen, the aborigines turned the machine and proceeded to trundle it towards the foot of the higher land. Flora slipped an arm through the doctor's and called to Bony to accompany them. And then when he was walking beside her she slipped her other arm through his. In step like soldiers, they walked towards the homestead, preceded by the suitcase carriers, escorted and followed by torch bearers. For Bony, too, it was a happy landing.

"Why ever did you take the risks of flying in the dark?" Flora asked Whyte. "You might easily have got lost."

"I intended coming in daylight, but I had to land miles south of Shaw's Lagoon and repair a broken oil pipe," he said in defence. "Time I'd effected the repairs it was almost dark. Just as easy to come on as to go back. The people at the township lighted a bonfire in the street to give me my position. I dropped my message there. You must have got it."

"Oh yes, it was telephoned through. We got quite a thrill preparing the fire and torches. We had no time to spare."

"I saw the light on the veranda from way back over the hills, I suppose old Jack took it out on to the lawn."

"And The McPherson?"

"He is out on the run," Bony cut in.

"Great man," asserted the flying doctor. "I'm glad he's not as tough as he looks, and that he doesn't look as tough as those birds in the dining-room. By hokey! He and his father have done a wonderful job of work out here, don't you think, Bony?"

"It requires time to get it all into proper perspective."

"It took me quite a time to realize that the place is almost in the middle of Australia," Flora confessed. "Uncle says it would not have been possible on the other side of the border in Queensland on account of the heavy taxation and uncertainty of tenure."

"I wonder what the devil they do with all the tax money they get," remarked the doctor. "You wouldn't think the politicians could spend it all, would you?"

"They give me some of it," Bony said, laughing.

He left Flora to take her guest into the house and himself went on to the office where he belatedly rang Nevin and told him the facts concerning McPherson. Now and then the overseer grunted his annoyance and impatience.

"I thought it was something like that," he growled. "The boss threatened to take it on last time the Illprinka raided the cattle and killed them two blacks at Watson's Bore. Why in hell didn't he let me go with him?"

"Possibly he thought of your wife and children and the aborigines out there," Bony said, soothingly, and Nevin immediately countered with:

"They could all have been shifted in to the homestead. Oh well, if he and the nigs shoot up them Illprinka fellers it'll do a lot of good and we'll have a bit of peace. Aint that Rex a devil! Cripes, I'd like to get a rifle sight on him. I'll call you first thing in the morning to hear the latest."

Bony was smoking his inevitable cigarettes when Burning Water entered the office and sat down at the table. Bony regarded him, and sighing, said:

"Did you see the manner in which the doctor flicked his eyeglass into his eye? If only I could do that. If only I could appear before my chief when he is angry with me, and flick a monocle into my eye and look through it calmly as though he were a beetle. Alas, my brother and my son and my father, we are but savages."

"He told me it took years of trying," Burning Water said with no envy in his voice. "But what of it? Jack Johnson, the Wantella medicine man, can cure as well as this white doctor. Doctor Whyte can't sit down by a little fire and send thought pictures to another man far away. He can't track anything save a horse. But he can fly a machine."

Bony blew smoke and regarded the chief through it.

"Tomorrow," he said, "I will get the doctor to fly me over the Illprinka country. From the air we could see wagon or truck tracks, and Rex must use one or the other to transport his petrol from somewhere. What d'you think of those smoke signals now?"

"I think they were a trick."

"Don't you think it seems to indicate that Rex wants us to believe his headquarters are at Duck Lake?"

"Yes, that may be so."

"And that it is likely, to say the least, that the huge area of cane-grass at the western end of the plain would be an excellent hiding place for him and his blacks and his aeroplane?"

Burning Water nodded agreement, saying:

"And after the trip over the Illprinka country what will you do?"

"After that, or it might be before, I am going to ask Doctor Whyte to join me in persuading Miss McPherson to leave with him for Birdsville. I have a sound basis for thinking she is in personal danger, worse luck, and I feel she is. I think that Rex baling up his father this afternoon was a hastily formed plan which has nothing to do with the threat expressed in his note and the plan he had conceived at the time. You and I will have to guard the girl as long as she is here."

"And after she has gone, what do we do?" insisted the chief.

"You and I will become two lubras who will stamp out a dangerous fire."

"That will be a good thing," again agreed Burning Water. Then he smiled, saying: "We may have to run about a great deal before the fire is put out. You will want your wind. Once I smoked many cigarettes, and I know."

Bony chuckled.

"Thanks for the advice, Doctor Burning Water. I'll certainly cut them down—after tonight. And now for this night. Will you keep watch on Miss McPherson's room until about three o'clock? That would give me a few hours sleep, and I shall want to be awake when in the air over the Illprinka country."

"As you wish."

"Have you a rifle?"

"No, but I have this."

Bony's eyebrows rose when with incredible speed an automatic pistol was snatched from the chief's dillybag and levelled at the window. For the second time Bony sighed with envy.

"It took years of practice," explained Burning Water. "I once read about the two-gun men in America. A motor-car explorer left the books with me, and I determined to be as quick on the draw as the two-gun men."

"Can you aim straight, you confounded enigma?"

"Straight enough, my brother who is another enigma.

Bony arose to his feet and stood looking down into the now humorous black eyes.

"Before this adventure is closed," he said, "I'm going to like you."

Flora saw no more of Bony that night, but Doctor Whyte did. He found him sitting in the darkness of his room when he retired.

"Hullo! Am I in the wrong room?"

"No, Harry. I want to talk to you, to explain fully to you why I am here at McPherson's Station, and why I am going to urge you to join forces with me in persuading Miss McPherson to leave with you for Birdsville tomorrow afternoon."

"Good! There's a spot of bother here I know, from what Flora told me. She seems anxious about the old bloke. There's a half-caste son of the old bloke in the background, isn't there?"

Dr Whyte was not much taller than Bony, but he was more strongly built. His face was marred by a scar crossing his forehead and another striking downward across the left side of his chin. His nose had been broken and badly repaired. When in a serious mood, as he was whilst Bony talked, his face was expressionless. The features, too, remained immobile for seconds together. The hands were passive. And yet about the man was an air of strength causing Bony to wonder if it was due to training or inherited from men born to command.

Presently Bony's soft voice ceased. He had permitted no surmise of the other's character and physical aspect to be betrayed by his eyes, and he did not know that Dr Whyte had been similarly employed. In the doctor, Bony had found strength. In Bony, the doctor discovered a combination of qualities which gripped his interest.

"You can count on me," he told Bony. "I'd like to stay on and help make the world hereabouts do a spot of humming, but, as you say, and I agree with you, Flora will have to go to a place of much greater safety."

"You appreciate the importance of the fact of McPherson

being away on his own business, leaving me tied here in case Rex makes a move in Miss McPherson's direction?"

"Of course. Why, Rex McPherson might even bomb the house. He must be mad, don't you thing?"

"He's an egoist who would be a danger to world peace if he was a national leader. I wonder now. Do you see this affair as McPherson apparently sees it. He wants to deal with it himself, to keep it a family secret."

"Quite! And you being a policeman will have to follow the rails and let it become a public entertainment."

Bony smiled.

"What would you do about it?" he asked.

"Keep it a family secret if it could be done," the doctor answered. "It's the McPherson family that's suffered—excepting, of course, Sergeant Errey and his family, and I've no doubt that the old man will provide handsomely for Errey's widow and the boy."

"That is one reason why I would like to forget I am supposed to be a policeman, but it is not the more important of two reasons supporting my intention to report Errey's murder as a car accident," Bony went on. "I would rather not state the more important reason, but should you ever visit the homestead cemetery, and gaze upon the tomb of Tarlalin, you may be able to make a good guess. Now I'm off to bed."

He rose and walked to the window.

"By the way. Would you be so kind as to take me up in your machine and show me a little of the Illprinka country—say tomorrow morning?"

"Certainly. I suppose there's plenty of juice in store here?"

"I saw several forty-gallon drums all full."

"Good! I'll be with you in the morning. Good night!"

Burning Water called Bony at three o'clock, and by eight the aeroplane had been refuelled and was left standing surrounded by the ever-curious aborigines, whilst its pilot and Bony rode back on the truck to the house.

Flora was waiting for them to come for breakfast.

"Bony and I are going aloft for an hour or two," the doctor told her, smiling into her eyes. "Then I must start for home and work. It's going to blow late today or tomorrow, and it might blow so hard as to make the trip unpleasant." ·

"Then you will be leaving this afternoon! Oh!"

The girl was dismayed. Bony was made hopeful and the doctor was gratified. He led the attack.

"Don't worry, Flora, me gal! You're coming with me. You're looking peaked and the change will do you good."

"Looking peaked!" she exclaimed and rose from the table to regard herself in the mirror above the mantelshelf. "Looking peaked, indeed. Why, you two have been conspiring."

"We have agreed that a short holiday would do you a world of good," Whyte said, helping himself to toast. " Convinced of it."

"Indeed!"

"I have tried to, Miss McPherson," Bony said gravely. "It concerns me that you are open to attack from a dangerous man who apparently will stop at nothing. Your uncle having gone off to carry out plans of his own, and Dr Whyte having to return to his patients, you are left in a not particularly secure position when Burning Water and I leave."

Setting down his cup, he produced an excessively grimed sheet of paper smeared with what even Flora could see was blood.

"When last night I told the story of what had happened to your uncle. I did not remember this note he left in his car. I will read it to you because it will, I hope, convince you.

"It begins: 'Dear Bony. Was bailed up at telephone break by Rex. Wanted me to speak into portable telephone box and get Flora out there alone. Look out for her. Get her away. Rex damaged my fingers and I can't write more.' It is signed D.M."

"Let me see it, please."

Bony rose and gravely placed the sheet on the table before her. She looked up at him after a swift glance at the note, saying: "That's not uncle's writing."

"We must not omit the damage done to your uncle's fingers," Bony countered, and returned to his chair. "Now, please, listen to me for a minute."

Swiftly he outlined the enormous difficulties of locating and arresting Rex McPherson, the dangers and hardships, the probable time that she would be almost defenceless.

"If you decide that you will not leave with Harry, then I will not be able to leave you alone here," he said, slowly. 'I think that those smoke signals have led your uncle on a wild-goose chase, and that he will fail in what he wishes to accomplish. In fact he and his party might well all be massacred. So, Miss McPherson. please go off on that holiday advised by your doctor and leave me free to stamp out a dangerous fire."

"But I can look after myself," Flora protested. "Rex wouldn't dare come here."

"He'll dare anything."

"Better give in and come to Birdsville with me," pleaded Whyte.

"No. I am not going to run away." Impulsively, she rose and passed round to stand close to Bony. "I know you can make me go away, Bony, but please don't make me. I'll promise not to be stupid or careless. You see, I fear Rex terribly, and if I ran away I'd begin to fear fear. Let me stay and fight it out with you and uncle. The Nevins could come in from the out-station and be with me. Tom Nevin would stand no nonsense from Rex, and besides his wife and children would be safer here. Please."

Bony's steady gaze wavered. Her intense earnestness defeated him, and he had not thought of bringing Nevin and his family in to the homestead.

"Women have ruled nations," he said. "I can well understand how they did it. I'll ask Nevin to come in today. If he will, you may stay. If he won't, you will have to leave with Harry. Is that a bargain?"

"Yes. Nevin will come for me if not for you. And don't worry about me, please. I'll be all right."

"You wouldn't hesitate to shoot—if necessary?"

"I would not," she answered, and he thought she had never looked more like those men on the canvases.

Nevin agreed to pack up and come in to the homestead. In fact, he seemed anxious to do so and promised to leave as soon as possible in order to complete the trip during daylight.

From the office Bony crossed to the blacks' camp and roused Burning Water per medium of the elder wife.

"The doctor and I are going up this morning," he told the chief. "It's a thousand to one that Miss McPherson will want to come along and watch the take-off. I've telephoned to Nevin and he's coming in at once with his family and as many of the blacks out there as can squeeze themselves on to the truck. I want you to come now to the ground, and after we have left to keep close to the girl until we get back."

"You are wise, my brother and my son and my father. So was Illawalli when he made you a great one," Burning Water said. "I'll come with you. Some of the bucks are down with the plane?"

"They were when we refuelled it. Yes, they'll still be there. I wonder where Itcheroo is this morning."

Burning Water went back and spoke with the elder wife for a few moments. On his return he looked worried.

"Itcheroo went early into the bush," he said. "Why not stamp out that dangerous fire before it becomes too fierce?"

"No, my brother. I have a use for Itcheroo."

As Bony had anticipated, Flora insisted on accompanying them to the aeroplane, and then stood with Bony and Burning Water watching the pilot swing the propeller and subsequently warm up the engine. When he was satisfied, Whyte got to ground again and joined them.

"She's all right," he said. "As sweet as a lady of my acquaintance. We'll get away when you're ready, Bony. Expect us back by noon, Flora, and as hungry as arctic sledge dogs."

"I'll be on the lookout for you," she promised. "Here Bony, you must put on the coat. You'll probably find it cold."

Bony slipped on the heavy serge coat belonging to McPherson, wished the girl *au revoir*, and left her with Burning Water and the small crowd of aborigines to walk with Whyte to the waiting machine.

The engine was purring softly and the propeller was reflecting a disc of colourless light. One of the blacks shouted, but neither Bony nor the doctor turned about to see the cause as the blacks had been shouting to each other.

Then above the purring of the aeroplane engine there burst on their eardrums a greater sound rising swiftly in crescendo. Bony spun round to face westward, to face the girl and the crowd of aborigines, to see above and beyond them the silver-grey aeroplane which had destroyed Sergeant Errey's car. With the wind behind it it was coming with terrific speed, coming down and towards them.

"Back!" he shouted to the doctor. "Come away. It's Rex and he might bomb your plane and kill us."

He dragged the reluctant doctor from the machine into which they had been about to enter. The silver-grey plane came down to a hundred feet, passed over their heads, then climbed a sky road as though it were a bouncing meteor. The blacks were stunned to silence whilst they watched the invader make a giant half-circle and return.

"Scatter!" shouted Bony, and running to the girl, he grasped her arm and urged her away from the crowd.

"Whatever is he going to do?" Flora cried.

"I don't know. He might bomb Harry's plane. He might bomb us if we bunch into a mass. Now wait. We've no cover. It is useless to scatter more than we are now."

The silver-grey machine was coming down and slowly, its engine ticking over. They could see the helmeted, goggled man in its cockpit. Then the great wings were spread above them, and the shining body passed comparatively slowly over them. They saw the bomb leave the underside of the fuselage, saw it fall like a drop of quicksilver to strike the cockpit of the doctor's aeroplane. Came then a loud report, a burst of flame, a gathering plume of smoke which the wind carried eastward.

CHAPTER 16

ANOTHER SPOKE IN BONY'S WHEEL

"WHAT a rotten sportsman—to kill a sitting bird!"

The flying doctor's voice was cool, a quality noted by Bony whose mind was concentrated on the wonder of a man being able to think along two lines of thought at the same time. He stood gazing upon the roaring flames and the vast black smoke clouds rolling over the claypans past the foot of the homestead garden. He was thinking what a pity it was that such an example of man's inventive genius could be so easily destroyed. At the same time he was thinking what a wonderful opponent this Rex McPherson was proving to be.

The flying doctor proceeded to step out of his flying suit, and Bony recalling that he was still wearing McPherson's heavy overcoat, removed it. Then, as though directed by an order, the three "fell in" and silently began the walk back to the homestead.

Presently the doctor said, conversationally:

"It's a great tragedy that that fellow wasn't born in time and in circumstances permitting him to take part in the last Great War. He's got guts. He's got flying temperament. He's got that valuable war-gift, ruthlessness."

"It is going to be a pity that he was born too soon to take part in the next war," Bony said so calmly that Flora flashed at him a resentful glance. "I am afraid, doctor, you will have to stay longer than was arranged."

"I'm afraid I'll have to slog you one if you call me anything but Harry—Mister Napoleon Bonaparte."

"That would grieve me, Harry."

Flora wanted to laugh, recognized the danger of hysteria, and controlled herself. That men suffering such loss and disappointment should thus speak to each other did not seem to be natural. She was furiously angry. The doctor said:

"It would give me tremendous gratification to slog someone hard and often. That crate was the best I've ever had, and I've only had it six months. It cost four thousand quidlets—Australian."

He uttered the word Australian as an afterthought, and Flora wanted screamingly to ask him what difference it made. If only she could see her lover "slogging" that hateful Rex!

"Insured?" Bony asked.

"Half. What's the odds? I'm stranded without a machine."

"We will go to the office and smoke a cigarette. Then we must bestir ourselves. Effects are the offspring of causes. The destruction of your machine was caused by two bombs. The bombs exploded because they were dropped. The dropping was caused by the release of mechanism caused by the hand of Rex McPherson. He was there in his aeroplane to drop the bombs at the right split-second because he knew your plane was there. He knew your plane was there because an Illprinka magic man told him, and the Illprinka man knew because Itcheroo, a Wantella magic man, told him. Itcheroo is the person fit and proper to take your slogs."

Dr Whyte stopped and turned and glared back at the aborigines still watching the metal twisting in the flames.

"Itcheroo is not there," Bony said. "Later I may introduce him to you." Following this half-promise they walked in silence, arrived at the road to Shaw's Lagoon and followed it up the steep slope to the office which they entered.

"What are we going to do about this business?" asked Whyte his voice still unruffled, his face almost without expression. Crises appeared to freeze him. Bony completed the making of a cigarette before he answered.

"It does seem that I continually make plans only to have them frustrated before they can be put into action," Bony said, slowly. "Were I not a patient man I would become angry. It seems, too, that I have been lethargic, and yet for this I have an excellent excuse. I hate to hurry or to be hurried. I decided that having accomplished what I came to do I would return to Brisbane and my wife and family. My wife will now be writing telling me how much I am missed and urging me to return as quickly as possible, and my Chief Commissioner will again be thinking of sacking me. But to revert. Having established the person who was causing a great deal of trouble in the Land of Burning Water, my mission was accomplished. Then I stood by the tomb of Tarlalin, and my plan to retire to Brisbane was discarded.

"I then decided to start out after Rex McPherson when Miss McPherson's uncle returned home. I could not do so because Mr McPherson did not return. I waited for the arrival of Dr Whyte —no slog, please, for I am speaking impersonally—and Dr Whyte's aeroplane is destroyed. These constant frustrations will have to cease."

Whyte stared at Bony fascinated and a little awed at a man whose ego was smarting under this challenge.

"As Miss McPherson will not run away, Harry, will you remain here for a week, two if necessary, and see to it that Rex McPherson doesn't steal her?"

The doctor considered and then assented.

"You see, Miss McPherson, what a problem you are," Bony continued. "However, I like problems, especially feminine ones, if genders can be applied to problems—which I doubt. Now I will plan again, and this time there must be no frustration. Pardon me."

Bonaparte rose and crossed to the telephone.

"Ah! This is Detective-Inspector Bonaparte speaking from McPherson's Station," they heard him say. "I want an urgent telegram dispatched. Will you see to it that it is sent off at once Thank you. Ready? Address: Captain Loveacre, Pacific Air Company, Brisbane. Message begins: You are urgently wanted McPherson's Station, via St Albans and Shaw's Lagoon. Remember my promise. Bring fast machine. Fuel supplies on hand. Excellent observer waiting join you. Bring tat-tat. Inform me when leaving Brisbane and probable arrival St Albans where flying instructions will await you. Message ends. Yes, from Inspector Bonaparte. What's that? Oh—tat-tat? T-a-t hyphen t-a-t. Good! May I expect a reply within two hours? Yes, I will be here."

Bony hung up and resumed his chair.

"Captain Loveacre!" exclaimed Whyte. "Not the ex-flying ace?"

"The same," replied Bony. "Captain Loveacre has on several occasions assisted me, or rather he has been associated with the background of several of my investigations. I like him. I once promised to call to him for assistance should an adventure offer. I am confident he will oblige me."

He blew a smoke ring towards the doctor and expertly sent an arrow through the ring.

"What is a tat-tat?" demanded Flora.

"Oh!" he said casually, "A tat-tat is a machine gun. It is

Captain Loveacre's word for it. When he knows my requirements he will beg, borrow or steal a suitable machine if he hasn't one of his own."

Dr Whyte relaxed and whistled. His mouth became expanded in a grin, so that the chin scar became more pronounced, but in his small grey eyes was the gleam of anticipation.

"When I was in Brisbane ten days ago—it seems ten weeks —Captain Loveacre took lunch with me," Bony said, reflectively. "After the war, when his services were no longer required by a grateful country, Loveacre formed a flying circus with which to make a living. Subsequently he obtained financial backing to form an air transport company.

"Now, Harry, you know more about the kind of machine Loveacre will bring to meet with my requirements, and you will know what supplies of petrol and oil Loveacre will need. After refuelling your machine there is now only some hundred and fifty gallons left in the store. How is petrol and oil usually brought, Miss McPherson?"

"When the truck is sent to Shaw's Lagoon for rations or supplies it always completes its capacity loading with petrol."

"And who drives the truck?"

"The men's cook."

"Where is the petrol obtained at Shaw's Lagoon?"

"From the store. There is only the one general store. The petrol depot is run in conjunction with an oil company."

"Then we must arrange with the store people to let us have as much petrol as possible, and further to have their stocks replenished as quickly as possible. Excuse me."

Bony was busy at the telephone for ten minutes, when he announced that the depot could supply up to a thousand gallons of first grade petrol. He was expressing his satisfaction when the telephone bell shrilly rang.

"That was Nevin," he said. "They are leaving the outstation now, and will be bringing all the blacks there with them. Now let me think. Yes, the two trucks can go to Shaw's Lagoon tonight. They cannot leave until after dark, and they must be back before daylight. We must think of a place to store the petrol and to camouflage the store to prevent Rex blowing it up. And tomorrow Harry, if Loveacre comes, which I am confident he will do, we must plan to construct a well camouflaged place to conceal his machine from the same destructive young man. Now we can but wait to hear from Loveacre."

The doctor rose saying:

"I feel younger, and I'm going over to the house to change into flannels."

"And I'm going over to see about a cup of tea. Will you come over to the veranda, Bony?"

On his feet, Bony was smiling at her.

"If you will excuse me," he said, "I would prefer to sit here and wait for Loveacre's telegram. But a cup of tea—here——"

"I'll have it sent over."

When, twenty minutes later, a lubra maid took to him a tray of tea she discovered him slumped into the swivel chair, a row of cigarettes on the table before him, the place filled with blue smoke, and a large sketch map drawn on sheets of writing paper pasted together. When she had set down the tray at his side he said to her:

"You are Ella, eh?"

"Too right, Mister Bony."

"Your totem is witchetty grub, I see. You know about Tarlalin who lived long ago?"

The black eyes widened and a smile flashed into the round and pleasant face.

"Tarlalin she live in that one sugar-gum tree beside cemetery feller. She wait there one time lubra go and sit beside it. Then she drop spirit baby beside lubra, and bime-by lubra she have little baby and little baby grow like Tarlalin. I bin sit there but ole Itcheroo he bad feller and little spirit baby he get frightened and run back into tree to Tarlalin."

"Itcheroo he bad blackfeller, eh?"

The girl "made a face" for answer.

"What totem Tarlalin? You know?" asked Bony.

"Too right. She witchetty grub like me."

"And Chief Burning Water—what totem feller him?"

"Burning Water he emu totem feller."

So the line of descent in this Wantella Tribe lay in the female side, and because Tarlalin's child father was a white man her male child would be given her brother's totem. Rex McPherson would be of the emu totem, and any emu man ought not to be led in battle against him. Bony wondered if McPherson remembered this when he took all the blacks with him from Watson's Bore.

Captain Loveacre's reply telegram arrived at ten minutes to twelve, and Bony was dictating a further message to be telegraphed to him when Dr Whyte entered the office, sat quietly down and studied the sketch map. Presently Bony joined him, saying:

"Loveacre will be leaving Brisbane first thing tomorrow morning. He will fly via Quilpie and St Albans where he will land for flying instructions. Those instructions I am going to leave to you."

"And the tat-tat?"

Bony smiled grimly.

"The captain says that his ta-tat is only too willing to accompany him."

"Good news! Let me see! Loveacre ought to get to St Albans with plenty of daylight to spare. What's this sketch?"

"It's of the Illprinka country. I have filled in the details as much as possible from information obtained from Burning Water. We'll get him to check it over later. Loveacre, or you as his observer, will want it. See, here's Duck Lake, and down here is the area of cane-grass. I've been thinking, too. Remember, Rex bailed up his father approximately nine miles from here about four o'clock yesterday afternoon. Here's the place on the sketch. This morning he destroys your machine here at nine o'clock. During the night where was he? Not such a great distance from the station boundary, and with his aeroplane I'm willing to wager. He's been close to us, Harry, and I think that the reason of that is to carry out a plan he conceived before he bailed up The McPherson, a plan he hasn't yet carried out. We will have to be extra careful tonight with Miss McPherson."

The instructions were dispatched to Captain Loveacre at the St Albans Post Office, and then Bony suggested that Whyte return to the house alone for lunch and ask Flora to have his lunch sent to the office. He did it in such a manner that the doctor did not suspect Bony's sentimental reason.

About three o'clock Burning Water came in and was asked to con the sketch map. He offered suggestions for several additions and one major alteration. Bony completed the work, and then he said, slowly, pointing to the area of cane-grass:

"That is where I think Rex McPherson has his headquarters. Those smoke signals were sent up for two reasons. First to allay suspicion of an immediate blow to be given by Rex McPherson, and, second, to create the belief that his headquarters, as well as the blacks' main camp, are at Duck Lake.

"See here. The difference in distance from here to Duck Lake and from here to the cane-grass at the western end of the plain is only forty miles, a bagatelle to the aeroplane. The cane-grass offers significant advantages over Duck Lake. Duck Lake is surrounded with sand-dunes and lines of box-trees bordering the several creeks emptying water into the lake. It's all bad landing country. The cane-grass, on the other hand, is bordered with wide claypan country, and also it would provide an excellently camouflaged hiding-place for the aeroplane and for all the Illprinka blacks. We must not omit from our plans the likely fact of Rex knowing the possibility of an attempt being made to arrest him."

"The cane-grass is where he would hide," agreed Burning Water. "It's a great place, the grass covering land half as big as McPherson's Station. I looked down on it once from the top of a high sand-dune. It stretches across the horizon. But the Illprinka people don't like it. They say that the Great Snake of the Alchuringa went into it one day and went to sleep and has never come out again. They believe that the Great Snake will be very hungry when it wakes and will run after any blackfeller it finds in the cane-grass and eat him up."

Bony pondered on this slight objection to his theory. Then:

"Still, Rex McPherson must be strong-minded, and I think he would be able to impose his will on the Illprinka people to the extent of persuading the bolder of them to stay with him at the cane-grass waterhole. By the way, Nevin is coming in today with every one at the out-station, and tonight I am getting him to drive his truck, together with the station truck driven by the men's cook, to Shaw's Lagoon for petrol. I want several of your best bucks to go with each truck in case of any hitch on the road."

"All right! I'll see to that."

"And there's another matter, too. Now that Dr Whyte and Nevin will be here my mind is relieved concerning the safety of Miss McPherson, and we can proceed to that dangerous fire and stamp it out. We'll leave immediately after Captain Loveacre has arrived. He is a friend of mine and is flying here. Meanwhile I think you ought to make us Kurdaitcha shoes. They will last longer than blood and feathers. What do you think of emu feathers?"

"They are good if the bird is young when killed."

"Good! Will you see to it now?"

"And Itcheroo?"

"What of him?"

"He went bush very early this morning and has not yet come back to camp."

"Oh! Well, I shall want him presently. Meanwhile let him alone."

When Ella brought the afternoon tea to him Bony was writing

a full history of the case against Rex McPherson, and he had not finished it when Burning Water returned.

"I have sent two bucks out to hunt a young emu, and when they come back an old man of my totem will make the Kurdaitcha shoes. I think I heard the out-station truck coming."

Shrieks and shouts drifted to Bony and the chief from the black's camp, and when the truck first appeared in the far scrub the homestead aborigines were running into sight to welcome the travellers: men, women carrying babies, and children of all ages.

Bony and the chief could presently see the fringe of black heads bordering the truck's cabin roof. The driving seat was exceptionally wide, and from both sides protruded gun barrels. The uproar increased: the homestead blacks dancing and shouting, those on the truck being as vociferous. Dust rose thickly from the stockyards as the truck ran past them, dust from the excited horses yarded that morning and not freed because The McPherson had not been there to issue his orders.

When the truck turned to draw in towards the side door of the house, the mass of black humanity it carried was such that one would have been pardoned for wondering how they all managed to retain their places. The vehicle stopped opposite the house door and the mass became black water falling to the ground like a waterfall.

Bony saw a white woman and two little children leave the truck and enter the house. Aborigines followed them with bags and cases. From the crush about the truck emerged a short man with flaming red hair, dressed in blue dungaree trousers and a black shirt. He was escorted by an aborigine extraordinarily dressed in a bright blue shirt only, and carrying half a dozen rifles. The blue shirt and the red hair formed a striking contrast.

A hand grasped Bony's right arm, and he turned to look into Dr Whyte's anguished face!

"Flora—I can't find her!" gasped Dr Whyte. "She's gone!"

CHAPTER 17

THE BLOW FALLS

BONY cursed himself for a dolt in not having set a rigid guard over the house night and day. He found no excuse for himself in the confidence he had had of Flora's safety whilst Dr Whyte was with her. Tight-lipped, he hurried to Nevin.

"Nevin—not a word, not a question," Bony cried. "Miss McPherson is missing from the house, and Dr Whyte fears the worst. Time and speed are vital. Get those horses saddled and bridled, and muster the best riders. Imagine the house to be on fire and you organizing the men to fight it. Spring to it, man."

Bony spoke with terrific intensity, and Nevin without hesitation did spring to it. He turned and raced to the stockyards, shouting to the blacks to follow him. For a moment they ceased their uproar, and then excitement regained ascendance and they ran pell mell after him.

Burning Water and the doctor followed Bony, who ran to the house, entering it by the front door. In the corridor beyond the hall he met one of the lubra maids, and at sight of him her smiling excitement changed to fear. He gripped her by the arm and she winced.

"Where's Miss McPherson?" he shouted at her, and dumbly she stared at him and over his shoulder at the two standing behind him. "Where is she?" persisted Bony.

"Missus she gone," wailed the lubra.

Bony turned to the doctor:

"When did you last see her?"

"We had afternoon tea together on the veranda," replied Whyte, his mouth grim. "She said she'd go to her room and change for dinner. Said she'd be only an hour at most. I stayed and read a book, and then, when she hadn't come out again ten minutes ago, I went to see where she was. I've searched the house. Ella went into her bedroom. She wasn't there either."

"You show me Miss McPherson's bedroom, quick," urged Bony. He was more controlled now. His voice was imperative.

She ran like a doe kangaroo along the passage and stopped outside a door. Without knocking, Bony went in. He stared about the pleasant room and swiftly appraised its contents and condition. Clothes lay on the bed, the kind of clothes suitable for evening wear. A kimono lay over a chair. The girl had gone to dress two hours before, and she had not even begun to dress when she had left her room. Bony bounded to the open French windows. Standing in the frame, he called:

"Burning Water, go and fetch the men's cook and Old Jack. Harry, get away across to the yards and hurry Nevin with the men and horses. See that horses are prepared for us three. Wait there with them."

His mind registered replies indicating obedience to his orders. There was no questioning Bony's authority in such an emergency. The first phase of mental excitement produced by the calamitous news had subsided, and now Bonaparte was calm and mentally taut.

Stepping beyond the windows, he found himself on the same west veranda upon which opened the windows of his own room. Recently this veranda had been treated with used oil from motor crankcases, and the wood was almost black. Now the wind of the day had deposited a thin layer of fine sand over the boards, and a lesser man than Bony would easily have seen the imprints of Flora's shoes on it. But a lesser man than Bony would not so quickly have read her recent actions in the footprints.

She was still wearing her house shoes when she passed out to the veranda, walked across it and stood talking with someone who stood on the path between the veranda and the lawn. Then she returned to her room, emerged presently and again crossed the veranda and stepped off it to the path.

The path, like all the garden paths, was composed of the "cement" of termite nests, broken and rolled level and further cemented with water. On this path, too, lay the dust deposited by the wind, and there Bony saw plainly the imprints of naked feet, and those of Flora's shoes.

With knees bent and arms hanging loosely, Bony crouched and stared over the paspalum grass short cut and evenly rolled. He could see nothing on it until his gaze extended to a wide circular patch recently drenched by one of the sprinklers, and crossing that patch went the man's foot-marks and the woman's shoe imprints. They had walked to the cemetery.

Bony ran to the door in the cane-grass wall, edged himself round it, stepped swiftly through the entrance into what he had termed a shrine. There was no one there. The fountain still played. A willy wagtail danced on the grass. In the wall on the far side was a hole large enough to permit a man to pass through.

Beyond this opening in the cane-grass the ground was dry and sandy. Naked feet imprints and those made by the girl's shoes extended to the bank of the gully below the great wall of the reservoir. Sinister fact that they had not crossed the gully over the wall—where they could have been seen by any one at the rear of the house.

Bonaparte turned and raced through the cemetery and across the lawn to the gate in the garden fence behind the house. There he was met by Burning Water, Old Jack, and the men's cook.

"Have either of you seen Miss McPherson this afternoon?" snapped Bony.

Old Jack shook his bald head. Alf, the cook, emphasized his negative reply with lurid language.

"Well, where have you been all the afternoon?" Bony demanded of the old man.

"When I had shifted all the sprinklers after lunch time, I went over to have a pitch with Alf. I ain't see Miss McPherson since afore lunch time."

"Well, have either of you seen any strange blacks about the place, or even any Wantella black being where he ought not to have been?"

"Nope," answered Old Jack, and Alf said:

"Now lemme think. No, I can't say as I have seen any strange nigs at all hanging around. I don't seem to have seen any nigs at all afore the truck came in from the out-station. Wait a mo though. I seen ole Itcheroo standing on the dam wall afore afternoon drink-er-tea time. He was looking at hisself in the water, admiring himself like. Why, what's the flamin' hurry?"

"Stow yer noise, you fool," snarled Old Jack. "Them Illprinka blacks have run off with Miss McPherson, and d'you expect all hands to stay talking to you about Itcheroo looking at himself in the dam water?"

Bony and Burning Water were racing across to the stockyards the former shouting for a horse. Aborigines were mounting and saddling and walking their eager horses. Whyte emerged from the press about the yards leading three horses, and Nevin rode out into comparatively clear air.

"Come on!" shouted Bony, and leaping into the saddle of a strapping black gelding that sawed at its bit savagely, he cantered him to skirt the garden wall and so come to that recently made opening in the cane-grass.

"Back a little," shouted Bony. "She's gone away with a black-feller—walked away—more than an hour ago."

Burning Water and Nevin and the doctor restrained their mounts to keep behind Bonaparte, to give him every chance not to lose those tracks. He rode his horse down the steep slope of the gully, and sensible of the situation, those behind him rode after him and not across the dam wall. The tiny stream down the gully bed—the overflow from the reservoir—was bordered with silver sand, and there deep and plain were Flora's tracks and the imprints made by the naked feet. Dr Whyte called ahead to Bony:

"Where's she going? What's she thinking about to walk away with a black? I don't understand it."

Without comment, Bony led the ragged cavalcade up out of the gully to the scrubbed summit of the next land shoulder to the west of the homestead. Here the ground was hard but covered with "fingers" of drift sand. Lying along his horse's neck as though anxious to place his head beyond the horse's nose, Bony kept the anxious beast back to a jog trot, for once he lost the tracks valuable time would have been wasted picking them up again.

For minutes Nevin lost them. For seconds Burning Water lost them. Then they would see the tracks ahead of Bony's horse ridden by a relentless human hound. Now and then could be seen southward through the scrub the vista of the great plain parallel to which the tracks were running on and on before Bony: now down into a gully, now over a sand-crowned summit where grew no scrub and from which vantage point could be seen the plain and the rolling border of the high land extending to the promised couch of the sun.

The leaders of the human pack were silent. So was the pack itself. Nevin's pale blue eyes were squinting into the sunlight. Hatless, Dr Whyte rode with the sun striking full upon his ashen face. Burning Water's face was calm, like the face of a sphinx, but his eyes were large black opals. Hoof thuds, creaking leather, the occasional snort of a horse were the only sounds to the rear of Bonaparte. Ahead lay sunlit silence. Ahead lay that fearful shadow in which lurked flame like a spider deep in its webbed tunnel.

Now the tracks led them out of the scrub to the ribbed slopes of the high land, led them downward to the lower and level country of the plain already beginning to be painted with growing sunset colours. Here the feet of the land shoulders were wearing shoes of green buckbush ending in curving edges of the claypans comprising the verge. The scene was not unlike that of a rocky coast. The buckbush might be imagined as the shingle beach, the claypans as the sand flats left dry by the receding tide, which in turn could be the herbal rubbish, capped by old-man saltbush. Ahead of Bony and his followers a great cape jutted far out on to the tideless, motionless land sea.

Abruptly Bonaparte reined back his horse and shouted for a halt. His mount circled like a sitting dog biting for a flea whilst he leaned out and downward from the saddle reading this open

page of The Book of the Bush. Presently he beckoned his lieu-
tenants to him.

"Here Miss McPherson refused to accompany any farther the
blackfeller she had been walking with from the house. Her suspicions were aroused, and here she realized the trap she had fallen
into. She turned to run back, then stopped and faced the aborigine. She fought him, and it seems, he knocked her senseless.
From here his tracks go on alone. He carried the girl. We must
———"

One of the aborigines shouted and slipped off his horse and
dragged it by the reins to a place several yards away where he
picked up something. On his animal's back once more, he rode
to Bony and held out a small automatic pistol.

"That is her pistol," Burning Water said, and took it from the
finder.

"The black knocked it from her hand when she was about to
fire, or he took it from her and threw it as far as he could," Bony
told them. "The tracks are going towards the foot of that headland. Spread out wide and keep your eyes on the ground in case
the tracks branch right to the high land again or left across the
plain. Come on!"

Wisely Bony permitted his eager horse only to canter. Red-
headed Tom Nevin rode on one side and Burning Water on the
other. Whyte kept close behind him, and behind the doctor
cantered the posse. Arriving at the headland, they began to skirt
its steep face, and again Bony saw the tracks of the man only,
tracks clearly indicating that the aborigine was carrying a
heavy burden. The land beyond the headland came into view,
the "coast" taking a wide northward sweep to form a deep "bay."
Like hounds seeing the prey, shouts of exultation came from the
blacks, a cry of savage despair was uttered by the flying doctor, and
a yell of rage from Bony.

A little more than half a mile distant, the silver-grey aeroplane
was resting on the wide claypan verge of the plain. Its propeller
was turning over slowly. By the machine stood a tall man facing
towards a naked aborigine who carried a white-clad form over a
shoulder. Bony estimated that the aborigine with his burden was
but twenty-five yards from the man standing by the machine. He
was staggering with fatigue.

Every one of these thirty or so horses had from early life been
accustomed to racing for the yard o' mornings before the cracking
whip of the tailer. This early morning race for the yards they
thoroughly enjoyed, and so it was that now they entered into this

race with shrilling neighs of joy and snorting nostrils. Very rarely were they given their heads by those who rode them, and now not only were they given their heads, they were urged onwards by yells, shouts, screams, and flailing hats and slapping hands. No man wore spurs: there had not been time to procure them.

They had to cover more than half a mile whilst a man carrying a woman covered less than twenty-five yards and handed her up to the airman now mounting to the cockpit of his machine Their riders, controlled by excitement of the chance, anguish and rage, laid themselves forward and settled down to win a sickening handicap.

The thudding of hooves rose to a dull tattoo. The wind sang in Bony's ears. The black gelding laid himself low. He became an effortless, well oiled piston.

A bay mare with white forefeet slipped up alongside Bony. Her rider was naked, black. His white teeth were bared in a terrible grin, and on his face was sketched the lust of the chase. The bay mare took him ahead and he shrieked with triumph. His flat feet left the stirrups and rose to feel backward for the rear of the saddle, the mind of the rider temporarily unseated. It appeared that he was about to stand on his horse's back when the animal suddenly crossed her forefeet. He flew from her back like a slung stone. to roll and roll over and over along the cement hard claypan. The rest thundered past his inert body.

Nevin appeared on Bony's left side, his red hair streaming behind him, a rifle grasped pistol fashion in his right hand. His eyes were wide open but his mouth was like a trap. Burning Water, mounted on a dapple grey mare, drew alongside Bony to the left side of Nevin, his plumed grey hair beaten flat by the wind, the reins in his teeth, his hands flailing the animal's withers.

Bony could hear Dr Whyte's sobbed threats and curses close to his rear the doctor's plaint being that his mount was only trotting. A chestnut gelding, riderless, swept past the leaders to take the lead, to kick his heels skyward, to pretend fury at the beating of the swinging irons.

He did not seem to be moving at all when that black figure burdened with a limp white-dressed form swiftly drew to the aeroplane's tail and began to move along the streamlined silver body towards the man in the cockpit waiting to take the burden.

The aborigine who had been wearing the blue shirt when he arrived at the homestead on the truck, now mounted on a stocky bay, passed Bony on his right side like a gust of wind.

He was standing in the stirrups, flailing his horse with a gum-tree switch. The shirt tail streamed outward above the empty saddle. He was screaming at the top of his voice and his teeth were snapping like those of a vicious dog. Steadily he drew ahead. He wore no trousers. Bony could see the horse's ears between the fellow's spindly legs. He never forgot the picture.

His own horse was running like a machine but could not take the lead from Blue Shirt and Burning Water. They could see, so close now were they, the helmet and upper part of the flying suit on the airman. The aborigine had reached him, was clinging to the fuselage, the girl still lying across his shoulder. The airman was leaning far over the side of the cockpit, placing his arms under the girl's arms. They could see his face, working with passion, as he urged the black to help him.

The thunder of the oncoming horses was beginning to rumble in his ears. Success or failure, for him, lay in the passing of seconds. Slowly he was lifting Flora McPherson up and up to the edge of the cockpit, the aborigine now pushing from under the limp form, energized by the oncoming avengers.

Blue Shirt still kept the lead. He still was screaming, riding his horse like a man will ride standing with each foot on the broad back of a horse. Burning Water was racing only a head behind, and a length behind came Bony, Dr Whyte, and a lubra riding a roan gelding with the lines of a racehorse.

Bony saw hope and triumph in the doctor's glaring eyes and pity filled his heart. His own horse appeared to be standing still. The lubra crept up and began to pass him. Her straggy black hair was lying out behind her head, straggly because of the demand for hair with which to make string. She was shrieking as though in the vilest of torment, but she rode hard to saddle and seemed to be but a back-muscle of the animal she rode. Nevin swung wide out from the lead, went away toward the plane, and Bony knew that he had estimated their chances and reckoned them to be poor. Then from behind them and planeward came the crack of Nevin's rifle, and beyond the aeroplane's propeller a bullet spurted dust.

Dr Whyte cursed him. Nevin fired again, and this time they saw the rent in the tail of the machine made by the bullet. The range was too short to miss-hit the girl and those with her, and too long to pick off either the airman or the aborigine hauling and pushing her into the cockpit.

Blue Shirt now was a length ahead of Burning Water, and the chief was yelling at him to ride full tilt into the tail which was the nearest part of the machine to them. Only a strip of Flora's white dress now was to be seen on the edge of the cockpit, and the aborigine was frantically jumping up to clutch the cockpit edge, ignored by the airman who was busy with the controls. Abruptly the engine roared and the machine quivered and began slowly to move forward.

There was no iron-bound emotional control of the doctor's features, no icy composure in the face of crisis, no cool calculation in the face of death itself. Training, hereditary reaction to personal danger was now non-existent. Hope had vanished. Triumph had become a mocking devil. His face was fearful to look upon.

Burning Water was yelling to Blue Shirt to ride straight into the tail of the machine which was moving forward with increasing speed. Blue Shirt gained on it, his horse making a mighty effort. Then he funked it when he might have ridden into the tail and smashed it and so have prevented the machine from rising. At the last moment he reined his horse to the side and rode for the aborigine.

The aborigine was now clinging to the edge of the cockpit. He looked back and they saw he was Itcheroo: His feet were jerking upward in vain searching for foothold. The helmeted airman turned to face the black hands clutching the cockpit. They saw the butt of the pistol rise and strike downward with fearful force on the black hands. Itcheroo screamed and let go his hold. He fell to the ground, and became a thing of arms and legs beneath the striking hooves of Blue Shirt's horse. Over went the horse and down went Blue Shirt in dust.

Nevin had stopped shooting. Burning Water held his horse's nose level with the aeroplane's rudder tip. The wind stream from the propeller raised dust which was blinding him, but he kicked his feet out of the stirrups, and hurled himself forward and sideways to the tail which was beginning to leave him behind. His hands struck the surface of the starboard rudderplane just as it lifted from the ground. The engine's roar increased to mighty volume. For three or four seconds he clung with his finger nails, and then was swept back to lie on the ground in the enveloping dust.

The race was over. Bony hauled back his horse, rage and disappointment a fire eating him alive. The plane was speeding away across the claypans. He saw its wheels leave the ground for a split second, saw them leave it again, seem to threaten to touch ground again, give up the attempt, rise and rise higher and higher. The machine climbed, came back to the east to fly by them at five hundred feet. Rex McPherson waved a gloved hand at them. They could see the white face of Flora McPherson on a level with the cockpit edge.

CHAPTER 18

BASE OPERATIONS

THE four men sat in the office: Bony, Dr Whyte, Nevin and Chief Burning Water. They had returned silently, and now they sat silently waiting for Bony to speak. Dr Whyte's hands were clenching and unclenching on the table desk.

Itcheroo was dead, killed by the flashing hooves of the horse ridden by Blue Shirt. A mind had perished possessing secrets many scientists would give their all to know, secrets many doubting Thomases in the scientific world refuse to credit because they have been unable to get under the skin of the Australian aborigine. No other suffered injury in that mad race, and now the body of the Wantella man of magic was being taken, tied with a covering of tobacco bush leaves, to the tribal death tree where it would remain for three months. The final rites would be performed that day, an arm bone was removed from the bundle and solemnly buried, rendering the spirit of Itcheroo no longer dangerous to the living.

"There is an old saying about worldly success to the effect that, 'if a man rises like a rocket he probably falls like a stick.' " Bony said, and paused to light the cigarette he had made. "Another saying is that, 'the higher one goes the harder one falls.'

"We are now confronted by a problem and we will fail in its solution if we are hasty, too ambitious, run when we should walk. That problem is not the capture of Rex McPherson. The problem is the ultimate safety of Miss McPherson. All other objectives must be set aside until our problem of the girl's safety is finalized.

"It is not a problem that can be solved by an air force and a military or police ground force. It is one which can be solved only by the employment of subtlety, and the word I use is the correct one because it implies intelligent cunning. To locate and attack Rex McPherson with superior force would inevitably result in the death of his victim.

"Let us first settle the question why he abducted Miss McPherson. I believe I can settle it. He has been and still is determined to force his father to retire and hand the station over to him. To achieve this unlawful ambition he has stolen his father's cattle, forged his father's signature to cheques, killed his father's stockmen, tortured his father with cane-grass splinters. So far he has failed. Therefore, he abducted Miss McPherson to ransom her for his father's station property.

"Do not think that this ambition is the final goal. It is but a lever with which to remove opposition.

"Having obtained the lever Rex will want to put it into use. He knows that his father has started off with a party of the Wantella aborigines in search of his headquarters and of him, for the dead Itcheroo will have told him. Rex will lose no time in communicating his recent success to The McPherson, who will doubtless be given a period of time to make up his mind to capitulate.

"Rex knows we know of the abduction. He will be uneasy concerning how we will react, and we may therefore believe he will do everything he can to persuade his father to communicate with us with the object of preventing any resolute action against him. In addition to the station property, he will demand our neutrality in exchange for the person of Miss McPherson."

"In that case he will have to have it," Whyte snapped.

"But——" Nevin was about to object.

"I agree that nothing must be done to prevent Miss McPherson's safe return," Bony cut in. "Which is why I stressed the urgent need for subtlety. If Rex McPherson found himself cornered he would destroy his captive. But, Harry, we cannot sanction neutrality, nor could we sanction The McPherson's surrender to the demand for his property. If the son's crimes had been committed only against the father, then we might have consented to act as the father wished, but, following the murder of three aborigines and Sergeant Errey, we have no choice. If the son's crimes had been confined to attacks on the father's property, and if meeting his demands would end the aggression, then we could agree to terms. But there will be no end to the aggression until the aggressor is prevented for ever from being aggressive."

"Giving in to the swine would get no one anywhere," asserted Nevin. "I know the swine. And I know, too, that he would kill Miss McPherson if he thought he was cornered."

"Well, what are we going to do?" demanded the flying doctor.

"This," Bony began in explanation. "Good team work is

essential for success. In effect if and when The McPherson is given the demands I have mentioned, he must enter into prolonged negotiations to gain time for us.

"Now this is my plan evolved from much thought and acceptance of all risks and chances. After dark you, Nevin, with the men's cook, will take the two trucks to Shaw's Lagoon for as much first grade petrol and oil as you can load. You must do the trip during the night hours, and you must be prepared to extinguish lights and stop at the first sign of attack by Rex McPherson in his aeroplane. Itcheroo being dead, I think you will have no trouble, but be advised to take half a dozen of Burning Water's reliable bucks.

"On your return the oil supplies must be stored in a secret place to avoid destruction. And then tomorrow you and every available man must construct a well camouflaged hangar for Captain Loveacre's aeroplane.

"You will know what has to be done about that, Harry. Meanwhile you must make all necessary preparations to receive Loveacre. You should get in touch with him as early as possible. He should reach St Albans sometime late tomorrow afternoon and be dissuaded from attempting to come on and arrive here in the dark.

"Tonight Burning Water and I will leave on foot for the Illprinka country to try and locate the headquarters of Rex McPherson. Our first objective will be the return to safety of Miss McPherson. We shall bother with nothing else until that is achieved. Once her safety is assured we can deal with Rex. but to do anything to reverse this procedure would I am afraid be fatal.

"Now let us clearly understand this vital point. The ground party, consisting of Burning Water and myself, will suffer certain handicaps. Our first objective is to be an area of cane-grass at the western extremity of the plain which is a hundred odd miles away. We will have to proceed with extreme caution in order to reach Rex McPherson's headquarters unheralded and, by the employment of subtlety, rescue the girl from him.

"Having done that we will be confronted by a hundred odd miles of open country to safety, with a hundred Illprinka men and Rex in his plane behind us.

"It will be Captain Loveacre's task to keep in touch with the ground party, but to avoid betraying it or its position through communicating with it, save if absolutely necessary. It will be his task to know where the ground party is from day to day without the ground party having to indicate itself. And it will be his task to be ready to pick up Miss McPherson as soon as possible after she is rescued. I trust you appreciate these several points, Harry?"

"I do," Whyte replied. "I think the plan is sound."

"It couldn't be sounder," added Nevin. "Intelligent cunning, as you said, Bony, is going to do the trick. After that trick is turned we then can get on with the clean-up."

"I'm glad you all agree," Bony said, and, glancing at Burning Water, he noted the faint smile in the eyes of the Chief of the Wantella. "Your particular job after you have brought the oil supplies, Tom, will be to keep ever at hand a supply of horses and armed aborigines in case a rescue of the ground party is essential.

"Well, there is the broad outlines of our reactions to Rex McPherson's latest crime. I am going to leave you two to control The McPherson who might return and express other ideas. You will have to keep to the plan as closely as possible, because Burning Water and I will be expecting your co-operation according to its details and we will be acting accordingly. The dinner gong was sounded two minutes ago. We had better have it, and then prepare for the night's work."

At half past eight Whyte and Bony saw the trucks depart for Shaw's Lagoon. At nine o'clock the flying doctor warmly bade *au revoir* to Bony and Chief Burning Water, Bony dissolved into the darkness beyond the garden fence as quickly as did Burning Water, for he was wearing black trousers and one of Tom Nevin's black shirts.

Again in the office, Dr Henry Whyte charged and lit a spare pipe and began the study of Bony's sketch plan and his fully detailed plan of operations, together with a list of signs to be made from Loveacre's plane and the ground party. Whyte's mind now was calm and cold, and he was feeling vexed that he had been conquered by fierce emotion.

The plan called every man to his trade. It called an aborigine and a half-caste to the trade of bushcraft. It called Nevin to the close command of men he thoroughly understood, and it called him, Henry Whyte, not to the profession of healing but to that of organizing base operations upon the smooth success of which depended everything. The lives of two men, and that of the woman he loved, were in his hands. Well, he had organized a medical service for a country as large as Great Britain.

This Bonaparte fellow was, indeed, an extraordinary man. Come to think of it, it was remarkable that he, one-time major in the Royal Flying Corps, and now a flying doctor who was regarded as a leader by people whose independence is a byword, should so quickly and easily have accepted a kind of second-in-command job and recognize as commanding officer an Australian half-caste. Wherein lay the power of the man? Whyte knew it did not lie in Bony's appearance, for Bony would not have been marked in a crowd of fellows. His voice was pleasing and perhaps a little pedantic, but the power did not originate in the voice. He was a puzzle defying the doctor.

Nevin was much more dynamic than Bonaparte but yet was commonplace when Bonaparte certainly was not. McPherson, as Whyte remembered him, was efficient but not outstanding.

Mrs. Nevin sent across coffee and sandwiches, and the doctor ate and drank and smoked and waited. Shortly after one o'clock Nevin called from the township to say he had loaded the petrol and oil and was starting back to the homestead. The trucks arrived as day was breaking, and their loads were dumped beyond the stockyards among the scrub. At seven o'clock Whyte and the overseer emerged from the house after having breakfasted, and stood on the south veranda smoking and reading the weather signs.

The sunlight falling on the plain beyond the garden appeared this morning almost colourless, and already streamers of dust were passing across the claypan verge. The wind was teasing the water spray from the sprinklers on the lawn.

"Blast!" growled Nevin. "The wind's going to come at last. When it shifts round to the west it'll blow hard. Captain Loveacre will meet it all the way. How far d'you reckon we are from Brisbane in a straight line?"

"Slightly more than thirteen hundred miles," replied the doctor. "Comfortable day's flying for a modern machine—in normal weather."

"Well, it's not going to be normal today."

"That's so, Nevin. I've been thinking that it might be a mistake to communicate with Shaw's Lagoon. Remember what Bony said about Rex having a portable telephone instrument? Supposing he's listening in waiting to hear what we're doing?"

"Hum! You sent Captain Loveacre his flying instructions yesterday didn't you?"

"Yesterday afternoon—to St Albans."

"I'm betting he won't get to St Albans today. The wind will be a howling gale by noon."

"Then we'll leave the telephone alone. If Loveacre sends a telegram no listener with a portable machine will get it. What about the hangar for the aeroplane? Know a good place?"

"The best. Let's go and take a look at it."

They crossed the garden, climbed over the fence and walked down the slope to the claypan verge, which they followed to the landing ground, where the flying doctor was met by naked men, women and children waving torches. Here and there along the slopes, rising to the high ground, were tree-lined gullies, and one of these was bordered by level ground, where it debouched to the plain.

"We could stretch wires from tree to tree and hang green branches on the wires to give a roof," Nevin pointed out. "All that would have to be done then would be to shift that sandbar, when the plane could be pushed in under the trees and the joining roof of branches. What d'you think?"

"Quite good."

"All right! I'll get the mob down here at once and fix things ready for the captain. We needn't worry about him getting here tonight. He won't reach St Albans. It won't matter much, as far as I can see, because Bony and Burning Water will only cover about thirty miles till daylight this morning, and I don't think they'll risk travelling in daylight."

Captain Loveacre left Brisbane in a fast twin-engined monoplane on the morning of 16 October. He had had the glass structure enclosing the cabin removed and wind shields placed, and on a specially rigged foundation he had had the machine-gun mounted for use by his promised observer.

The loan of the machine-gun had been facilitated by Colonel Spendour, the Chief Commissioner, to whom Loveacre had gone to explain as much as he could the telegram received from Bony. Alterations to the machine and the loan of the gun and requisite ammunition from the Defence Department had been completed in six hours, but after all the haste had been unnecessary because Loveacre got only as far as Roma that first day on account of the head wind and dust.

The same flying conditions were experienced the next day, and it was late when Loveacre reached St Albans where he read and mastered the instructions given by Dr Whyte.

The following morning he landed at McPherson's Station at seven-thirty, to be welcomed by a crowd of aborigines and two white men.

"Glad to see you, Captain Loveacre. I'm Dr Whyte," the flying doctor greeted him as they shook hands.

Together, there was a certain similarity about these two men. They were of the same build although Loveacre was shorter. The actions of both were swift and yet not nervously so. Their eyes were keen and steady and bright, like the eyes of birds. Had it not been for the facial scars Dr Whyte would have been as strongly good looking as the man he welcomed.

"Glad to be here," Loveacre returned. "Head winds kept me back. Why, what the devil's the hurry?"

His plane was being rushed towards the trees by every aborigine directed by red-headed Nevin. Whyte indicated the skeleton remains of his own aeroplane. "That was my machine. We are opposed by a gentleman who bombs."

"Ha! ha!" exclaimed Loveacre. "That sounds interesting. Where's Bony?"

"He's away on the job. Come along to the house to wash up and breakfast. I've a pretty long story to tell you."

Captain Loveacre stepped out of his flying suit and flung it over a shoulder.

"Great feller, Bony," he said when they were walking towards the house. "The Police Heads think the sun shines out of his boots. He wants me to fetch a machine-gun, and he wants it fetched like you or I would ask for a match. How the devil am I to get a machine-gun? They don't sell 'em in pawnshops. I charges off to interview the Chief Commissioner who's one of the hardy damn and blast you, sir, warriors. 'A machine-gun!' he says, looking at me as though I were nutty. 'Bony wants you and it, eh?' he goes on. 'All right, Captain. I'll get one delivered to you tonight by the military, but for heaven's sake don't let Bony start a war or a revolution.'"

"He's trying to prevent a revolution and a war combined, I think," Whyte said, thoughtfully. "I don't get him. He's the first man who has ever made clay of me."

"He puts me in the same boat," Loveacre confessed. "I'm reminded of a bar of iron wrapped in velvet."

"I can't understand the source of his strength."

"Can't you? I can. It lies in the victories he has won over himself. Get him sometime to tell you about the war going on inside of him, the war of influences exerted to control him by the hereditary instincts of the races from which he has sprung. Think of the fearful handicap of his birth, and then remember the position he has gained by sheer intelligence and a diplomatic mind. He didn't get to where he is by fair competition with equals."

Dr Whyte told the story whilst acting host at the breakfast table, and now and then Captain Loveacre nodded his head but said nothing to interrupt the narrator. When they rose from the table, Whyte suggested they pass to the office and study Bony's sketch plan, his table of signs, and the general plan of action.

"The proposition is attractive but hellish for you, Whyte," Loveacre said whilst leaning over the rough sketch plan. "We've got to go slow, I can appreciate that. If you and I meet this bird in the air, and he's alone, we've got to send him down for keeps. But until your girl is rescued we've got to go so slow that we'll have to keep our feet wide to avoid tripping. Any idea where Bony and his aborigine chief will be right now?"

"Nevin says they won't risk travelling in daylight, and that they ought to cover thirty miles a night. That places them within twenty miles of that cane-grass swamp."

"Yes, that'll be it," agreed the captain. "It's a likely place, too, for a man with an aeroplane. Always plenty of claypan country bordering that kind of swamp. You know, Bony's handling this business in his usual far-seeing manner. Think of the uproar if he had called in the police and the military. It would have been a war without doubt, and gentle Rex McPherson would do in your girl when his back was to the wall. Hullo!"

Both men turned to stare at the apparition standing in the door frame.

"McPherson!" exclaimed the doctor.

The cattleman's face was unshaven, dirty with grime. His eyes were bloodshot and singularly void of expression. His clothes were shapeless, torn and stained. On his left hand was a dirty bandage in tatters.

"Hullo, Whyte!" he said, mechanically, whilst staring at the captain.

"This is Captain Loveacre who has arrived this morning by air from Brisbane," Whyte said in introduction. "Loveacre, this is Mr McPherson."

"Glad to meet you," Loveacre said easily. "Take a pew. You look tucked up. Shall I go across to the house and bring you a drink?"

"Nevin's coming. He can go. What's he doing here? Where's Bony?"

"You heard about Flora?" asked the doctor, and Loveacre went out to meet Nevin. McPherson nodded, and Whyte proceeded to tell him of the abduction, of Bony and Burning Water having gone to locate the abductor's camp and rescue the girl from him, and of the preparations for Captain Loveacre's operations. During the telling, the captain entered with Nevin and the drink, and the squatter was given a stiff glass of whisky.

"So, Captain Loveacre, you are an airman?" McPherson said, having put down his empty glass. "Your trip will, I think, be for nothing. My son has won the game he's been playing with me. I've no option but to surrender."

The flying doctor sat down on the corner of the table desk and lit his pipe. He foresaw the battle ahead.

"Bony predicted that Rex would communicate with you. I assume that he did."

"He did. We were half way to Duck Lake when he flew over before we could take cover. He dropped a letter. He knew the moment we passed off the station land. He knew where we were from hour to hour, for his blacks dogged us. I lost three of my men and brought back two who were badly wounded. As the boys say, I'm getting old and done for."

"Not a bit of it sir," Whyte said, roughly.

"Well, anyway, Rex has got the upper hand with me, and with you too. If I don't send up my surrender smoke before six o'clock the day after tomorrow he'll marry Flora—black-feller fashion. How does that strike you?"

It seemed that already McPherson was sensing opposition to his determination to submit. Whyte accepted the letter offered him, and noted the fearful condition of the fingers of the right hand. Aloud, he read:

DEAR FATHER:
  I have Flora. I admire her immensely. She is more beautiful than ever, but I am willing to exchange her for the station, lock, stock and barrel, as grandfather would say. If you send up the surrender smoke before six p.m., 20 October, I will return her safe and sound. If not, then I marry her according to the somewhat casual custom of the blacks. What was good enough for my mother will be good enough for my cousin.

                               Your affectionate son,
                                                    REX.

Loveacre lit a cigarette. He was the least depressed man there, and he said:

"Well, there's still two days left before the proposed marriage. Bony, and the black with him, will be within twenty miles of that cane-grass swamp. They ought to know by tomorrow morning if Rex is living about that swamp."

"What swamp are you talking about?" demanded McPherson.

"The one at the western end of this valley, according to the map Bony drew and left with us. To me, as an airman, it seems the most likely place for Rex to have his headquarters. Bony must have his chance."

"Have his chance!" shouted McPherson. "He had his chance to stop Rex taking Flora, didn't he? He knew what happened to me, because in spite of the wind my bucks read his tracks. He knew what happened to the doctor's aeroplane. He knew that Rex was after Flora because I wrote a note and left it in the car at Watson's Bore telling him so. And yet he goes to sleep and allows Rex to walk off with her."

"If there's any blame to be handed out, I'm to take it," rasped Whyte. "Bony was here that afternoon working on the map and plans. He thought Flora would be safe enough over in the house with me. She simply walked off with Itcheroo."

"And Itcheroo's a corpse," Nevin interjected.

"More's the pity," McPherson ground out. "Anyway, matters being like they are, I'm going to send up the surrender signal."

Dr Whyte spun round in the doorway to shout passionately:

"No you don't. We're not going to give in to that black devil. Flora's my life, but as Loveacre points out we've got two days yet and Bony's getting near that swamp."

"Two days' grace," the squatter said. "If you two knew Rex like I do you wouldn't accept two minutes' grace from him. The smoke signal is going up today, this morning. Rex wouldn't expect to see it before this morning on account of the wind. He's got to see it, or be told about it by his people, before tonight. Decent men don't offer a baby to a tiger."

"You'll wait two days before sending up that signal smoke," the doctor said, levelly.

McPherson lurched to his feet.

"I'll do what?" he shouted. "Who the devil are you to dictate to me in my own country?"

"I'm O.C. Base Operations," came the reply spoken with such steel coldness that McPherson winced despite his rage. "You blamed Bony for letting Rex take Flora. What kind of an ass are you to go off with a few blacks who were tricked by fake smoke signals? Your place was here keeping an eye wide open to counter just what did happen to Flora. You can't accept terms laid down by an outlaw, a murderer, and possible madman. As Bony said, the only chance of getting Flora back is to employ subtlety. That's what he's doing. He and Burning Water are risk'ng their lives. You are not going to act independently any more. If you even threaten to I'll chain you to a tree."

CHAPTER 19

THE LIZARD AND THE SNAKE

THE water gutter came down from the slope from the higher land, deep and sharp edged, passed beneath the massed top branches of a fallen gum-tree, thence zig-zagged wide and deep like a military trench far across the valley. It carried water only after heavy rain. The bed of coarse-grained sand now was dry and hot to the touch, for the sunlight fell directly upon it. Only beneath the fallen tree was there coolness and dark shadow. It was not unlike a war dugout, and there slept Burning Water and Napoleon Bonaparte.

Now and then a blowfly droned in the shadow created by the compressed leaves of the fallen tree, clinging to the coolness, waiting until the evening to venture farther afield. Other flies, too, were grateful for the cool shadow, the little flies which are a torment to the new-chum. The only living thing appreciative of the heat of the open gutter was a small lizard no larger than a pencil and five inches in length. Down its back lay a bar of old silver. Its little legs and underside were clothed in the softest of dove-grey. Its eyes were pin heads of bright jet.

It emerged from its hole in the side of the gutter, walked slowly down the side to the bottom and there halted and poised its head as though listening. It may not have been doing this, but undoubtedly it heard the occasional buzzing of a blowfly and the whirring of the wings of the smaller flies too faint to be within the scale of sound registered by human ears. The lizard ran along a straight course till it passed just inside the edge of the shadow made by the fallen tree.

Much like a cat, the lizard began to stalk a fly. The distance between it and the fly gradually lessened until it was a bare three inches. Then the fly began to move its wings as though loosening muscles preparatory to instant flight. It still thought itself safe, remained grandly confident of its power to escape a thing that had to remain on the ground. And then the lizard jumped, and the fly was between its jaws.

During the next hour it captured a dozen flies and made only two misses. It was a wonderful life, warm, crowded with good sport. Ah! There came another of the poor suckers to dance and mock. Down it came to alight on the earth. The lizard crouched and began to stalk, its attention concentrated on the victim. Eventually it leaped and caught the fly, and in that same split second saw its own doom in the slate-coloured eyes of the thing which had been stalking it for an hour.

The saltbush snake paralysed its victim with an injection of poison, just enough and no more to effect a paralysis. Then slowly the lizard disappeared down the snake's gullet, to swell a little a short section of the eighteen-inches-long, light-grey body.

It will be recalled that the great Alchuringa ancestor of this saltbush snake had been made by Pitti-pitti's evil son. This specimen proceeded to investigate the interior of the dugout and those who inhabited it. The kangaroo hide dilly-bag suspended from Burning Water's neck, and now lying on the ground, provided much interest for the snake. It put its head into the opening of the dillybag, thought better of it and passed on to investigate a partly filled sugar sack. The contents did not appeal, and anyway it was not so very hungry. It crossed the sandy floor to reach the huge Kurdaitcha boots removed from Bony's feet. The smell of blood and musty aroma of emu's feathers was truly delightful, and in and out among these boots the saltbush snake moved like a playful mouse.

Of course everyone knows that a Kurdaitcha man is an evil spirit always wandering about the poor blackfellows' camp at night. His evil is not very potent, but his presence is annoying and often has to be chased away. Sometimes he leaves behind one of his boots, the boots made of birds' feathers and worn so that he will leave no tracks.

Anthropologists tell us that the Kurdaitcha boots in the possession of the aborigines are too small for the ordinary man's feet, and that in any case the wearing of them would not prevent another aborigine from easily tracking the wearer. This would be so were the wearer a white man, for a white man would walk like a bull buffalo and with about as much intelligence, treading down grass stems, turning over sticks and stones and so forth. Properly made Kurdaitcha boots will enable any wily aborigine to escape a tracking avenging party.

The hours passed away into a cosmic silence broken only by the muttering of passing willi-willies until Burning Water yawned and stretched himself. He then had been awake fully three minutes, listening intently not for sign of hostile blacks for he would not hear such signs, but the alarm notes of birds. The birds were quiet or busy about their own affairs, and before he went outside he knew by their voices that the sun was going down.

Quietly he rose and crawled on hands and knees down the gutter, passing from under the fallen tree roof, until he reached the butt of a solitary currant bush. Here he slowly raised his head above the rim of the gutter. First he examined with eagle eyes the flat expanse of the valley, and then regarded intently the scrubbed slopes rising to the high land east and west.

He saw nothing of interest, no uneasy frightened birds telling of hidden aborigines, no smoke signals in the clear sky, no kangaroos running because they must. The hill range beyond the valley was painted with russets and purple. He could see no shadows, but shadows lurked in this bright world, shadows with flames in their hearts. The splashes of colour were vast. Away to the east ten thousand acres were covered with yellow butter-cups stretching up the bordering slopes. The green buckbush covered thousands of acres lying towards the centre of the plain, and a tiny purple-flowering creeper lay like a magic carpet of old Arabia over the summit of one of the distant hills.

When he returned to the dugout Burning Water was satisfied there were no enemies close to them, and certainly no enemy aware of their presence within twenty miles of the great cane-grass swamp. Carefully choosing his material, he made a fire which produced no smoke, confident that the hot air produced by the flames would be so diffused by the tree roof as to escape observation. On the fire he boiled water for tea in the only quart-pot they had with them.

As Burning Water had done, Bony lay still, listening for a minute or two before finally sitting up. Suave and polished when in contact with white civilization, he was able when in his beloved bush to tense his senses to the acuteness of the aborigines, to see and hear and reason as they do, to be as close to their background as they themselves.

This evening however his body was feeling the unusual strain of passing over eighty miles of bushland in three nights. He had been soft, he admitted freely to his companion, but he had not lagged. He had suffered much from the rigid rationing of his cigarettes, but he knew this rationing was doing his health enormous good. He had had to drink tea without milk or sugar, to eat flapjacks made only of plain flour and water, and once the roasted meat of an iguana, and even this spartan fare was not excessively distasteful to him because he dreaded a waistline.

"Ah!" he murmured, and Burning Water glanced round at him and smiled in his solemn manner. "How does the world look to the birds and the ants, and the Illprinka men?"

"It is a fine world and everything in it is peaceful," the chief replied. "The sun will set in an hour. The land seems empty of Illprinka men, and the sky is empty of their smoke signals. How are the lungs?"

Bony distended his chest before saying:

"They feel as elastic as toy balloons. Phew! It has been a torture, the craving for tobacco smoke. I have tobacco sufficient only to make three cigarettes. If I cannot find friend Rex and obtain tobacco from him, if I have to go without cigarettes for, say, three days, I'll be either fit for an asylum or able to run a three-mile race. Do you know exactly where we are?"

"Yes. I came this way several years ago on a visit to the Illprinka. There was peace between us then. I should say we are not more than twenty miles from the cane-grass. When day breaks tomorrow we ought to be able to look down on it from one of the great sandhills bordering it along the south."

"Should there be much water in the swamp after the wet winter?"

"Not as much as after some wet summers, but there will be plenty of water well inward from the outside. I have given much time to imagining I was Rex McPherson, as you told me to do, and the most likely place for a camp close to where he could hide his aeroplane. I think that where the hills end and the swamp curves to the south will be a likely place. There the cane-grass and lantana is thick and very high, and between it and the sandhills lies a wide claypan flat that would give plenty of room for the aeroplane."

"Good!" Bony said approvingly. "We'll have a look at that place as day dawns tomorrow. What's for dinner? Flapjack? I'm becoming meat hungry. That iguana was all right. It tasted like fish, but I want steak half done, with the blood dripping from it."

"We eat too much," Burning Water said unsmilingly. "Our bodies get heavy with fat. It is good sometimes to live on the fat."

Bony accepted the cup of the quart-pot filled with tea, then broke the flapjack in two and proffered a part to his companion.

"It is as well that we have good teeth," he said, smilingly, adding: "Otherwise we'd want gizzards like the birds. I knew a man who once suffered fearfully with rheumatism. Do you know how he rid himself of it?"

"By taking a gum-leaf oven bake."

"No, by fasting. He wasn't a doctor, of course."

"What was he?"

"A——Listen! I hear an aeroplane."

The chief froze. Presently he nodded affirmatively, saying:

"It's coming this way."

"We'll go down the gutter," Bony said. "It might be Captain Loveacre."

Crouchingly, they passed out of the shelter and down the winding natural gutter, careful not to raise their hatless heads above the level ground, peering upwards into the ribbon of sky their confined situation permitted. The machine was somewhere to the north-west beyond the edge of the high land towering above them two to three hundred feet. From that quarter they risked observation by Illprinka scouts, and, having gone a hundred yards beyond the fallen tree, they lay and covered themselves with the sand of the gutter floor. Until they saw the machine they could not be sure.

Their problem was first to see possible scouts and not first to be seen by them, hence this clinging to the bed of a water gutter well below ground level. If the plane proved to be Loveacre's machine, then the problem was to disclose themselves to the airmen without betraying themselves to chance enemy scouts.

"Look!" exclaimed Bony. "It's Captain Loveacre flying one white streamer which means he wants to communicate to us important news. Lie down and wiggle about, comrade."

To ask a man like Chief Burning Water to lie and "wiggle" about at the bottom of a gutter would in other circumstances have sounded absurd. Burning Water "wiggled", and Bony produced a white handkerchief and waved it energetically.

Whyte saw the signal in time to drop a small calico bag filled with sand and containing a message. He made no sign whatever. His message fell within a hundred yards of the gutter. Continuing its course, the plane flew across the valley.

"Mark the position of the bag of sand," Bony urged, softly,

bringing his eyes to the ground level. "We'll wait till dark before we get it. Now watch for a possible scout who saw the bag and might be tempted to leave his cover."

They both guardedly watched the calico bag lying white on a grassy bed of everlasting flowers, and at the same time scanned the surrounding country for sign of an enemy. They watched for fifteen minutes before deciding that the message had been dropped unseen by others. The sun was then about to set, and Bony went back to the temporary camp and added dry wood to the small fire for the purpose of baking flapjacks. A few moments later Burning Water joined him.

The flapjacks were baked hard just when the sun had vanished, and, with the quart-pot and the remainder of the flour, they were packed into the sugar sack which the chief would carry slung from his shoulders. With whisks of leafy twigs they smoothed out all signs on the ground betraying their presence there, and then Bony proceeded to put on his pair of the Kurdaitcha boots.

He uttered a sharp exclamation.

Burning Water looked up from lacing his own boots of emu feathers. He saw the saltbush snake fall from Bony's right foot held high off the ground. He saw the snake glide swiftly away and enter its hole at the base of the gutter wall.

CHAPTER 20

INTRUSION

"LIE still," hissed Burning Water.

His big black body appeared to hover over the slighter man. Seizing the ankle of the bitten foot, he dragged Bony from under the fallen tree and into the clear light of early evening. From his dillybag he snatched his blade razor and opened it with his teeth as his left hand remained fast to the ankle to stop the circulation. He cut twice, deeply. No more than four seconds had passed.

The dusk was deepening, the walls and floor of the gutter becoming a pasty, shadowless grey. Bony lay passive, fear of death submerged by the greater fear of being unable to go on to Flora's rescue. Burning Water crouched over the foot and sucked and sucked till the muscles of his mouth ached.

"Give me the handkerchief," he urged. He knotted the hand-kerchief with his free hand and his teeth, then twisted a stick in it to tighten it. "The snake missed biting a vein by the width of a finger nail. How do you feel?"

"All right. The poison is very rapid."

"A few minutes at longest if not conquered."

Slowly he raised himself and peered across the flat expanse of the plain and upward at the land slope. The colour of the world now was the uniform pale purple of the great patches of the tiny creeper-flower. The only living things he saw were two eagles floating like sand-grains in the green sky and the rabbits in the vicinity of their burrow. Then he ducked down into the gutter.

Beyond the nearest angle of the gutter a black head had begun to rise above ground level. Round that corner was at least one Illprinka man. Burning Water bent over Bony to whisper.

"Illprinka man just round the corner. He must have come along the gutter from the middle of the valley. He saw the aeroplane drop the message, or rather he saw something drop from it, and he's been watching it and waiting for dark to get it. Lie still. You've got your pistol. I'm going to see how many there are."

"All right. No shooting if possible."

On his hands and knees Burning Water crept along the gutter. When he reached the corner he rose on bent legs and crept slowly forward round the angle. Inch by inch he negotiated that angle until he saw two naked aborigines both standing with bent legs and staring over the ground towards the message in the bag of sand. Beyond them the gutter ran straight for thirty odd yards. There were only the two Illprinka men.

It was probable there were no others in the gutter beyond the next angle, but, as it was possible there were others, Burning Water did not delay. When he leaped forward he disappeared from Bony's sight, and this moment was the termination of Bony's inactivity. With the ligature about his right ankle his foot was "dead" and useless. He moved fast, however, on his hands and knees, looking not unlike an ungainly spider. Beyond the angle he saw a writhing man on the ground and two others in desperate struggle beyond him. The writhing man lurched to his knees, clawed his way to a standing position against one of the gutter walls, and then began to struggle to climb out. He certainly had received serious injury, and his mind was made up to escape injury even more serious.

Bony grasped his legs and hauled him back. He snarled like a dog as he fell on the half-caste, and then proceeded to try to gouge out Bony's eyes before Bony's fingers choked him. His breathing was a harsh rasping noise. His eyes were small black discs swimming in seas of white. And then something thudded, and he collapsed on the fighting Bony, to be dragged off by the panting Chief of the Wantella Tribe.

"There's no others," asserted Burning Water. "If there were others this fellow would have shouted. His companion didn't get the chance to shout. I'll get the plane message."

It had now become so dark that he had no fear of being observed from an appreciable distance. Back in three seconds with the message, he proceeded to drag Bony under the tree roof.

"I have it," he announced. "As you said, it is a small bag filled with sand and will certainly contain a message."

"Block up the gutter entrances to this hiding hole," Bony suggested. "I'll have to use the torch to read the message."

"And I'll want a fire—for your foot," added Burning Water.

Lying on his side, Bony saw his companion fill the quart-pot with water and then place the utensil on a foundation of burning sticks. That done, Burning Water continued the blocking of the two entrances with leafy branches from the roof. Within the bag Bony found the sheet of paper and read, slowly, his lips bloodless, pain indicated on his face:

DEAR GROUND PARTY:

This is the eighteenth of the month. Loveacre arrived this morning, having been delayed by that windstorm. McPherson got back today, too, after having a lot trouble with the Illprinka. He was half way to Duck Lake when Rex flew over them and dropped word to say he had got Flora and would hold her in exchange for the station until six p.m. on the 20th. If by then McPherson has not sent up his surrender smoke, Rex threatens to take Flora blackfellow fashion.

McPherson wanted to do this, but Loveacre and I dissuaded him. If you get this we will, of course, know your position today. We have two days to locate Rex's headquarters and rescue Flora. The old man says we're a couple of fools because, not knowing Rex like he does, Flora won't be safe from him, station or no station. But we felt we must give you and ourselves a chance to rescue Flora and defeat him. Remember what you promised me if he harms my girl, so don't be hasty and kill the blackguard. It'll be my right to stamp out that dangerous fire.

PS: Adding this whilst in the air. Have been over the canegrass swamp. It's terrific. Big enough to hide a million men. Saw no indications of any camp. Three smoke signals away to the north-west where that Duck Lake must be. We'll come out again tomorrow, but won't communicate without urgent reason. If you want us to pick you up you know what to do. Loveacre sends regards. He's got the tat-tat mounted and I'm the gunner. Feels like old times. Good luck."

"Two days, eh," exclaimed Burning Water, evidently impatient. "Better make yourself a cigarette. Lie back. I want your foot. If Rex harms Miss McPherson, the doctor will certainly be given the chance to stamp him out. Come on, now, you'll want the cigarette."

"I'm going to wait," Bony decided.

"Quiet. Too much time lost as it is. Lie still."

Burning Water pulled Bony's naked feet close to the fire. Then he crammed his mouth with young gum leaves. Bony bit back a cry of agony. A sizzling sound opening the lips of the wound made by the razor. Into the wound he poured cold water from the canvas bag to cleanse it. Then with the finger and thumb of one hand holding open the wound as much as was possible, with the fingers of his left hand he picked up a red-hot wood coal and dropped it squarely upon the open red flesh.

Before the pain was registered by Bony's brain, he had grasped the ankles of both feet to hold them immovable, his jaws working on the mastication of the gum-leaves. Bony bit back a cry of agony. A sizzling sound came from the living coal, and a smell of burning flesh began to fill the chamber. Bony groaned. The agony seemed eternal and too much for his will to remain passive.

Then with a forefinger Burning Water flicked away the blackening wood coal, and with his tongue and lips pressed the mushed gum-leaves hard into the wound. Off came the handkerchief to bandage the foot. Off came Nevin's black shirt to add to the bandage, and then, whilst returning circulation increased the pain, he pushed Bony's feet into the Kurdaitcha boots.

"How d'you feel now?" he asked.

"Give me a drink."

"I'll make the tea. The water's boiling."

The tea was made. Sand was thrown over the fire. In the darkness Burning Water squatted beside Bony and blew upon the tea to cool it.

"Here. Take the cup and sip it. It won't taste too nice. I've put in half a handful of box-tree seeds. They'll act like a double dose of painkiller. Where's your tobacco."

"I don't want to smoke," Bony asserted, his voice weak and filled with pain.

"You will moke a cigarette. And you will drink my medicine. Then I'll bring in the dead men and clean up. We have twenty miles to travel before daybreak."

"I don't know which is worse, the pain of my heart or the pain of my foot."

"Are you drinking the medicine?" insisted Burning Water.

"Yes. It doesn't taste badly. It's warming my stomach."

"Good! Here's the cigarette. I'll strike a match. Ready?"

"Thank you, enigma," Bony said.

Burning Water tore down the screen of branches from the lowerside entrance and passed out to bring in the two dead Illprinka men. The doctored tea was pleasurably warming Bony's stomach. He felt this heat attacking the constricting pain about his heart. The pain in the foot was subsiding, the searing burning being submerged by a pleasant glow.

"That's done," Burning Water said. "How now?"

"Better."

"I thought that would be so. A little of the poison did get into the blood stream. I was too slow, and then those Illprinka men coming when they did delayed me more. I'm not as good a doctor as Jack Johnson, but you're lucky after all. The medicine man bites the bitten part right out."

"Like chopping off a man's head to cure his headache."

"Nearly as bad. Now, I'm taking you out of the gutter before cleaning up."

Burning Water assisted Bony from the shelter and to the level land, and then with a switch of twigs he smoothed away from the gutter floor all trace of their presence there.

Bony could place his injured foot to ground only at the expense of additional pain. A strong black arm was round his waist, helping him forward on a tramp of twenty miles, to be accomplished before the next day lightened the sky.

CHAPTER 21

FLORA'S AWAKENING

WHEN Flora McPherson regained consciousness she found herself lying between cool and clean sheets on a soft mattress supported by a brass-mounted bedstead. The bed was flanked by a table on which burned a petrol lamp, and by a dressing-table bearing a large mirror, and which obviously was a wood packing case covered with pale blue cretonne.

The same coloured material draped the walls, being stretched from the ground of termite nests to the ceiling of what appeared to be stretched white canvas. On the floor beside the bed were blue grass mats. In a part of one wall the cretonne was raised to reveal a wide doorway and no door.

Flora could hear distant voices but could not understand the language being used. A nearer sound, and one more persistent, was a continuous high-pitched whine which originated in the walls of the room. It was not sufficiently loud to be irritating, but was omnipresent and not to be shut away.

Behind her eyes was a dull ache, and she closed them to find relief from the pain and so slept again. She dreamed fearfully of Rex McPherson standing over her, and of an enormous lubra dressed in scarlet, who was wearing a crown of white marble. It was when she awoke free of pain and normally refreshed that she knew she had been lying in the bed for a long time.

The room was exactly the same. The walls were singing a little more loudly than she remembered them to have done. Nothing was altered, but there was an addition in the person of the enormous lubra sitting on the chair. She was dressed not in scarlet but in vivid green material which appeared to be wrapped about her huge body. Her crown of marble was her white and frizzy hair.

On observing Flora looking at her, she rose with much difficulty and panting breath, and trotted out of the room, giving Flora a glimpse of another room beyond the curtained entrance.

Rex McPherson! If the lubra had become real then Rex could become as real here in this very room. Flora's heart began to pound, and that terrible fear, reborn, hurt her pounding heart. Her world of unreality was invaded by a cawing crow that came and passed on, sounding to her as it would had she been sitting on the south veranda at home.

Then her mouth opened wide to scream, and her right hand flew to her mouth to stifle the scream. In the doorway stood Rex McPherson. Sight of him raised the girl high on the pillows. She rested on an arm in an attitude clearly indicating the urge to escape.

He was dressed in a suit of white duck cut in military style. He was wearing white tennis shoes and he was hatless. His straight black hair was immaculate, in keeping with his immaculate clothes. There was no ignoring his undoubted good looks. Six feet tall and yet not lanky, he carried himself with the grace of his maternal forebears.

Seen in the light produced by the petrol lamp, his eyes were black beads resting on beds of white velvet. His mouth was revealed by the white teeth bared in a smile. His nose was long and straight and his forehead was broad and high. There was strength in his chin. By comparison Bonaparte would appear nondescript, but Rex McPherson's skin was much darker and appeared like chocolate laid on a base of crimson.

"Well, my beautiful cousin, how are you this afternoon?" he said in tones like velvet.

Flora's heart was beating so rapidly she felt she was stifling. No longer wildly longing to scream, recognizing the futility of trying to escape, she drew the clothes higher about her and regarded Rex with that McPherson chin of hers most prominent.

"Where am I?" was naturally her first question.

"You are in the house of Rex McPherson," he replied, continuing to smile at her. "I am delighted to see that you have recovered from the effects of the nasty blow given you by that scoundrel Itcheroo. I told him not to treat you roughly, and I regret not having taken him aloft before rapping his knuckles as he clung to the side of the cockpit. Would you like a cup of tea and something to eat?"

Without waiting for her reply he clapped his hands and a moment later the enormous lubra entered, bearing a tray of tea and biscuits. Rex lifted the table and lamp to the side of the bed and told the woman to set down the tray. He whisked the chair to the opposite side of the table and sat down in it. Then he poured tea with the elegance of a lounge lizard. Rising to his feet, he leaned towards Flora, placed a filled cup near her and the boat of biscuits beside it.

"I remember you like sugar," he told her. "Two spoonfuls, isn't it? Dinner won't be ready for two hours and so we must satisfy ourselves with the biscuits."

Laughing, he sat down. When he laughed his face changed to emphasize, or rather to take on, distinctly aboriginal features. While sipping his tea, he said:

"Now compose yourself, Flora, and don't have hysterics. Drink the tea. Perhaps you would like a couple of aspirin."

He produced a packet and offered her two tablets, saying:

"Three are too much for sober young women."

Without comment the girl accepted the tablets and swallowed them with a draught of tea. Her left arm pressed to her side, informed her that the pistol in the soft leather holster was gone. Her eyes were big and round despite her effort to control her beating heart, and between herself and Rex appeared the ghost of Itcheroo. His face was awful and he held high a mulga waddy. She saw her own ghostly hand and knew that the automatic pistol had been knocked away from it. Then the ghost vanished and in its place was the smiling face of a black devil. As though someone else was speaking, she heard herself ask for a cigarette.

"Pardon!" her bedside visitor murmured and, again on his feet, he was offering an opened cigarette case and a burning match. "I did what I could for your head," he went on conversationally. "I was obliged to cut the hair from the contused part of the scalp to place on it a salve in which I have great faith. You certainly received a nasty crack."

"I don't understand," she told him. "I can't remember how I came to be about to shoot Itcheroo when he clubbed me."

"Oh—it will all come back, Flora, my dear. I sent Itcheroo to tell you that the dad urgently wanted you. In fact, I wrote a letter in the dad's handwriting. My women found it in your blouse, where you must have put it after reading it. In the letter I—or rather the dad—asked you to accompany Itcheroo to Big Cape, where he and the blacks were camped, as he wanted you to carry out an important plan which would reconcile us. This plan would exclude further action by that detective fellow, who was to know of it only when it succeeded. It was quite a long letter. I'll read it to you sometime."

"Don't!" Flora snapped. "I don't want you to remind me I've been taken in by such a simple little trick. I should have had sense enough to remember that forgery is second nature with you."

"Yes, dear Flora," he said, purringly. "I am delighted to feast my eyes on you again. Your beauty is breath-taking, and it hasn't reached its zenith. Damn it, I'm sorry I made you a pawn in my grand game with the old man. Still, even yet I may raise you from a pawn to be a partner, for the dad may continue to be obstinate."

"And if he is?"

"Oh—I don't think he will be."

"But if he is?"

"If he is obstinate, if he does not send up a smoke signal

announcing he will give me my inheritance now by six o'clock on the evening of the twentieth, I am going to make you my wife. I told him so in a note I dropped to him."

"And where was he then?"

"About half way to Duck Lake. I tricked him with smoke signals, indicating that the Illprinka were about to hold a corroboree at Duck Lake. He fell for the trick even after I held him up on the road and tried to persuade him to call you on the telephone."

"That was the time you tortured him?"

"That was the occasion," Rex answered. "If father was only as wise as he is courageous, everything would be right in this very bad world."

"And you are going to marry me? Supposing I refuse."

"A lubra doesn't refuse. She may resist—but not for long."

"A lubra! Me a lubra!" exclaimed Flora.

Rex smiled and blew a smoke ring.

"The word lubra translated is woman," he said. "All women, black, white, and er—brindle, are lubras. As a matter of fact, my father and mother were married blackfellow's way when they were children and when neither of them participated in the ceremony. Having foreseen the possibility of your uncle being obstinate, the Illprinka blacks were persuaded by me to marry us some weeks ago."

Flora's eyes became hard and her mouth like the grim mouths of her ancestors whose portraits hung on the dining-room walls.

"Well, then supposing uncle does surrender the station to you in exchange for my safe return. You couldn't accept the property. You couldn't live on it. You'd be arrested for the murder of Sergeant Errey and Mit-ji."

"Not a bit of it, Flora," he countered swiftly. "Who saw me bomb that car? Why, only a half-caste detective, who's little better than an ordinary police tracker, and old Burning Water. What they might say wouldn't carry any weight against my word that I wasn't near the confounded car. The car accidentally caught fire and the driver became panicky and sent it over the edge of the road and down into the gully. I can lay my hands on eight Illprinka men who would swear they saw it happen.

"Oh, I'll be safe enough, because when father makes the exchange, the station for you, he'll swear not to prosecute me for forging his signature to cheques, and that's the only thing he can prove against me. Then, when I own McPherson's Station, I'm going to take in all this open country, or a big slab of it, and I'll be the biggest squatter in Australia and will be known as the Australian Cattle King. And then you might consent to marry me white fellow's fashion."

So confidently did Rex talk that he almost convinced Flora by his argument. Come to think of it, only Bony and Burning Water saw the sergeant's car bombed, and there *were* Illprinka men near the place, for hadn't they tried to obtain the sergeant's attache case from Bony?

"You think all that over, Flora," he said, slowly. "As I have just told you. I am going to be a somebody in the not distant future with or without your uncle's submission. As my wife, married white fellow's fashion and not blackfellow's fashion, you'd be a somebody too. Make things easier, you know."

Then she read the look in his eyes. He wanted to marry her with her willing consent: he would take her without her consent and without proper marriage if——

"Then I have really three days, this being the seventeenth I think you said?"

"Yes, three whole days," he said, to add: "Three long days and nights, dear. Well, I must be off. I've had to take the plane engine partly down in an overhaul long overdue. I'll tell Tootsey to bring you a bath and your clothes. Dinner will be served at seven, and the cook is really good. A Chinaman and more a friend than a servant. Accept my advice. You are free to go where you wish. But don't be so silly as to try to escape. There is a hundred miles between you and the homestead. You wouldn't get far before my people caught up with you and brought you back with aching feet. They are fine trackers, you know."

Nodding coolly and smiling, he walked from the room and disappeared beyond the curtained entrance. She could hear him calling for Tootsey, and presently Tootsey came in, carrying a canvas bath and a huge bucket of hot water.

Refreshed and dressed in clothes which had been washed and ironed, having used a man's hair brushes and a silver backed comb, all Flora wanted was a pinch of powder.

She had three days. And Rex's aeroplane was temporarily grounded by an engine overhaul. And he didn't know about Bony having sent for Captain Loveacre. So conceited was he that he hadn't even asked her what Bony had done after Dr Whyte's plane had been destroyed. He was so in love with his own vaunted cleverness that he considered Bony to be only a black tracker employed by the police. In that frightful conceit lay hope of salvation.

She passed from her "room" into the larger one, where she stood with astonishment whilst regarding its details. Scarlet cloth was stretched from floor to ceiling. The ceiling was of the same material and colour. Scarlet grass mats were plentiful over the hard termite cement floor. A polished table was flanked with polished oak chairs. A standard petrol lamp supported a giant red shade. There was a large bookcase filled with volumes, and two massive screens composed entirely of mirror glass.

The wide but rather low entrance to this room attracted her. Standing there, she gazed across a half-mile expanse of level claypan to the bordering range of high sand-dunes. She saw no one, but she could hear the soft clank of iron on iron. Stepping out from the room she looked back at the "house" to see only the waving tops of cane-grass and lantana teased by the high wind, the "house" entrance but a shadow.

CHAPTER 22

ZERO HOUR

THERE was in Rex McPherson much of the material with which great men are fashioned, but his vanity upset his judgment in the valuation of the details of a scheme necessary for its success.

Was he not Rex McPherson? Had he not destroyed opposition by destroying Dr Whyte's aeroplane? Was not the possession of Flora a loaded gun in his hands pointed at his stubborn parent? Was he not secure from assault with his outflung Illprinka scouts before and the cane-grass swamp behind him? The next move in the game would have to be played by his father: meanwhile he could conduct an overdue overhaul of his aeroplane engine.

With Mit-ji dead and Itcheroo either dead or hostile to him, his source of information from the enemy's camp was stopped. Even this he regarded as of little importance. He took no steps to learn the reactions of those at the homestead to his theft of Flora, believing as he did that he was truly master of the situation. Thus he had not tapped the telephone line to Shaw's Lagoon, and he knew nothing of the coming of Captain Loveacre with a machine-gun mounted on an aeroplane.

He had placed a screen of almost a hundred aborigines in a great arc between himself and the homestead, being fully confident that these wild blacks would be more than a match for the softer and more civilized Wantella aborigines who might be employed by his father. But Burning Water had made an opening in the screen by killing two of the Illprinka men, and the opening was sufficiently large to permit a thinking aborigine and a subtle half-caste to pass through.

Rex had, too, placed certain men to relay back to him his father's signal of surrender which surely would be made when the high wind gave place to a calm. Having done all this he was content to glory in his own cleverness and to remain inactive.

Flora he treated with suave politeness, but it was rather the politeness of the cat that knows the mouse will inevitably make a fatal mistake. He found no reason to be crude as a host. He saw no reason to press advances because, so he had decided, Flora was merely a stepping stone to the realization of his great ambition to be somebody. Should his father continue to be stubborn, then would be the time to take Flora, with her consent if at all possible, without it if not. Meanwhile it would be foolish to antagonize her.

Flora had awakened the day before Loveacre flew from Roma to St Albans. It was the second day of high wind and rolling dust clouds. Other than the vast lubra, ironically called Tootsey, Flora came into contact with no other native. Unable to concentrate on the books in the bookcase, wanting to escape her horribly apprehensive thoughts, she wandered about the "house" and even walked outside it.

At the close of each of the two days of wind Tootsey beat the walls and the ceilings with a leafy branch to remove the dust which had penetrated through the walls of cane-grass packed between wire-netting. She dusted the furniture and watered the floors of the large living-room and Flora's bedroom. Flora could find no other rooms, and she never found the kitchen. But when she visited the hangar she saw in one corner of it a stretcher bed and dressing-table, and then understood that she was occupying Rex's bedroom.

The hangar was farther within the fringe of the cane-grass and lantana. Its open front was semi-masked with curtains of cane-grass woven by the Illprinka women. Within she found Rex working on his engine, and so bored was she with her own company that she talked with him for an hour on the subject of aeroplanes. When she left him she realized that on one matter he was profoundly learned and sane.

Early the second evening after a day of wind she walked as far as the sand-dunes, climbed them and gazed north-westward over the great swamp. It effectively hid the "house" and the hangar from her, for even the entrance to the house appeared to be one shadow of many. From the sky no house or hangar, or any other object could be seen.

Now more confident in herself, and feeling that Rex's interest was impersonal, her hope of being returned to the homestead rose higher. She was sure her uncle would capitulate and retire to the city, and although she liked the inland the prospect of living with him in the city was not distasteful. Anyway, she could look after him better down there, and he could even live with her and Harry when they were married.

Came the morning of the eighteenth when Rex greeted her at breakfast with:

"Hullo, cousin! Good morning! You look charming. Try these duck eggs and bacon. Tea or coffee?"

"Coffee, thanks," she said, guardedly returning his smile. "Engine work finished yet?"

"No. I've to fit together two parts of the wrong size. Can't trust people to do anything right. Order a particular size and they'll send another size. A pilot has to be an engineer and fitter these days."

"You're remarkable in your way," she told him.

"Of course," he agreed. "I'm going to rise high, dear. There is nothing a man cannot do if he makes up his mind to do it. I made up my mind I'd fly a plane. I then made up my mind I would know all about an aeroplane and its engine. Then I decided that in case of a forced landing in the bush I had better know how to effect repairs."

"No signal yet from uncle?" she asked.

"No. And I haven't expected it. This wind will prevent smoke signals, you know. Don't worry. The dad will give in and go down to the city to live. He'll feel a little lost, but he will get over that. You will look after him, I suppose."

"And what will you do?"

"I shall be the boss of McPherson's Station which will be four to five times bigger than it is now when I've taken up much of this open country. I am going to be the biggest squatter in Australia. I'm going to be somebody."

Be somebody! Was that the force driving him? Was the universal dream of men and women of being somebody in this man a force, a fire, sending him along the road to destruction? Flora regarded him wonderingly, and, he thought, admiringly.

She spent the morning doing nothing. The day was calm and cool, for a light breeze came from the south. She wondered if Captain Loveacre had reached the homestead, and what Bony and Dr Whyte were doing and thinking. Like Rex, she was confident her uncle would surrender his station in exchange for herself. After lunch, taken alone, she retired to her room where she lay and read by the light of the lamp.

At three o'clock by the little clock standing on the makeshift dressing-table, Tootsey entered her room with a tray of afternoon tea. This was unusual. Tootsey had never been communicative, but now she said:

"Missis stay here. Rex boss say so."

To Flora's questioning she merely shook her white-crowned head. And to Flora's astonishment she took the chair and, placing it square in the doorway, sat down. Frowning, Flora said:

"Go away, Tootsey. I don't want you there."

"Missis stay here. Rex boss say so," repeated Tootsey, and Flora knew the lubra had been taught the two phrases.

An hour later another lubra appeared and stood guard at the room's entrance. She was certainly Tootsey's opposite number. She, too, had fattened on good living. But she was naked save for the pubic tassel, and she was armed with a waddy fashioned from a mulga root. Tootsey was not particularly ugly, but this woman was hideous. Fat and sand mixed solidified her scanty hair to hanging rolls. Her body scent was appalling. Flora asked, sternly:

"What are you doing there?"

She received no reply. The lubra's stare was steady and hard. She held the waddy as though it were made of paper. So Tootsey now was her gaoler, and this naked savage woman was Tootsey's assistant.

Flora was confined to her room for the remainder of that day and succeeding night, but the following morning when Tootsey awakened her with a cup of tea, she said:

"Missis eat with Rex boss. Missis go out."

Rex was already at breakfast when she entered the living-room, and Flora now understood that when Tootsey said she was to go out she meant only to go out to the living room, for there standing in the uncurtained entrance was an armed aborigine.

"Morning, Flora," Rex greeted her, and his phrasing as well as his face told her that something had happened.

"There's a strange aeroplane flying around. Do you know anything about it?"

He was again the old, passionate, fiery Rex.

"I expect it's the aeroplane flown by a Captain Loveacre," she said. "Inspector Bonaparte sent for Captain Loveacre that day you destroyed Dr Whyte's plane."

"Oh! That's news. Why didn't you tell me before?"

"Because I had forgotten about it."

"What else haven't you told me?"

"Nothing else that you don't know," she answered, pretending indifference though feeling the shock that the old Rex lurked below the suave personality of the new. "It was Inspector Bonaparte who asked Dr Whyte to come. He wanted the doctor to fly him over the Illprinka country. When you destroyed the doctor's aeroplane, he thought of Captain Loveacre."

"Loveacre, eh, my dear! I have heard of Captain Loveacre. He's quite a somebody, too. Well, he won't do any harm. He won't locate my headquarters." Rex leaned back in his chair and laughed, and Flora was reminded of the aborigine standing in the doorless entrance. "All the aeroplanes in the Commonwealth wouldn't find us. And supposing they did, what then?

"If this place was located from the air and they sent a ground force against us, that ground force wouldn't get within eighty miles of us before we would know about it. Think I haven't thought of the possibility of an invading ground force? I have, indeed, my sweet. I have planned for all eventualities. Long before the ground force could arrive we would have left, retreated to an even more secret place."

He expected her to ask where, and she asked the question.

"Do you know how much there is of this cane-grass and lantana swamp?" he inquired, flashingly. "I'll tell you. At its widest point it is eleven miles across. It is forty-two miles in length. For months water will lie over great areas of it making it impassable almost to dingoes. My secret place is in the middle, and the road to the secret place is a secret, too. You and I, dear, would be undisturbed there for ever."

In the middle of the afternoon she heard the aeroplane coming fast towards the swamp. She ran into the living-room governed by the idea of running out of the "house" and attracting Captain Loveacre's attention. But there was the guard standing just inside the entrance, and now masking the entrance was a curtain of woven cane-grass.

All the following morning she sat in the living-room with her back to the guard. It was like waiting for the executioner. Time by the large clock paradoxically raced and yet stood still. The ticking of the clock became a torture, and yet she knew she could not bear to see it stopped.

She drank her afternoon tea in her room but could not eat. Her ears ached through straining to register the sound of an aeroplane engine. All she heard was the whine of the light wind in the cane-grass walls. The large clock in the outer room struck the hour of five. After the passing of an eternity, it struck six. Time stood still. Flora sat on the bed waiting, her nerves tortured. The outer clock struck seven.

Then she heard movement in the living-room and could wait no longer. She had to know if the smoke signal had been received. The suspense was no longer to be endured.

In the living-room Tootsey was setting dishes on the table. The aborigine was still guarding the entrance. It may not have been the same man. They looked alike to Flora. And then she was staring in Tootsey's black eyes and knowing she was deserted by her uncle who loved his station better than her, deserted by Harry and by Bony and Burning Water, deserted by the world and all that was decent and worth living for. For Tootsey was smiling at her like a woman who is jealous.

Like an animal forced from one cage to another, Flora turned back to her room. Whatever should she do? What on earth *could* she do? There was only the chair with which to defend herself. Her pistol was gone. A knife! Probably there were knives on the table in the other room. She could hear Rex speaking to Tootsey, and then he called her.

"Come on, Flora! Dinner is served!"

"Go away!" shouted Flora. "Leave me alone."

"Don't be damned stupid," Rex called back. "Come on, now! There's grilled chops and mashed potatoes, a fruit pie and custard made with condensed milk. There's coffee and biscuits and nuts. I have brought a bottle of brandy to mark the great occasion."

The great occasion! She was saved. She was going back to the homestead. Her uncle had capitulated to Rex.

Flora ran to the entrance, stopped. She gulped air into her lungs. She patted her hair and squared her shoulders. Then, lifting the curtain, she passed into the living-room.

Her lower jaw almost dropped. Rex was in evening clothes. He looked magnificent. He would not be in evening clothes if he was going to fly her back to the homestead.

Slowly Flora approached the table. There were no knives on the table. She sat down to look at Rex, and Rex lifted a cover to disclose curry and rice. On the table were only spoons. Even the bread was cut. Rex said:

"I'm sorry. I thought it was to be grilled chops. But Ah Ling can make curry, real curry. There's wild ducks in this one. Will you take a little rice?"

"Thank you," replied Flora, and her own voice sounded distant. "Didn't uncle send up the smoke signal?"

"Er—no, dear. He forgot to make it, or he has gone on a journey, or he has even decided to keep his station."

"Then—then——"

"We meet at last—as husband and wife. You will remember I told you we had been married by the blacks some time ago. You know, dear, I'm not a bit disappointed that father is stubborn. Not a bit. I shall have to apply the pressure in some other way. Water?"

Silently now the girl ate dinner, refusing to speak, to warm to his gay blandishments, armoured by the ice of despair. She accepted his suggestion of a little brandy in her coffee, abruptly determined that she would not submit without fighting. Tootsey came in, summoned by Rex's clapped hands, and removed the dinner things. Rex spoke to her in the Illprinka tongue and the huge woman nodded her understanding. Then he spoke to the man on guard, and he grunted and vanished beyond the dropped curtain of woven cane-grass.

The alleged husband and wife were alone.

Flora accepted a cigarette, but would take no more coffee.

"Do I really look objectionable?" Rex asked.

"You look nice in evening clothes," Flora admitted, and knew she spoke the truth.

"Then why can't we be good friends?" he asked. "Nothing is going to stop me from being a somebody, nothing at all. I'm not really bad. I've been misunderstood, frustrated. I am ambitious. And I am deeply in love with you."

"I don't love you."

"But that should not be sufficient reason."

"Well, then, because I am not an aboriginal lubra."

"Nor is that sufficient reason."

Flora sighed and stood up. She saw the unguarded but curtained entrance. It was dark outside. The guard would certainly be standing outside. She sat down in one of the cane chairs. Rex placed another opposite her and sat down and offered her another cigarette. He began talking of his ambition and his schemes, like a man talking to an audience of many people. He was going to become Australia's Cattle King, and then he'd work the oracle and get himself knighted and be called Sir Rex. Flora would be called Lady McPherson.

"And so, dear, you will not be tied to a nonenity," he concluded, and came and sat on the arm of her chair. "You and I are going to be somebodies. We're going to count in the scheme of things. Your beauty allied to my brains will raise us high. Beautiful Flora! Dear, I love you so, and you must love me."

"No!" The girl suddenly screamed. She slipped from his hands and stood facing him. "I tell you no! Let me alone. Let me alone, I say! If you touch me I'll blind you with my finger nails."

The old Rex flashed uppermost. He laughed and his face broadened until again it resembled the features of an aborigine. Like the fly-catching lizard he sprang to her, knocked down her protecting arms, swept her close to his scented person and, forcing upward her face, kissed her repeatedly.

Flora wanted to scream but could not. The terrible fear was gripping her heart, paralysing her tongue. She fought with all her strength—and knew she was doomed. Then above the torment of her mind she heard the voice she had longed to hear:

"Pardon me! Kindly desist, Mr McPherson."

CHAPTER 23

GREEK MEETS GREEK

"THANK you, Mr McPherson. Remain quite still," Bony requested. "The reason why I am refraining from pressing hard on the trigger is not because I have strong views against capital punishment. Thank you, Burning Water. Make very sure that Mr McPherson has no other weapon about his clothes. To continue: I always have great sympathy for the dependants of murdered people, and none whatever for the murderers. I regard the life of a murderer as of no more value than the life of a snake."

Burning Water had taken from Rex's hip pocket a dainty but efficient automatic pistol, and now with practised hands he examined the weapon and found it was fully loaded.

"Now, my brother, maintain strict attention to Mr McPherson.

I am aware you want to shoot, but don't forget the inconvenience which might follow the report of a shot," urged Bony.

"Charming fellows," sneered Rex.

Bony turned now to Flora who, still breathing rapidly and white-faced, was staring incredulously from Bony to Burning Water and back again to Bony.

"A little sip of brandy, eh, Miss McPherson?" he asked. "Two sips for you: six for me."

She tried to speak, failed, and began to cry. She was suffering from terrible reaction. Her hands were trembling.

"You will be better in a minute," Bony predicted. "It is seldom that I touch spirits, but this evening I must take a glass of Mr McPherson's brandy. I am not so well as usual. Ah, that's better! Now for a cigarette. Ah, that's still better. We aren't out of the bog yet, but you are comparatively safe. You are going home with Burning Water. Tonight you will have to travel far and fast, and you will require all your strength. Will you take another sip or two of brandy?"

Flora shook her head. The trembling of her hands had subsided. There was growing colour in her ashen face.

"Oh Bony, thank heaven you've come. I—I——"

"Trust old Bony to do his stuff," he said, smiling. "That is not my expression. It has been used by those of my critics who are more direct than elegant."

Now he knelt before her and, without asking permission, proceeded to remove her shoes and place on her feet the Kurdaitcha boots he slipped from his own feet. The shoes he joined together by knotting the laces, and then placed them in her hands, saying:

"You must take these with you. Burning Water and I have planned every detail of your escape, and you must try to ask no questions because time is of vital importance."

He stood up and regarded her with an encouraging smile.

Looking up at him, Flora was startled by his appearance. He was wearing only a pair of trousers. Nevin's black shirt was wrapped about his right foot, and she had seen him limping badly when he went to the table for the brandy and the cigarettes.

"Go on, Rex, do something," Burning Water urged.

Rex McPherson laughed, and he laughed as Flora had heard him laughing in the old days.

"You'd like to shoot, wouldn't you," he said, with his teeth bared. "You'd be signing your own and Flora's death warrants if you did. But my turn will come again."

"I doubt it, Mr McPherson," Bony said.

Now he proceeded to examine the walls behind the stretched scarlet cloth masking the wired walls of cane-grass, making himself sure there were no other exits from the room other than that by which they had entered. He moved the table and set two chairs opposite each other. The brandy and glasses and the box of cigarettes he placed to his satisfaction.

"If Mr McPherson would take the chair opposite. Back, Mr McPherson. Careful, Burning Water. Conduct Mr McPherson until I take over."

"Quite like the pictures, isn't it?" Rex sneered.

"More so, Mr McPherson. Much more so. On the screen the guns aren't really loaded," Bony told him, continuing to place emphasis on the title. "Kindly keep your hands on the table and remember that any involuntary contraction of my forefinger will cause an explosion. Burning Water you must start without further delay. Bring my rifle and place it against my left leg. Good! I can now keep my eyes on Mr McPherson and the entrance. We shall be quite comfortable."

"What kind of game are you playing?" asked Rex.

"I will be happy to explain it later. We have plenty of time. Now, Miss McPherson and Burning Water, off you go."

The girl came and stood behind Bony.

"But why aren't you coming, too?" she asked. "You can't stay here. There's at least twenty Illprinka men about. You'll never get away from them once they know you're here."

"There is little reason to be concerned about me, Miss McPherson." Then in tones she had never heard him use, he added: "Now be off. You are wasting time, Burning Water! Get going at once."

Rex watched the chief and Flora pass out by pushing aside the edge of the cane-grass curtain, and then he laughed.

"How far d'you expect Flora to get tonight? She'll drop with fatigue when they've travelled ten miles. And if she's able to get twenty miles before sun-up my bucks will catch up with them. You must be a fool if you think those Kurdaitcha boots will stop the Illprinka tracking them."

"Thank you for your cigarettes, Mr McPherson. I was perishing for a smoke. You may be correct in your prognostications, but their fulfilment or otherwise will hardly concern us. Of more immediate concern is ourselves. We have a long night to get through without boring each other. I overheard you telling the guard he could go to his quarters and camp for the night. The lubra was less willing to obey a similar order. She hung about outside the curtain for some considerable time. and I was beginning to think it necessary to club her when she departed and later her snoring could be heard. Now, provided you behave yourself, we can be assured of peace and content till breakfast time arrives."

"Then, I think, we will both die—you first."

"Melodramatic, eh?"

"Life itself is melodramatic."

"There's comedy, too. Why are you staying here? Why not have trussed and gagged me, or, as Burning Water suggested, have taken me some distance away and then murdered me?"

"There are objections to either course," Bony replied. "Two days ago I was bitten on the foot by a saltbush snake. Burning Water was quick but not quick enough. Then, whilst he was attending to me, there was an intrusion by two Illprinka blacks who had to be dealt with. I am, in consequence of the snake bite and the condition of the wound, almost too lame to cross this room. My forced role is to keep you entertained as long as possible."

"We must talk about something, I suppose."

"By all means. Let's talk about you, shall we?"

"If the subject interests you. Make a start."

"Thank you. Tell me how you worked Itcheroo to steal from my swag Sergeant Errey's attache case."

"Yes, that's a beginning," assented Rex. lighting a cigarette of the dozen Bony pushed towards him from the box. There was vibration in his voice betraying seething anger, and the struggle to speak calmly evidently was made in order to maintain equality with Bonaparte's self-control.

"When a magic man of the Illprinka party I had on hand to make sure no evidence survived the tragic accident to the car, informed me through another magic man that you had been a witness, and that you had picked up from the ground a flat and square object, I knew it must be a case of some kind. I then sent a communication to Itcheroo about it. telling him to meet you and Burning Water and see if either of you carried such a case. If not, then the case would be in your luggage. He was to obtain it if possible and burn it.

"I understand that he. having great power over a housemaid named Ella, persuaded her to take it from your swag whilst you were in the bathroom. Itcheroo subsequently burned the case and its contents. How did you come to associate Itcheroo with the theft?"

"I found Itcheroo the following morning sitting beside a little fire and sending thought messages. In the fire were still remnants of the case and the sergeant's notebooks."

Rex regarded Bony steadily. He was beginning to understand that this quiet man was superior to a police tracker. Contempt was being replaced by a degree of respect which in turn aroused fear.

"Itcheroo got a nasty crack from one of the horses, didn't he?" he asked.

"Itcheroo was killed."

"Oh! Well, perhaps that was fortunate."

"I am inclined to think it was for you less fortunate than you believe."

The clock chimed ten and Rex glanced at it.

"Itcheroo could have told many tales. So could Mit-ji. I am like all the great kings. When a man becomes dangerous, remove him. If one doesn't he will remove one. I would have brought Itcheroo here in the plane, but he was tired or something and you people were in a great hurry. It was quite an exciting finish, that race, wasn't it?"

"Very. I am glad to know that Itcheroo did not kill Miss McPherson. She was, of course, unconscious when he was carrying her?"

"Of course. He clubbed her. Too severely, the fool. Flora was unconscious for two days. Poor girl!"

"I agree, Mr McPherson. You know, you puzzle me. You were reared by two doting grandparents and an easy father. They provided you with plenty of money. You could have gone high, and yet you threw it all to the winds. Seldom has any boy and young man been so greatly favoured."

"Favoured!" sneered Rex, leaning towards Bony. "Favoured, my foot! How the hell d'you make that out?"

"Even when your income was stopped through the action of a dishonest trustee, you could eventually have become your father's partner, and then owner of McPherson's Station."

The crimson base of Rex's complexion was swiftly more evident when at last anger was beating down his self-control.

"It all sounds all right, doesn't it?" he said, heatedly. "Money! Money can't make our skins white, can it? Money can't even prevent us being insulted, regarded either as dangerous animals or pet poodles. You know that. You must know it. We can't mix on equality with white people."

"But," interposed Bony, "you and I and others like us can put on the ar,nour of pachyderms. People who try to insult me because of my birth never hurt me. In fact, they provide human study that interests me. I am always interested by the unfortunate people who suffer from the inferiority complex which they so clearly reveal by using insulting words and by being snobbish. Far from being hurt, I am always pleased because it is an acknowledgment of my superiority to them. I still don't understand why you, having the advantages you did have, should have cast yourself outside the pale."

"No? Then you must be dense or ignorant, or satisfied with being a lackey to the whites," Rex said, still heated. Bony was not to know it, but Rex was now become the old self known to Flora. His eyes were flashing. "The money was a curse, not a blessing," he went on. "When I first went to school and they knew I had money to burn, my school mates crowded me like the born spongers they were. I was invited to their homes, but if I smiled at their sisters the girls would vanish. Behind my back they called me the nigger. I was worse off than if I'd been a full blood. And, to get down to a base, whose fault was it? Is your father still alive?"

"I never knew him," Bony answered. "Keep your hands well forward on the table."

"I know mine," snapped Rex. "For what I am he is to blame. I hate him. I've hated him ever since that day I really saw myself for the first time. A fellow called me a dirty half-caste and we fought. I sent him to hospital, but he mauled me and I was attending to my face with the aid of a mirror. I wasn't dirty, but I was a half-caste. I hated myself that day, but I hated my father much more.

"Why did I run off with Flora? Why did I get money by forging his name to cheques? Why did I come here and carve for myself a station and steal the old man's cattle to stock it with? Why—oh blast! Why everything? Because I hate him. Because I am going to force the whites to respect me. Because I am going to make them acknowledge me as an equal. A dirty half-caste, eh? Well, I'm going to prove that a half-caste is as clever as any white man."

"How?" asked Bony, and with his left hand he reached for the brandy and a glass. It was eleven-thirty, and he was feeling deadly weary.

"How!" Rex almost shouted. "To date I haven't been ruthless enough. From now on I'm going to have no mercy on anyone. I'll have no mercy on Flora tomorrow when my bucks fetch her back. As for you, you interfering fool, your finish will come in a way you won't like. Then I am going to get McPherson's Station and add all this open country to it. After that I'll join the Illprinka to the Wantella people. I'll train the bucks to be soldiers. And then, if the government sends police or soldiers against me I'll engage in a war.

"I won't have a chance, eh? I'll have every chance to win. What about the Boers? What about the Abyssinians and now the Chinese? They weren't licked easily. And even if I lose I'll go down as the man who avenged the aborigines.

"Why should the damn lordly whites take all Australia from the aborigines?" he demanded to know, and would not wait for an answer from the man opposite him who was himself fighting to subdue the mental lethargy threatening him.

"But I'm not standing for it, d'you hear?" Rex banged the table with his clenched fists. "I'm going to hit back before I'm finished. I'm going to leave my mark on Australia, to be remembered for hundreds of years either as the Australian Cattle King or the Avenger of the Aborigines. And you—well, as you're in the same boat with me, I'll give you a chance. What about joining me? What about being my Chief of Staff? Your name, too, would be remembered."

Bony was perturbed by the necessity of bringing his mind to bear on the suggestion. Reaching for a cigarette, he said:

"If you hadn't attempted to run, if you had been content to walk, you would have gone far towards achieving that ambition of yours. Where you have failed——"

"I haven't failed," shouted Rex, springing to his feet, oblivious of the automatic pointed at him. "I haven't started yet."

"Where you have failed," continued Bony, "is by not recognizing forces which neither you nor I, nor a million like us, can withstand. I refer to the forces of human evolution. Just wait and let me have my say. Sit down. I'm not forgetting to watch you. That's better. Why have the Australian blacks become submerged? Why have the Abyssinians been conquered? Because humanity is no different from the animals and the insects in the jungles. There the strong devour the weak. It is the same in the human world. The weak go to the wall. Those who will not struggle to survive, will not compete with competitors, must go under.

"You cannot, as one man, realize that fantastic dream of yours of avenging past crimes against the aborigines. You can't as Rex McPherson, ever become the Cattle King of Australia. You have incurred a debt for the murder of Sergeant Errey and those others, and civilization will exact payment. You will ask me to join you. My dear fellow, I understand your hatred of the whites, even your hatred of your father. But you have tried to conquer your enemies with bombs and you threaten to try again with guns and trained aborigines. I have conquered my enemies with my mind as a gun and knowledge as ammunition. You have tried to move a mountain; I have succeeded in moving a grain of sand."

"Give me a drink, as I suppose I mustn't reach for the bottle," Rex urged. The tip of his tongue was passing across his lips and on his wide brow glistened drops of perspiration.

"Water?" asked Bony.

"A little."

There followed a long silence, punctuated by the ticking clock. They smoked incessantly and occasionally drank. Then the clock struck twelve, and presently Rex said:

"Why be a fool? If you joined up with me we could do great things. You're a thinker. I can see that. You can have no hope of getting away from here, even if you shoot me."

Now before retiring to her bed of gum-leaves, Tootsey had eaten an enormous dinner. Her dreams, therefore, were of violence so terrible that she awoke at last and lay trembling and cold. And in this state of wide wakefulness, she heard Rex McPherson's shouted speech, not a word of which could she understand. Despite the colour of her skin and her race, she was naturally curious, and the shouted words she could hear indicated that Rex boss was taming the white woman. Tootsey decided to observe how the taming was proceeding.

Leaving her bed of gum-leaves, she tip-toed to the curtain of cane-grass which she found being gently swung inward by the light south wind. By lying down she could see into the living-room everytime the curtain was swung inward, and what she saw interested her exceedingly. The magnificent "boss," arrayed in resplendent evening clothes, was certainly in one of his tempers, but what intrigued Tootsey was the fact that he did not seem to be angry with the strange man who was seated at the table pointing a pistol at the boss.

The absence of Flora did not have much weight with Tootsey, but the fact that Rex boss was standing when a pistol was aimed at him had great weight. Tootsey knew that pistols could send men back into the trees and stones from which they had first come as spirit babies, and she didn't want Rex boss to be sent back into such a place.

Back in a tree, or a stone, or an ant hill, Rex boss could not provide her with such lovely dresses, and she was sure that if the strange man killed him the supply of white man's tucker, especially the sugar, would end. That must not be, and she crept away to arouse the Illprinka men.

The chief and two others accompanied her back to the entrance and looked under the curtain when the breeze lifted it. Being a crafty man, the chief clearly foresaw what would happen if they rushed into the room. Rex boss would go back into a stone or something, and no longer would he be head man, because under Rex boss's protection he had committed many tribal crimes.

Motioning those with him to withdraw, he conscripted an aborigine who had assisted Rex boss to build the "house" and who knew how to use wire-cutters and wire. With this man, he went to the back of the room in which Flora had slept, and ordered the other to make a hole through the wall of wire-netting and cane-grass. When he crawled through the opening into the bedroom, the clock in the outer wall struck twice.

"Oh yes," Rex was continuing, his voice raised almost to shouting. "After my plans mature I'll be strong enough to defy the government. In this heart of the continent, I'll be supreme. If I'm let alone I'll be peaceful: if not, I'll sting worse than a million scorpions."

He could see the Illprinka chief creeping soundlessly across the floor towards Bony. Bony was sitting listlessly with his back to the stalker, the night taxing his endurance weakened by pain and fatigue. Rex went on, now smilingly:

"I think I'll take you to about five thousand feet and tip you out, my friend. Then you will have time to think of your stupid refusal to join me. I'll do that with Flora, when I'm tired of her and old Burning Water, too."

The Illprinka man made no sound when he rose to his feet at Bony's back. Had Bony been normal he would have "sensed" the presence of the man. He was too late.

A black arm flashed over and down one shoulder and swept aside the pistol. Another encircled Bony's neck and pressed hard against the powerful chest.

Rex pounced upon the pistol, and then danced away from the table, shouting threats and oaths and commands. Bony struggled to rise but failed. The lamplight flickered. The ticking of the clock became the sound of a hammer in his ears.

CHAPTER 24

FLIGHT

FLORA'S reactions to the immediate prospect of escape and the distant prospect of safety and assured security were akin to the beginning of intoxication. She wanted to laugh, to shout, even to dance. Then she wanted to shriek with laughter at the absurd shoes of emu feathers on her feet. Fortunately for her, Bony's feet were small and their use of the shoes had shaped them almost to fit her.

"Quiet!" breathed the Chief of the Wantella Tribe.

The stars were bright. The new moon hung low above the cane-grass and lantana country behind them. The walking was easy, for Burning Water kept to the claypans. He walked fast, and the girl was obliged to step more quickly to keep with him. When they had been walking for half an hour, he said:

"We expected difficulty with dogs, but Rex must have been afraid that dogs about his camp might betray it. It was good for us."

"That's strange," Flora said. "Only now do I remember never having heard a dog bark once all the time I was there. But never mind the dogs, or their absence. Tell me what Bony is going to do back there with Rex. Why didn't he come with us?"

"It is wise not to talk too much when it is sure an avenging party will come after us," Burning Water said, and Flora knew by his voice that the subject of Bony was painful to him.

Despite the rubbing of the Kurdaitcha shoes every time her feet passed each other, despite the fact that they were so light and the ground so smooth, already her feet were beginning to ask for the accustomed leather shoes with cuban heels. Sinews and little bones in her feet were beginning to ache a little when Burning Water stopped.

"We will sit down and rest," he said, and squatted on his heels.

"Rest!" she echoed. "Not yet, surely?"

"For five or ten minutes. It will help to keep strength."

She sat on the warm ground beside him. Then she asked: "Are you tired?"

"No." After a short period of silence he added: "But my heart is tired."

"For Bony? Do you fear greatly for him?"

"Chief Illawalli was wise when he made Bony a great man among us, Miss McPherson," Burning Water strongly affirmed. "Two nights ago a saltbush snake bit him: bit him on the foot. I did what I could—quick. Before I could finish with the treatment, I had to kill two Illprinka men who were waiting for dark to go and get a message dropped from Captain Loveacre's aeroplane. The delay gave the poison a chance. Last night we travelled twenty miles to the cane-grass. Bony was very sick, and towards morning his foot pained much."

"A saltbush snake! They're deadly, aren't they?"

"Yes. All today he lay deep in a fox hole which I covered with bush. I went looking for Rex's house. We had no water. Then I saw the clothed lubra come out of one place and go into another place in the cane-grass, and I knew that was where you must be. I saw Rex come out and go into a big shadow, long and fairly low, and I knew that was where his aeroplane was. After dark I got water and took it to Bony. We waited. We daren't make a fire to make tea. Then we crept close to the camp and began to watch."

"Oh! Being so sick he ought to have come with us."

"It is what I told him," asserted Burning Water. "He said no. He said we would have to travel far and fast before day broke. He said he'd only be a drag on us, what with his sickness and bad leg. So he is staying behind to keep Rex from giving the alarm as long as possible."

"How will he escape from Rex and the Illprinka men?"

"I don't know. I don't think he'll be able to. I wanted to take Rex some way into the bush and cut his black throat, but Bony said that would be murder. I suppose it would, white-fellow law, but I don't think it would be murder when it means Rex or Bony. In the morning that clothed lubra will find him there and tell the Illprinka men. He's hoping to keep Rex from doing anything till morning comes. We must get on."

"How far have we come?"

"About six miles," he replied.

"Six miles! Only six miles! What is the time? Do you know?"

"By the stars I should say it is about eleven o'clock. Would you like a drink of water?"

"Please."

Soon after the beginning of the third stage, Flora felt yielding sand beneath her Kurdaitcha shoes, and she felt herself walking up an incline. Presently she saw the curved back of a sand-dune against the sky. The hand clasping her own tightened, and her guide said:

"Walk on your toes and lift your feet high. We are crossing the rump of a great headland. We'll come down to the valley again in about half a mile."

When for the third time Burning Water stopped to rest, she asked if she might wear her leather shoes inside the masses of feathers. Burning Water took time to consider the matter. He found grounds for arguing for and against, and he decided in favour because speed was the first essential. On his knees, he assisted the girl with her footwear. Then:

"A little water?"

"Please: I wish it were coffee. Don't you?"

"I do. But we daren't make a fire to brew coffee. And I could never brew coffee like old Mrs McPherson used to."

When for the fourth time they stopped, she said weakly:

"Oh, my feet are terrible. My legs are all stabbing pains."

"Lie still, Miss McPherson," he urged. "We'll stay here for about twenty minutes, no longer. We have come only about eleven miles."

"Do you know where we are?"

"Oh, yes. We are close to the south side of the valley. We'll have to cross the valley presently to gain the north side, and then we will have to look out when walking through the bush not to step on an Illprinka man. On the claypans it's safer, because the blacks won't be camped so far from shelter from the night wind."

"O-o-h! My poor feet!" Flora softly exclaimed. "I'm sorry, Burning Water. I've no right to complain."

"I am hardened to walking, Miss McPherson. It makes a great difference. I'm sorry, but time is up."

Her own shoes certainly gave her a measure of relief, and now Burning Water pulled her arm through his crooked arm, and although she tried hard to maintain independence of action, she found herself increasingly placing her weight on him. The travelling became rough, deep water gutters barring their passage, and down and over and up these gutters Burning Water carried her. Save for the gutters the way was ever clear, for although she was blinded by the darkness, he appeared able to see as well as a night animal.

She had lost count of the number of short halts, but actually it was at the termination of the sixth halt, when they had walked seventeen miles and it was three o'clock in the morning, that her legs refused longer to serve her.

"I can't—oh, I can't go on," she sobbed.

"Don't worry, Miss McPherson," he told her, although he was beginning to dread seeing the first sign of approaching day. He slung the rifle across his back and then, stooping, he lifted her in his arms.

"Let me down, please," she requested without a trace of urgency. "I mustn't give in. I mustn't be a child. Let me down."

"Lie quiet, Miss McPherson. You are not heavy."

"Aren't I? You're so strong, Burning Water, and so kind. And don't call me Miss McPherson. I would rather you call me Flora."

"Thank you—Flora. Perhaps tonight it would be all right. Tomorrow, when the day is bright, you will again be Miss McPherson, the mistress of McPherson's Station. I will be just Burning Water. You know, away back in the old days, when I called the McPherson Donald or Don, and we used to fight and make our noses bleed, old Mrs McPherson would say: 'Now, you boys come into the kitchen for a scolding.' And we both would say, 'All right, mother, and after the scolding will you give us a slab of toffee?' She always did."

She could see his head silhouetted against the sky, the head crowned by the tufted hair, but when she closed her eyes it was so easy to forget that he was an aborigine. Grave and thoughtful, he yet could delight in playing that game with a small child, when his task was to blow down a "chook house" of matches built on his stomach. He carried Flora fully half a mile before he put her down.

"We mustn't stop," he told her, his breath hissing. "Now please don't think I'm being familiar, but I am going to put my arm round your waist and help you along."

There began again the agonizing torture of lifting her feet, pushing them forward, putting her weight on them.

"Are we going to any particular place?" she asked.

"Yes. A place where we can defy all the Illprinka men and wait for Captain Loveacre and Dr Whyte to find us and pick us up in the aeroplane. We have to get there before Rex's Illprinka bucks catch up."

"Is it—is it much farther to go?" she asked, dully.

"Another seven miles."

"Seven miles. Oh, I can't. How far have we come?"

"Nearly eighteen miles, I think. We have travelled fast, as Bony told us to. You have done well, Flora."

Time came to have no meaning. She was dimly conscious of walking on a treadmill, and suddenly this stopped and she found herself lying on a soft mattress. She thought she was on the south veranda of the homestead, and she tried to recollect when she had had the mattress taken there. Then she saw the silhouette of Burning Water's head and realized she was being carried. Presently that period passed into blissful sleep which in turn passed to the consciousness that again she was being held up whilst her legs were moving and her feet were scuffling across hard claypan.

She was amazed to find it was daylight. The sky ahead was rose-tinted, and in the rosy glow were tiny puff clouds stained all gold. The valley lay stretched to the far horizon which was on fire. They were skirting the feet of the bulging slopes rising to the northern high land. The sun was about to rise.

"How much farther?" she asked piteously.

"Less than three miles," Burning Water replied, his voice anxious, his magnificent body drooping. "You see that headland beyond the tobacco-bush? That's sanctuary."

He had carried the girl for half-mile stages, and had been obliged to support her and almost drag her in between those stages. It made no mark on Flora's mind that they were following the centre of a long line of claypans, that the walking was easy on this cement-hard surface. She did not know that keeping to the bush towards the centre of the valley were several stalking Illprinka men, members of Rex's screen, that these men were fresh and strong and that their own pace was less than a mile an hour. Nor did she see those men, five in number, leave the bush and begin to run towards them as though intending to prevent their further advance. Abruptly Burning Water lowered her to the ground.

The sharp report of his rifle galvanized her into full consciousness. She saw Burning Water lying full length on the claypan and cuddling the stock of the weapon which discharged a devastating bullet at point blank range for three hundred and fifty yards. She saw a black body stretched on the claypan about a hundred yards away, and four others armed with spears and shields fleeing towards the bush.

Then Burning Water was bending over her and lifting her in his arms to stand her on her awful feet. The walking began again and now memory of those black forms energized her mind to will effort. How long the walking continued did not interest her. It appeared to be hour after hour without pause, without rest, and then she found herself being lifted and wanted to protest at being "slung" across a broad shoulder.

Her annoyance, however, was nothing compared to the relief her feet and legs received. She heard Burning Water utter a sharp exclamation, and she felt his body exert greater effort. She wondered but was too exhausted to ask him the reason. She did not see what he saw when, glancing back, he saw far away along the claypan verge of the villey a large party of naked aborigines running like hounds.

At the foot of the headland there was a sandy slope falling gently to the claypan verge. It was little more than a hundred yards in width, and when Burning Water reached it the Illprinka men were a mere three hundred yards behind and screaming their excitement and blood lust.

Half way up the slope Burning Water staggered and fell. His mouth was wide open. His face was contorted by the agony of terrific effort, and his eyes were red discs. Up he lurched to stoop and raise Flora, to heave her across his shoulder with her face to his back. She then saw their pursuers less than a hundred yards behind them. Some were fitting the hafts of their spears into the sockets of throwing sticks: others were yelling and lifting high their feet like the emus.

When Burning Water fell again it appeared to Flora that her fatigue vanished beneath the appalling fear. She was on her feet when Burning Water rose to his, and he flung an arm about her waist and dragged her on up the slope of yielding sand towards the base of the headland. In front of her was the usual line of debris, and among this jetsam from the cliff face was a huge boulder standing like a monument to mark the very front of the headland. Burning Water was urging her to run. A spear passed them and buried its fire-hardened point in the deep sand. Flora guessed that behind the boulder must be a cave in which they could shelter, and she was astonished when Burning Water voluntarily flung himself, and dragged her down with him, to the base of the stone.

Down at the foot of the sand slope the Illprinka men had halted, and stood staring at them. The great stone stood guard over the tribe's sacred treasure house, and even within its shadow there must be no violence. In the shadow of the stone was sanctuary.

CHAPTER 25

SANCTUARY

NONE but a few old men of the Illprinka tribe would ever dare approach near the great boulder fallen from the face of the headland in the dim and distant past. For any unauthorized buck, any woman or child, to be found near the stone would inevitably mean sentence of death, from which there could be no escape even from the protection of a friendly tribe.

When it feil the impact had cracked the rock, the extent of the crack being about two feet in width and seven or eight in length. The interior had been made weather tight with termite cement, and periodically the old men visited the sacred place to effect repairs or to remove objects necessary for their ceremonies.

The boulder was the bank of the Illprinka Tribe. Here were kept the tribe's churinga stones, the head of the sacred pole decorated with birds' down and hair alleged to have belonged to the tribe's Alchuringa ancestor, bull-roarers and other sacred objects.

Normally Chief Burning Water, of the Wantella Tribe, would have avoided this place as he would have avoided a saltbush snake. By bringing a woman to it he could not increase the penalty he himself had incurred, the penalty of death which even in his own country would be meted to him. That he, an unauthorized person, had desecrated the Illprinka's sacred store-house with his presence would not mean the desecration by·the Illprinka people of the sacred store-house belonging to the Wantella Tribe. There would be no such retaliation.

Burning Water had taken Flora to a place where she would be safe not only from the Illprinka men but, also, from Rex McPherson, for even he would not dare defile the precincts of the sacred store-house with violence from the sky.

Presently Burning Water regained his wind and sat up. His action was watched anxiously by the old men who dreaded that he would open the "bank" and handle the "cash." Had they known that Burning Water knew the locality of their sacred store-house, and that he would have dared to violate it with his presence, it is doubtful whether they would have pursued at all. They would have preferred to face Rex's anger because of failure to capture the fugitives.

The sun's heat was increasing, and Burning Water lifted Flora and carried her into the still long shadow cast by the boulder. He reassured her of their complete immunity from attack, and, having laid her down, he removed the Kurdaitcha boots and her own shoes. She thanked him wearily. The boots of emu feathers added to those removed from his feet provided for her quite a comfortable pillow.

"It's all right now, Miss McPherson," he told her. "We are safe here, and presently, perhaps, the flying doctor and the captain will come in the aeroplane and see us and take us back to the homestead."

The extremity of safety about the sacred store-house would be fifty yards, and within fifty yards of their side of the boulder was an abundance of shrub providing wood for a fire. Burning Water gathered some of this wood to light a fire close to the store-house. Whilst the water in the quart-pot was coming to the boil, he gathered dry wood for a signal fire and fresh boughs to create the dense smoke.

Flora was sleeping despite the flies. Burning Water brewed the tea and then sat beside the fire on his heels. While waiting for the liquid to cool he watched the old men clustered together and all facing towards him. The younger men had disappeared into the distant bush, no doubt sleeping and recuperating from the run of twenty-five miles, but Burning Water dared not lie down for fear he might sleep.

The shadows shortened. Now and then the leafy twigs waving above Flora's face would fall to rest upon her for a space. Then Burning Water would rouse himself and perk them upward. To maintain wakefulness, he cleaned the rifle and his pistol and then kept loading and unloading the weapons.

He was thus engaged when he heard the sound of the aeroplane engine, the sound he had been longing to hear. At first he could not locate the machine's position in the glaring world of sunshine. The valley was now partially filled with mirage water which distorted the waiting and watching Illprinka men into a high black mound.

Then he saw it. It was to the east, approaching fast, following the course of the valley and a mere thousand feet above it. He snatched a burning stick from the fire, waved it swiftly about his head to produce flame, and applied the flame to the signal fire made ready. When the smoke from the fire began to rise the machine had passed, but those in it had seen the group of aborigines sitting in the hot sunlight on the claypan verge, when normally they would have been in the shade.

"Let's go back and see what those fellows are doing down there." Dr Whyte said by telephone to Captain Loveacre. "There's a black at the foot of the headland, and—why—there's Flora lying down there with him. Bring her round, man. Slight wind from the south."

The twin-engined machine vanished from Burning Water's eager eyes, only to come again to view farther away. It returned and flew past him over the excited Illprinka men, who now scattered and raced for the bush. Burning Water saw Dr Whyte waving to him. He waved back vigorously and lifted Flora and implored her to wake.

"Miss McPherson!" he shouted unnecessarily. "It's Doctor Whyte and the captain. They're landing. Open your eyes, please and look."

"What is it—the Illprinka men?"

"The aeroplane. It's the captain and the doctor."

Not an Illprinka man could now be seen. The machine touched ground and began to taxi with whirring propeller blades towards the place the old men had occupied and keeping parallel with the face of the headland. Then it stopped opposite Burning Water, who began to carry Flora down the sand slope to the waiting flying doctor.

"Watch the blacks!" shouted Burning Water.

Whyte nodded. He reached down and took Flora up into the roofless cabin. Burning Water climbed up to join them. Flora was crying and stroking Whyte's face whilst she lay in his arms.

"Grand work, Burning Water," shouted the doctor to make himself heard above the engine noise. "Where's Bony?"

Burning Water described Bony's situation when they parted and Bony's probable desperate position at the moment.

"I want the captain to fly me over to the other side of the valley and put me down," he went on. "All the Illprinka men will be this side. Perhaps if the captain could fly me nearer Rex's camp and put me down it would be better still. I must go back for Bony, my brother, and my son and my father."

"On your own?" asked Whyte, amazed.

"Alone," asserted Burning Water more grammatically. "Tell the captain. It wouldn't take you long to fly me nearer to the cane-grass. S﹒ ten or twelve miles, or even fifteen. I must reach Bony quic﹒ly. Then, perhaps you and the captain could come out this way again and see what might be seen. Have you any tucker?"

Whyte nodded and pointed to a locker. He spoke to Loveacre and the captain revved the engines and set the machine along the ground in gathering speed.

Burning Water passed sandwiches and then proceeded to eat hurriedly. He found bread and meat in the locker and placed the food in the sugar bag suspended from his neck, and then he felt the plane bump on the ground and begin to run along the claypan verge bordering the southern edge of the valley. The machine stopped and the engine roar subsided sufficiently to permit talking by shouting.

"I go back," he told Whyte. "From here I should reach the house in the cane-grass by two o'clock. All the Illprinka men may be out there where you picked us up, and if so I'll get Bony from Rex. I'll make a fire to tell you where we are. Goodbye, Miss McPherson."

He smiled into her wide eyes, wide because his leaving and the reason were fully understood. Then he disappeared from her sight over the side and dropped to the ground. Whyte, leaning over, saw him lacing on the Kurdaitcha boots. He spoke to Loveacre and the machine began to move away. Burning Water vanished among the scrub.

CHAPTER 26

CURTAINS

IMMEDIATELY Rex McPherson obtained Bony's pistol he shouted to the Illprinka man to release his stranglehold.

"Keep still, Mister Napoleon Bonaparte," he ordered, emphasizing the prefix as Bony had done. Maintaining aim at Bony's heart and his gaze at Bony's eyes, he gave orders to the Illprinka man, who ran outside and could be heard shouting in the native dialect. Tootsey came in, accompanied by the naked lubra.

Outwardly calm, Bony was warmed by self-reproach for the easy manner in which the initiative had been taken from him.

He had given Flora and Burning Water a five hours' start, but he planned to give them at least eight hours' start, representing twenty miles before the inevitable pursuers were unleashed.

With half-inch rope used for lashing camel packs, the Illprinka men swiftly and efficiently secured Bony to his chair, and then departed with Rex. They could be heard outside shouting eager assent to Rex, who was telling them not to bother with tracking the fugitives, who would be certain to keep to the valley and head for the homestead. Like a pack of dogs giving tongue, they set off on the hunt, their voices rapidly dwindling. Tootsey lowered herself into one of the cane chairs and the naked lubra squatted at the entrance. Within fifteen minutes Bony was sleeping.

When he awoke sunlight was streaming in through the wide entrance, from which the cane-grass curtain had been removed. Tootsey was setting the table for breakfast. The pain had gone from Bony's right foot, but he could not be sure whether this was due to the numbness produced by the rope binding the leg to the chair or if it indicated that the wound had discharged all the poison. He certainly felt very much better, mentally and physically, and he was wondering if he would be given breakfast, when Rex McPherson entered.

"Good morning, Mr McPherson!" he said.

"Ha, Mr Bonaparte! Good morning! I trust you spent a comfortable night," returned Rex, unsmilingly. "Well now, as this will be your last day, and as I want you to be feeling very well, I suggest that you join me at breakfast. Tootsey! Unbind Mr Bonaparte's arms, but see that his feet and legs are secure. Now, Mr Bonaparte, grilled chops and coffee. Don't attempt to throw the knife."

"Your kindness would not permit such a display of bad manners, Mr McPherson," Bony said lightly, adding, when his arms were free: "Ah! That's better. In a moment the circulation will return. That coffee smells delicious."

"I never fail as a host," boasted Rex, still without smiling. His body was passive and he had control over his face and tongue, but his flaming eyes betrayed the unbalanced mind. Bony took up the coffee cup with fingers aching with returning circulation and drank. The question he put might be supposed to have been the last to interest him.

"You own sheep as well as cattle?"

"Yes, I have a small flock," admitted Rex. "Mutton sheep are more economical than store cattle when there are only two of us —myself and the cook. The blacks have their emus and kangaroos. As I mentioned last night, I have a plan to deal with you in a manner which should interest us both. I am going to take you up five or six thousand feet and tip you out over the swamp. You will have time to reflect, on your way down, on your stupidity in interfering with what didn't concern you."

"What time is this interesting event to take place?" inquired Bony, already experiencing the glow produced by good food and drink.

"Probably this afternoon," Rex replied, and Bony could see he was enjoying the thrills of the sadist. "I have a little more work to do to my engine, tuning, you know. Then I have to extricate Flora and Burning Water from a stalemate."

"Indeed! You have, then, had news of them?"

"Yes. I kept an old man back from the chase to receive progress reports, and a mulga wire was received an hour ago saying that Burning Water had taken Flora to the Illprinka's sacred storehouse. Do you know what that means?"

"It means that the Illprinka will not attack Miss McPherson and Burning Water while they remain in that sanctuary."

"Just so. It means also that Burning Water has condemned himself to death, and henceforth not for a moment will he be able to consider himself safe from an Illprinka spear. Even in his own country he will not be safe, for his own people will do nothing to protect him, even to warn him. I suppose you planned for them to reach that sanctuary?"

"Only as a last resort. Burning Water must have been hard pressed."

"Yes. He beat my bucks by a head, as it were."

"Fine fellow, isn't he?" Bony said.

"Damn fool to condemn himself like that. But he was always a little soft. Used to be the little Lord Fauntleroy I understand. His sacrifice, as I suppose he'll think it, will be in vain because the blacks will watch until he and Flora are driven from the place by thirst."

"They may be picked up by Loveacre," suggested Bony. "I understand that a plane could be landed quite close."

"There is just a chance of their rescue by Loveacre, but only a chance. I'll be out there by twelve o'clock, and then I will destroy Loveacre's plane with a bomb or two. That done we can leave them to the Illprinka, and you and I will go up over the swamp. I have heard it said that a man falling from a great height loses consciousness, but I don't believe it. You will be conscious until the moment of impact.

"I am going to have you taken to the hangar where I can keep my eyes on you whilst I work," he said, and gave Tootsey an order. "I shall be behind you all the time, and should you make a break, I'll shoot you not through the head but through a kidney. You are going to take that journey into the swamp where you'll never be found."

Tootsey and the naked lubra freed Bony's feet and legs, but for several minutes he was unable to stand. Then, with a lubra either side of him and grasping his arms, he was semi-dragged from the room and along the skirting claypan to the hangar. There they bound his wrists behind his back, bound his arms to his sides, pushed him down on to the stretcher bed, bound his ankles and legs, and bound him from neck to ankles to the stretcher itself.

The place both astonished and interested Bonaparte. There stood the beautiful silver-grey aeroplane revealing with its shining surfaces the devoted attention of a man whose reason was certainly unseated by the obsession for power. The recent high wind had smothered parts of a long bench with sand grains, but no dust was now adhering to the aeroplane. Rex, dressed in mechanic's overalls, was working on his engine from a wheeled platform. Bony could see a lathe and a tool rack, and there was a handcart loaded with cased petrol, which indicated that the petrol store was not inside the hangar.

An hour passed, during which Rex never spoke. The lubras had gone. The wind maintained its soft whine in the walls and roof, and other than the occasional cawing of a crow and the clink of metal against metal this world of shadow and sunbars was, indeed, peaceful, until a naked aborigine entered and ran to speak with Rex.

His news was serious, for Rex got down from the work platform to question him. Questions and answers passed between them for several minutes. Then the aborigine went out and Rex crossed to Bony who noted his flashing eyes and the dull-red base of his dark skin.

"Loveacre and Whyte have picked up Flora and Burning Water," he said, savagely. "You've won that trick, Mister Napoleon Bonaparte, but I'm going to win the next one. Those fellows think themselves smart, but I'm going to disillusion them. I've got an hour or two's work yet to do, and then I'll destroy Loveacre's plane and give the old man ten minutes to make up his mind what he'll do about the station."

"How would that forward your schemes?" asked Bony.

"It won't. But I won't care once I'm sure the old man refuses to give in. When that happens I'm at war with him and with the world. I'll go down in the end, I suppose, but it will be a glorious end and I'll be remembered for many a long year."

Turning about, Rex almost ran to the aeroplane and sprang to the work-platform, where strangely enough the nervous reflexes of his body subsided and again he moved with the deliberation of the surgeon.

Time passed slowly for Bonaparte. The sun-bars gave him the hours, and when Rex finally completed the engine tuning it must have been after three o'clock. He had worked without lunch, and now he clapped his hands when on his way to the washbasin beside the stretcher bed.

"Now I'm ready for the air again we'll see what's doing," he told Bony. "First a little lunch, then to load the bomb rack and fill the tanks. I should be back inside the hour, and then up you go to six thousand feet. I did think of taking you with me and doing all three jobs on the same flight, but first things first, eh?"

Tootsey came in with a large tray loaded with tea and sandwiches. Seated on the stretcher Rex ate and drank and sometimes paused to describe what he intended doing and how he would wage warfare with the world. He offered Bony neither food nor tea. He did not offer him a cigarette.

To open and pump the cased petrol into the plane's tanks took quite some time, but his task was presently finished and then he carried his small thermite bombs from the back of the hangar to load beneath the fuselage. This done he came towards the stand near the stretcher to wash his hands, and his face indicated intense satisfaction.

"*Au revoir*, Mister Fool Bonaparte," he said whilst assuring himself that the ropes were tight and the knots secure. "You'll do until I get back. Meanwhile pleasant thoughts."

Rex had donned his flying suit and was adjusting his parachute when Bony felt hands touching his bound wrists.

"It's me, Burning Water," he heard a voice say. "I came in by making a hole through the wall. Where's he going?"

"Where! Why he's off to bomb Captain Loveacre's aeroplane and then destroy the homestead," Bony cried, confident that the running engine would prevent his voice reaching Rex McPherson who was about to climb up into the front compartment of the cockpit. "Quick, Burning Water. Stop him. Shoot him. He's mad."

The pressure of ropes vanished from Bony's body, but he was helpless to move either his arms or his legs.

"Haven't you got your pistol?" he asked, despairingly. "Didn't you bring your rifle? He's loaded the machine with bombs and he's off to destroy the homestead and perhaps all those there. Stop him! Shoot him, man!"

Rex was in his seat. The engine was accelerated and the plane quivered. The propeller swept dust from under the plane against the rear wall. Tootsey was hauling on cords to roll up the grass blinds from the entrance.

"I can't shoot him," Burning Water said, steadily. "It's not my way. My rifle is beside you. Here's my pistol. You can easily escape. There's only the two lubras here. I've accounted for the cook and one old Illprinka man."

The plane was moving to the open entrance when Burning Water raced from the stretcher, reached the tail of the machine and then clambered along its gleaming body to the step insets serving the rear compartment. Tootsey had withdrawn to one side of the entrance and outside. Rex was concentrating his attention on taxi-ing the plane from the hangar, and besides he was sitting low down behind the front windshield. The tail bar had not left the ground and he neither saw nor felt the additional weight when Burning Water climbed into the rear compartment and slumped down.

"There's that Illprinka store-house place where we picked up Flora and Burning Water," Dr Whyte told his pilot by leaning forward in his seat and shouting at the top of his voice.

Whyte continued to use the glasses, searching the sky for the silver-grey aeroplane. He knew from Flora that the machine was grounded in its hangar, but even she did not know for how long.

From the horizon now emerged a ribbon dark-brown in colour, uniform, unbroken. The aeroplane "drifted" southward to cross the valley whilst it headed for the broadening dark-brown mass slipping beneath them. This was the cane-grass and lantana swamp, and when its nearest edge was but a mile distant the airmen could not see its farther side. Nothing stirred on it or beside it. There was no sign of life. A minute later Loveacre pointed downward and Whyte brought his glasses to bear in the direction.

"He's just taking off! By hokey, Loveacre! Now's our chance. Remember, he's faster than we are. Get alongside him for only one minute, and leave the rest to me."

"Hope he hasn't a gun, too," Loveacre shouted back. "He's climbing fast, but he's headed east. I'm going down now."

"I'm sure he didn't have a gun when he bombed my crate," Whyte asserted and then for the hundredth time manipulated the Lewis gun on its railed mounting.

"He's fast, all right," shouted Loveacre, and on his face was a kind of glory. "Like old times ain't it, comrade? Bust him wide open when we get alongside. We probably won't get another chance, for if he hasn't a gun he'll get away from us. Mind your head!"

Loveacre was beginning to flatten out his machine and to utilize the speed gained by the dive to take it alongside the silver-grey. They could see Rex McPherson looking at them. In another half-minute the machines would be flying side by side and then Whyte could take his gun into action. Then they saw a grey-tufted black head emerge upward from the rear compartment of the cockpit, and Dr Whyte swore and Loveacre shouted:

"Curse it! There's Burning Water!"

Whyte groaned. In another three seconds he could have sped bullets into the silver-grey's pilot, and now he was paralysed. Rex saw the gun aimed at him and he shook his gloved fist and turned his ship away. Loveacre's plane followed, rapidly losing position.

They distinctly saw the astonishment Rex McPherson felt when, on looking back at them, he saw Burning Water occupying the rear seat. They saw him jerk his body forward to reach a weapon. They saw Burning Water raise himself and smash the windshield in front of his compartment and then, against the pressure of the wind, force himself forward to grasp the edge of the front compartment. Now he was almost out of his compartment, hanging with one hand, the other grasping the pilot's flying suit at the chest. The plane lurched, began to slip to starboard.

Rex fired his automatic pistol but it did not appear that his aim was true because Burning Water now had both hands on the pilot and was pulling him toward himself. Rex was standing and smashing his assailant with the pistol. The plane was slipping down, its wings almost at right angles to the ground. Burning Water had his arms round Rex's middle, and Loveacre and Whyt could see that the pistol arm was crushed against Rex's side.

Then both men in strong embrace appeared to "drift" from the silver-grey aeroplane which went into a nose dive. Down and down through the crystal clear air they fell, clasped together slowly turning over and over.

The pilot chute appeared like a puff of smoke. Then like pricked balloon the main parachute appeared to follow the tw bodies earthward. Abruptly it bellied, mushroomed, held for an instant, seemed to explode and then follow on down with the men all tatters and ribbons. Neither Whyte nor Loveacre continued to gaze that way. They watched the silver-grey aeroplane till it struck ground and became the base of a vast column of writhing black smoke.

"He had bombs on that ship," Loveacre told Whyte. "What do we do now?"

"Try to locate Bony. Yes, he had bombs on board. But he didn't know that Burning Water was aboard till he looked back at us. The black must have stowed away on his plane."

Loveacre turned his ship towards the swamp. They were in time to see the birth of another smoke column at the southern edge. Its growth was amazing. Within three minutes it formed a giant black shadow confronting them, and down at the foot of the shadow they saw figures running across the claypan road to the red dunes. They now saw other blacks emerge from the scrub of the valley and run towards the same dune.

"There's Bony!" shouted Whyte. "He's holding up the crowd from the summit of that sandhill. Land for him, Loveacre, and leave the mob to me. Looks like he fired the blasted camp."

The plane dropped down the face of the rising black smoke that looked like a cliff of coal. It passed southward for a mile, turned and came northward, then sank till its wheels touched the claypan verge between the conflagration and the sand-dune range. Bony was lying on the summit of a whaleback. Father along the range black figures were moving like ants against the slopes, and one of these ants was a brilliant scarlet.

Now Bony was running down the dune towards the ship. The Illprinka men, among whom was Tootsey, came slowly towards the running man, fearing rifle fire; a burst of machine-gun fire sent them racing for cover among the dunes.

Although he was limping badly, Bonaparte gained the side of the machine. He was hauled up and into the roofless cabin, and they were confronted by his passionately angry face.

"That was Burning Water with Rex McPherson," he shouted. "Didn't you see him? Why did you shoot the plane down?"

"We didn't, old man," Whyte said. "Rex didn't know Burning Water was in the observer's seat behind him until he turned to look back at us. Then Burning Water grabbed him and they fell out together."

The anger faded from Bony's eyes.

On the way back to the homestead they sat together and Bony

told them about Burning Water refusing to shoot Rex McPherson, explaining how by taking Flora to the Illprinka's sacred store-house he had condemned himself to death, and how he had decided to stamp out a dangerous fire to relieve his friend and chief of the trouble.

"It might have been better to go out that way than to be always expecting a spear in the back," Loveacre said. "But I don't think I could have chosen that way."

Six months had passed and again Captain Loveacre had flown to McPherson's Station, this time with Napoleon Bonaparte as his passenger.

It turned out a wonderful day, a soft and cool wind blowing from the south, Dr Henry Whyte had come in his new aeroplane, and his passenger had been the minister from Birdsville. The minister had conducted the marriage in the dining-room from the walls of which hung the pictures of the bride's magnificent ancestors.

And now The McPherson stood with Captain Loveacre and Bony and the parson and Old Jack and the men's cook at the fence at the bottom of the garden. And down the slope were grouped all the members of the Wantella Tribe, hushed, expectant. Old Jack was relating stories of the old days to Loveacre and the minister, and Bony was saying to the squatter:

"Looking back on that terrible business I find it hard to believe that my visit here from first to last was only nine days. It is as well for me that it was only nine days, for I could find no fitting excuses to offer my Chief Commissioner for having made the decisions I did make. He proved very . . . difficult. Of course, he is always difficult, but this time he was more so."

"You had a good deal of trouble, too, in hushing it all up, didn't you?" asked The McPherson.

"As a matter of fact I very nearly lost my job over it," Bony replied, smilingly. "It was quite impossible to convince a man like Colonel Spendor of the poetry there is in the name Tarlalin. It was difficult to convince him that, the dangerous fire having been stamped out, there could be no justifiable reason in making the affair public and thus causing the innocent to suffer. The fact that you intended to, and eventually did, bestow a handsome annuity on Errey's wife certainly assisted my efforts."

"I did what was right: neither more nor less," claimed the squatter. "Before you go, I would like to take you along to the cemetery. I have something to show you."

"I would like to accompany you. It sounds as though Harry's plane is taking off. Ah—yes! Here they come."

From the direction of the landing ground a sleek, modern, low-wing aircraft came roaring over the claypan verge and passed those on the slopes and at the garden fence on the same level. They could see Flora waving to them. The aborigines leaped and yelled and shrieked. The white folk waved and cheered. Then the machine had passed, was climbing steeply and, after circling the homestead once, flew away over the valley of burning water towards the radiant hills.

"Well well!" exclaimed Loveacre. "That's the end of a story I like. Fine fellow, Whyte, and dashed lucky, too. What a bride! And now I suppose, we must be off, too."

"Yes, I suppose you must, but I do wish you would stay the night," McPherson said, regretfully.

"Sorry, but I simply must be in Brisbane tomorrow."

"All right, captain. But just a moment. I want to show Bony something."

Together Bony and he walked over the thick lawn so ably preserved from the hot winds and the scorching sun by Old Jack. They skirted his sprinklers and his beds of standard roses, and passed through the door in the cane-grass wall into the shrine. McPherson conducted Bony to the three slabs of red granite under the centre one of which lay Tarlalin, and standing at her feet pointed to the left hand slab, but did not speak. And under the original name cemented in, Bony read the deeply chiselled words:

Burning Water
Chief of the Wantella

"The McPherson's justice," murmured the squatter. "I had him brought and placed there. I could have done no less. The other was buried where he fell, but I got the minister to go out and read the service over him. When my time comes I shall die content in the knowledge that I shall sleep with Tarlalin, my wife, and Burning Water, my friend."

Bony nodded that he heard. He made no comment. He refrained from saying that the unfortunate Rex McPherson was greatly to be pitied. The squatter would not understand the influences that had warred for the mind of Rex McPherson. No white man ever would understand those influences, which were so well known to Detective-Inspector Napoleon Bonaparte.